"I KNOW YOUR KISS."

Startled, she stepped back.

"You couldn't possibly." There was no way she was acknowledging what had happened at Haunt. "We met yesterday at Driscoll Financial."

"Kisses are like fingerprints—no two are alike."

He was scaring her now. "There have to be similarities."

He shook his head. "You could blindfold me and have every past lover kiss me. I'd recognize each one, as far back as sixth grade."

Panic squeezed Cat hard. The floor seemed to shift, and she clutched the wooden bin for balance. A lick to her lips found them warm and swollen. She tasted him on her tongue. "You're mistaken. Perhaps in sleep—"

"You're more than a wet dream," he said, cutting her off. "Lips don't lie, sweetheart. I've kissed you."

BOOK YOUR PLACE ON OUR WEBSITE AND MAKE THE READING CONNECTION!

We've created a customized website just for our very special readers, where you can get the inside scoop on everything that's going on with Zebra, Pinnacle and Kensington books.

When you come online, you'll have the exciting opportunity to:

- View covers of upcoming books
- Read sample chapters
- Learn about our future publishing schedule (listed by publication month *and author*)
- Find out when your favorite authors will be visiting a city near you
- Search for and order backlist books from our online catalog
- Check out author bios and background information
- Send e-mail to your favorite authors
- Meet the Kensington staff online
- Join us in weekly chats with authors, readers and other guests
- Get writing guidelines
- AND MUCH MORE!

**Visit our website at
http://www.kensingtonbooks.com**

Sweet Spot

KATE ANGELL

KENSINGTON BOOKS
http://www.kensingtonbooks.com

KENSINGTON BOOKS are published by

Kensington Publishing Corp.
119 West 40th Street
New York, NY 10018

All Kensington titles, imprints and distributed lines are available at special quantity discounts for bulk purchases for sales
promotion, premiums, fund-raising, educational or institu-
tional use.

Special book excerpts or customized printings can also be created to fit specific needs. For details, write or phone the office
of the Kensington Special Sales Manager: Attn. Special Sales
Department. Kensington Publishing Corp., 119 West 40th
Street, New York, NY 10018. Phone: 1-800-221-2647.

Kensington and the K logo Reg. U.S. Pat. & TM Off.

ISBN-13: 978-0-7582-6918-8
ISBN-10: 0-7582-6918-8

First Printing: May 2012

10 9 8 7 6 5 4 3 2 1

Printed in the United States of America

To my editor, Alicia Condon.

You are appreciated.

WELCOME
TO
JAMES RIVER STADIUM

HOME OF THE RICHMOND ROGUES

Starting Lineup

25	RF	Cody McMillan
18	C	Chase Tallan
11	3B	Jesse Bellisaro
21	CF	Risk Kincaid
9	SS	Brody Jones
15	1B	Rhaden Dunn
46	LF	Kason Rhodes
1	2B	James Lawless
53	P	Brek Stryker

Prologue

Orange strobe lights. Pumpkin-scented incense.
Glow-in-the-dark spiderwebs.
Evil-faced jack-o'-lanterns.
Ouija board and tarot cards.
Inhibitions were left at the door, along with the cover charge. The adult Halloween costumes guaranteed anonymity. Everyone wore a mask.
Pheromones heated the crowded club and sweat trickled down chests and between thighs. Anticipated sex throbbed as insistently as Michael Jackson's "Thriller."
Captain America stood against the wall and took it all in. On the dance floor, Darth Vader fondled Scarlett O'Hara. At the corner of the bat-shaped bar, a sexy skeleton stroked Jesse James's revolver. The outlaw was cocked.
A well-oiled Tin Man felt up Dorothy beneath an

exit sign. Her red heels clicked as he kissed her back
to Kansas.

In a darkened corner, Zorro twisted more than the
fringe on a flapper's costume. Behind the buffet, a zombie
unwrapped an Egyptian mummy down to her thong.

It was a night to get laid.

Captain America shifted, adjusting his patriotic
bodysuit, a replica of the original American-flag motif.
His blue mask had an *A* centered on his forehead, and
gold poly-foam wings were clipped on his shoulders. His
red boots reached his knees. His red gloves cleared his
elbows. He was armed with an indestructible shield that
could be thrown as a weapon.

"This is one hell of a party." The Incredible Hulk
handed the captain a Samuel Adams. "I'm glad you
wanted to check out the club. Haunt has real investment
potential."

Captain America nodded his agreement. The renovated warehouse sat on a prime piece of real estate in
downtown Richmond. Its notorious adult Halloween
parties drew celebrities, athletes, models, and executives all year long. The waiting line wrapped an entire
city block every single night. Customers sold their
souls to the devil at the door to enter.

"I meet with Driscoll Financial tomorrow," the captain reminded Hulk. "My offer will have been presented to Dan Hatton and I hope to close on Haunt."

Hatton was the present owner of the club. He'd recently suffered a minor stroke. The man had worked
hard all his life, and on his eightieth birthday, his heart
had warned him to slow down. As a result, he'd begun
selling off his holdings, starting with Club Haunt.

The hot property was a diversified venture for Captain

America. If all went well, he would soon own the trendy night club, and his adrenaline rushed at the prospect.

Midnight, and the music built. The sounds became darker, kinkier, more suggestive. Haunt pulsed, and bodies ground against one another. The air vibrated, and the sexual tension pumped toward orgasm.

Hulk took a long pull on his beer, then caught the eye of a Victorian vampire. She flashed her fangs at him. "Lady wants to bite." Hulk grinned.

The captain watched as the mean, green fighting machine in the torn purple pants sauntered toward the goth-looking woman in a tight black leather bustier and flowing skirt. Her auburn hair fell to her waist and her bloodred fingernails were as long and sharp as her fangs. Her white face powder gave her an eerie glow.

Captain America's testicles tightened. The vamp wouldn't have been his first choice for a hookup. She looked damn scary. The Hulk, however, liked the dark side.

An enormous T. rex lumbered past, and the sweep of his thick, spiky tail tripped a dozen people in his wake. Only Wonder Woman avoided the collision. Her red satin cape swung wide as she hopped over the tail and landed lightly on the balls of her feet.

The captain stared at the woman in the red bustier with a blue bottom patterned in white stars. He noted their costumes were quite similar, even though he was an Avenger and she fought for the Justice League.

He admired her endless legs, a hint of pale hip bone, and the slight dip of her belly. The heels of her knee-high red-and-white vinyl boots added five inches to her height. She proved a true Amazon Princess, and one fine DC Comics heroine.

Wonder Woman had curves. High, full breasts and

one hell of a nice ass. A wide gold belt cinched her waist and a silver cuff bracelet banded each wrist. A sparkly golden headband contained her dark curls and a red-winged mask hid half her face. She tapped her Lasso of Truth against her thigh in time to the music.

The captain liked what he saw. He handed his empty bottle of beer to a cocktail waitress, then elbowed his way through the crowd. There was no direct path to Wonder Woman. He was stopped twice—once by a flirty, cotton-headed female Q-tip and a second time by a Barbie doll in a cellophane box. While both women drew his smile, it was Wonder Woman who held his interest. He pushed forward, filled with purpose and curiosity.

Wonder Woman was partied out. It was time to call it a night. She had a big day at work tomorrow. Her boss had suggested she attend the club in costume to evaluate its market value. The warehouse was worth its asking price, she'd decided. Haunt had a sexual mystique no amount of publicity could buy. It was the hot spot of the city.

From what she'd witnessed, the club was a gold mine. Her boss had a client ready to invest. According to her audit team, Haunt turned a solid profit. Her recommendation was to buy quickly. The club showed no signs of slowing down.

The nightly Halloween celebrations masked reality. People gravitated and gyrated to the unknown. Wonder Woman had lost two boyfriends to Haunt. They'd both entered the club monogamous and left for a ménage.

Anonymity turned partiers into players.

She wasn't a fan of the place.

The club's cardinal rule forbade sex on the premises, but what happened in the parking lot stayed in the parking lot. Though this wasn't her personal playground of choice, those around her were having a hell of a good time.

Wonder Woman stifled a yawn. She wanted to get out of her costume. The brown wig had begun to itch and the curls had lost their bounce. The bra cups on the bustier pushed her breasts up, doubling her cup size. The blue bottom was as skimpy as a pair of bikini panties. She was totally out of her element.

The crush of the crowd made her claustrophobic and the noise level was deafening. Her eyes burned from the candle smoke and her lungs demanded fresh air. She was exhausted from turning down the advances of amorous costumed characters. Bozo the Clown's big, floppy feet had stepped all over her boots when he'd requested a dance. Gumby had twisted his body around her like a pretzel.

She scanned the room. The warehouse was enormous, and there was no immediate sign of a black-and-red Ladybug. She and her friend Carla had agreed that should they get separated, each would find her own way home. The Ladybug had hoped to get lucky, and she'd had her eye on Daffy Duck.

Wonder Woman turned to leave, only to run smack into Captain America. *Could the man stand any closer?* His proximity smothered her.

All sound in the club receded, and it was only the two of them in a sea of costumes. Stillness, stark and indefinable, embraced them both until someone jostled her elbow and all the noise crashed back. Instinctively, she raised her indestructible bracelets to ward him off.

Behind his mask, daredevil dark eyes gleamed at her and his lips curved in a slow, sexy smile. "No need to defend yourself against me, babe. We're both superheroes on the side of justice." His voice was deep yet distorted against the background noise.

Wonder Woman swallowed hard. She was certain she'd need protection against this man—he was one fine Avenger. She couldn't fully see his face, yet she instinctively *knew* he'd be handsome. No doubt too handsome for his own good.

There was no padding to his costume; his bodysuit fit like a second skin. He was six feet of broad shoulders and ripped muscle. Tight spandex cupped his groin, leaving little to her imagination.

Captain America leaned in, his power raw and tangible. His cologne was designed to arouse desire and passion, an orgasm in a bottle. "Are you here alone or in the company of Superman and Batman?" he asked.

Alone made her available. While the pulse of the club had gotten under her skin, she wasn't looking for a one-night stand. Not even with a Marvel comic book hero who'd mastered the martial arts and was known for his intelligence, strength, and super reaction time.

"The members of the Justice League are always close by." She raised her voice above the music, letting him assume the trinity was in attendance. "Are you here with the Avengers?"

"Only the Incredible Hulk," he stated. "He hooked up with a bloodsucker."

The Victorian vampire. Wonder Woman had noticed the vamp circling the crowd, looking for her next victim. The Hulk would get fanged.

The captain's gaze narrowed and his jaw shifted. "Are you a regular?" he wanted to know.

Was he wondering if she was a serial dater; if she slept around?

"This is my virgin haunt." She strained her voice to be heard. "How about you?" She roped his arm tightly with her Lasso of Truth so he could not lie.

"First time for me, too," he said.

"You're not into nightly costumes?"

His gaze glittered behind his mask. "Only if my woman wants to dress up privately for me in the bedroom."

Her lasso went slack. She could imagine a very naughty nurse stripping for this man, as well as the hot, sweaty sex that would follow. He'd have satin sheets and skilled hands. He was satisfaction guaranteed.

She blushed, and desperately hoped it was too dark in the club for Captain America to witness her embarrassment.

His grin revealed dimples, and her whole body flushed. The man was a mind reader.

"Have you eaten?" He nodded toward the buffet. "There's chicken witch-fingers, miniature bat burgers, and Bloody Marys."

"I've had dinner." Her throat was so raw from shouting, she now sounded like Minnie Mouse. She'd soothe the scratchiness later with a cup of tea with honey.

The music soon turned eerie and hauntingly slow. The floor reverberated with a deep, sexual bass. Goose bumps skated down her spine. All around her couples pressed together and kissed as if it were New Year's Eve.

Boldly, the captain propped his shield against the wall. His hands now free, he made his move and drew her body flush against his. Her booted heels raised her to his height. Her palms splayed across a chest as solid as armor plate. Her lasso dangled dangerously near his groin. She inhaled their closeness.

They shared air, breath, and heat. The darkness

captured and seduced; their intimacy was compelling. Her heart slammed hard and her stomach shimmied. He consumed her.

The man was physical perfection. For one hot moment, she savored the superhero. They swayed together, their attraction dominant. Her inhibitions slid down her legs like a pair of silk panties.

She could handle one dance before she sneaked into the crowd and out the side door. She'd hail a cab and disappear into the night. Too bad she didn't have her invisible plane.

Beneath the orange strobe lighting, Captain America's strong hands now spanned her waist, then worked higher. He brushed the underside of her breasts and her nipples tightened in response. She ached to be touched further.

His warm breath fanned her cheek, a forewarning of his kiss. He claimed her mouth like a conquering hero. The man was all touch, tongue, and temptation. His stubble scraped the soft curve of her chin.

He stroked down her ribs, thumbing her navel.

He squeezed her hips with sexual urgency.

She sighed, and he swallowed the sound.

Wild currents built within her as she wound her arms tightly around his neck. Her fingers dug into his back.

He grabbed her bottom and their bodies were grafted. The spandex made them fluid and seamless as they simulated sex. She rolled her hips to feel him fully, and his bulge pronounced him supersized.

Friction sparked, and their chemistry shot through the roof. Desire zinged between her legs. She went damp for him.

Time swelled, and his kisses deepened. He bit her

lower lip and sucked her tongue. The moments seemed surreal. Caped in darkness and anonymity, they groaned and grew impatient. She clawed his shoulders and he stroked the crease of her ass.

The rhythm of the night overtook them. They dry humped, harder, faster, all control lost to her wetness and his rigid inches.

Her skin stretched, taut yet tender.

His erection strained.

His heart seemed to beat in her breast. They were as close to being one as two people could get without being naked.

Sensations fogged her brain. His desire branded her. There was no delaying the inevitable.

The intensity was insane.

So crazy, she climaxed.

She came apart in his arms on the dance floor.

Spasms of release left her body liquid, but shame soon cleared her head. What had she done?

She'd humped a comic book hero at a club known for anonymous pleasure. He'd teased her and turned her on. She'd let herself be taken. She'd fallen to the darkness and decadence and one erect Avenger.

This was so not her. She needed to leave.

Hand-to-hand combat was Wonder Woman's specialty, and a strong elbow to the captain's ribs freed her. She forced long, deep breaths into her lungs and clutched the golden lasso protectively to her chest.

His brow furrowed beneath his mask; obviously, sex fuzzed his brain. She hated to be his buzz-kill, but her night ended right here, right now.

She backed away from him; one step, then two.

His gaze held surprise and hunger. He spread his hands wide, openly confused by her departure.

She couldn't explain her feelings, how she'd foolishly lost herself in him. She'd walked the dark side and experienced the sexual mystique of Haunt. But instead of satisfaction, she felt hollow and numb. And embarrassingly easy.

Humiliated, she turned toward the exit. King Kong provided the perfect cover and she darted behind him. She pushed past a Chicago gangster and a samurai warrior. A glance over her shoulder revealed no sign of Captain America. She picked up her pace, moving faster through the crowd.

A whirling, twirling ballerina knocked the Lasso of Truth off her wrist. It whipped beneath the feet of a dancing bear. Wonder Woman didn't stop to pick it up; it would only cost her time.

The side exit was in view. A final dash and she cleared the dance door. The bouncer flagged down a cab.

She was gone.

Captain America caught the taillights of her taxi. He imagined her taking off in her invisible plane. She'd fly full throttle into the night sky. Far away from him.

His gut wrenched over his inability to stop her. He and his overactive libido owed her an apology, yet she'd run off while he'd been bone hard and unable to give chase.

On his way to the exit, Little Bo Beep had snagged him with her pink staff and requested a dance. He'd waved her off. A nun in full habit had invited him to sin. Had he not met Wonder Woman, he might have taken the nun up on her offer.

The comic book heroine had hit him low and left him hard. He wasn't a man to bring a woman to orgasm on the dance floor. He preferred his privacy. Yet she'd gone off on him, a woman with a short sexual fuse. He'd absorbed her climax, then her uncertainty. She seemed to hate herself for letting go.

He flat didn't understand.

They'd been damn good together.

A part of him hoped she wasn't a tease. Or a good girl gone bad for the night. He liked his women stable and sane.

He reentered the club and was immediately propositioned by Olive Oyl and an Indian maiden. He chose to go home alone. His desire for the Amazon Princess held strong.

Head down, he crossed the dance floor. A golden rope was being kicked about by the dancers, and it nearly tripped him. He bent and retrieved the Lasso of Truth. Her scent lingered on the golden lariat: patchouli and spice.

He smiled slowly. His life had taken a turn for the better. Wonder Woman had lost a part of her costume. He'd have his administrative assistant contact every Halloween shop in Richmond until he located the customer who'd returned her suit without the lariat.

He'd soon know her true identity.

He had every plan to see her again. If the lasso fit, she'd be forced to tell the truth. He wouldn't let her run a second time.

Chapter 1

"Dude, you've got green paint behind your ears." James "Law" Lawless, second baseman for the Richmond Rogues, stared at the back of Brody Jones's head. The shortstop hadn't fully scrubbed the Incredible Hulk from the back of his neck.

The men had arrived early at James River Stadium in preparation for their upcoming game against the Ottawa Raptors. They'd worked out in the weight room for an hour and now pulled on their uniforms, preparing for warm-ups on the field. The remaining team members would be arriving shortly.

"Hickeys, Brody?" Law caught the bites and bruises on the shortstop's neck and shoulders. Red scratches ran up his spine. "Your vamp played rough."

Brody jerked on his sliding shorts and adjusted himself. "Lady was in character."

Law shoved his arms into his jersey and buttoned it down. "Did you get her name, her medical history?" In case she carried rabies.

"She called me Hulk and I called her Vampira."

Brody was a nooky junkie. He preferred nameless sex. No ties. No good-byes. No morning-afters.

Law shook his head. "You're fuckin' crazy."

"So screwed up, I plan to see her again."

"Do you know where she lives?"

Brody shrugged. "East of Haunt. It was hard to drive and pay attention to street signs. She was all over me in the car." He grinned widely. "She sucked more than my blood." He kissed and told.

More than Law needed to know. "Did you see her face?"

"Nah, we stayed in costume," Brody said. "My green body-paint didn't sweat off during sex. Her white the-atrical makeup glowed in the dark."

The Hulk and his vampire had chosen anonymity. Had Law and Wonder Woman connected, he would have stripped off her mask and learned her name. Set up a second date.

Brody pressed a shoulder to his locker and yawned. "Did you hook up?" he asked Law.

Law continued to dress. He wore old-fashioned short baseball pants and high socks in homage to the baseball greats who'd come before him. As he looped his belt, he was slow to say, "I met Wonder Woman."

Brody scratched his belly. "Did you join the Mile High Club in her invisible plane?"

The lady had climaxed and he'd suffered blue balls. "She booked." Law found it hard to admit. "I lost her in the parking lot."

Brody snorted. "That has to be a first. Women swarm you."

"I was in costume," Law said, defending himself. He'd dressed as an Avenger, not as a Rogue.

"You should've gone as Batman or Iron Man," Brody

pointed out. "Their rich alter egos, Bruce Wayne and Tony Stark, are closer to your lifestyle. Richie Rich or Scrooge McDuck would've fit, too."

Law ignored him. The majority of the Rogues didn't give a shit about his birthright or inheritance. It was a known fact, though seldom discussed, that he came from money. He could pay a team's salary for an entire season and not make a dent in his trust fund. As long as he gave his all on game day, no one cared that his grandfather, Randall Burton Lawless, was ranked fourteenth on the Forbes 400. At eighty-six, the hotelier and CEO of Grace Hotels Worldwide allowed Law to be an athlete first and heir to the hotel chain second.

Brody grunted as he snagged a white T-shirt from his locker and pulled it over his head. "Captain America put patriotic on the map. Every woman wants a super-hero."

"Wonder Woman has her own sense of justice." Law dropped onto a long wooden bench to tie his athletic shoes.

"We could hit the club again tonight," the shortstop suggested. "Maybe she'd show a second time."

Law doubted it. Wonder Woman had left so abruptly, he had the gut feeling she'd rush to return her costume and attempt to erase all memories of their dry hump on the dance floor. She'd write off her lasso and pay the rental shop for its loss.

At that moment, Law couldn't commit to another night out anyway. "We've got nine innings on a ninety-degree field. After the game, I meet with Zen Driscoll. If I'm not wiped out—"

"Don't go old on me, man," Brody said as he smeared black grease under his eyes to cut the glare of the sun.

"My costume's rented for a week. I'd like to get some use out of it." He grinned. "If not Haunt, I could be Hulk at Hangovers."

Hangovers was a sports bar two blocks from the stadium, where crowds flocked nightly and the players got their egos stroked. Brody had proved an instant favorite. While Law had cut his teeth on the majors right out of college, Brody had spent three years in the minors. Nothing came easy for the West Virginian. Fans saw him as scrappy and persistent. He'd bled for his spot on the team roster, a position vacated by Zen Driscoll.

Zen had broken his ankle the previous season. The bones had healed nicely, but he'd lost the jump and pivot needed to play shortstop.

Fortunately, Zen had skills beyond baseball. He was also a financial genius. He'd left the Rogues and opened his own firm, dealing in investments, savings, stocks, bonds, annuities, mutual funds, government securities, and real estate. His specialty was matching properties and corporations to potential investors.

All the Rogues had tattoos on their groins, and Zen's read EINSTEIN. He was competent, trusted, and never let his dick think for him. Most of his teammates had sought Zen's assistance at some point to pad their retirement portfolios.

As the season progressed, Law planned to strong-arm Brody to meet with Zen. It was time the rookie invested his money in more than his dates.

Zen had given Law a list of potential investments, including Haunt. No one else knew the club was up for sale. Law hoped to close the deal today. He even had the perfect manager in mind.

Afterward, he'd look into smaller investments. Zen had assisted Law in establishing Prosper, an organization that supported graduates from the Richmond Business College in starting their careers as small-business owners.

Josh Prosper had inspired the foundation. He'd been a loyal fan of the Rogues for more than four decades. He slapped every player on the back after a game, win or lose. He went so far as to meet the team at the airport for out-of-town games, wishing them well on their departure, then welcoming them home on their return. Josh became the Rogues' good-luck charm, up until the day he disappeared.

The players had been puzzled over his unexplained absence. A month passed, and Law, Kason Rhodes, and Risk Kincaid searched him out. They'd found him sitting on the steps of his home, a foreclosure sign in the yard. Depression had wiped all expression from his face. Law had never seen a more vacant stare.

After a little nudging, Josh pressed the heels of his palms to his eyes and fell apart. He'd lost his job to downsizing and his wife to divorce, all in the same week. Bills had stacked up and credit agencies hounded him. He was close to jumping off a bridge.

He had a high school education, but company managers were looking for college graduates. Josh had filled out two hundred applications and no one had called for an interview. He no longer gave a shit.

The three Rogues came up with a solution. Kason wrote Josh a check to clear the foreclosure, which Josh insisted he'd pay back. Risk lined Josh up with a job at Jacy's Java, his wife's gourmet coffee shop. Josh was soon a barista with a cash flow.

Law went for the long-term solution. He helped

Josh apply to the local business college. Once Josh graduated, Law helped him start his own business.

Josh now owned All-Sports Memorabilia. From baseball cards to autographed hockey sticks, he covered every professional sport. He'd become a new man with a bright future.

Law knew several of the professors at the college. The screening process for Prosper was rigorous. Law remained anonymous, no more than a silent partner, while those students who qualified went on to work and repay their loans. Once paid in full, each took ownership of his new business.

Many of the students were in their late thirties to early fifties, all good people with bad credit. Most had faltered under the poor economy and were trying to regain their footing. Law believed in second chances. He became their banker so they didn't have to jump through all the mortgage-lender hoops. They didn't need the humiliation of being denied credit. People deserved their dignity.

He was gratified to have sponsored twenty-two individuals, and he valued each success story.

Stretching now, James Lawless pushed to his feet. He needed to get his mind off Wonder Woman and Prosper and onto the game. The Rogues were currently second in the National League East standings, just behind the Marlins.

A commotion at the locker room entrance drew Law's attention. He glanced up to see the Bat Pack shoulder through the doors. Tight as brothers, third baseman Jesse "Romeo" Bellisaro, catcher Chase "Chaser" Tallan, and right fielder Cody "Psycho" McMillan could power the ball out of the park on just about any given pitch.

Behind the Pack came Kason Rhodes, the Rogues' intense left fielder. Team captain and center fielder Risk Kincaid sauntered in next. Starting pitcher Brek Stryker brought up the rear.

All the men were tough, dominant, and competitive. They owned cocky. Over the past four years, many of them had married. The bad boys of summer had become good husbands. While they kicked ass at the stadium, outside the park they were making babies. They'd soon be family men.

"Anyone have two lines on his pregnancy test?" Psycho asked the room at large. He stood before his locker and rolled his navy T-shirt off his shoulders. The shirt pictured a large white sperm and the words VARSITY SWIMMING.

When the players all shook their heads, Psycho pumped his arm. "Ante up then." He slipped a hundred-dollar bill from his wallet. "It's Psycho Daddy any day now."

Risk Kincaid fished out his own Benjamin Franklin. "My swimmers are faster than yours."

Psycho smirked. "I'm Olympic freestyle, old man, and you're dog-paddling."

Law shook his head. The men were betting on who would get his wife pregnant first. He watched as Psycho collected money from those in the baby pool. Psycho would later deposit the money in a savings account.

Psycho looked at Risk. "You're paying for my son's Harvard education."

"You'll have all girls." Risk's prediction made Psycho shudder. "You'll go to ballet recitals and play with dolls while I attend my son's sporting events."

"Bullshit." Psycho flipped Risk off. "I won't do *Swan Lake* or Barbie."

"I can picture you at a tea party," Romeo said. "A pink boa around your neck, pearl necklace, fake press-on nails."

"Asshole." Psycho shot the third baseman a dark look.

Law stood silently, taking it all in. Times had drastically changed. Not so long ago, the locker room echoed with talk of sports, booty calls, bars, and fast cars. Now fertility was the hot topic. The men were turning OB-GYN. It was weird as hell. Law couldn't wrap his head around the conversation. He had nothing to contribute.

"Boxers drop my stones," Chase Tallan grunted as he shucked his navy polo and jeans. He stood in loose blue cotton. "Jen swears Jockeys hold too much heat."

"You've got to let your boys breathe," put in Psycho, a known nudist. The man had never worn underwear.

Chaser frowned. "My wife drained our hot tub. I'm sworn to cold showers."

First baseman Rhaden Dunn sauntered into the locker room and took up the conversation. "It's abstinence at my house until Revelle ovulates."

Law listened with one ear as the men talked basal body temperature and fertility charting. They were definitely into their women. Brek gave his opinion on prenatal vitamins and folic acid while Romeo and Psycho moved to baby names: Axle McMillan worked for Psycho, but not for his wife, Keely; Romeo favored MacGyver, Mannix, or Magnum. His spouse had pulled the plug on all TV reruns.

Law found it unsettling. He missed the old locker

room rants, rages, and sex talk. Single players were in the minority this season, and he felt odd man out.

"Jacy's grandmother recommended Geritol for getting pregnant," Risk announced.

Psycho stood naked before God and his teammates. "Sounds like an old wives' tale."

Romeo cut Psycho a look. "Bet you're the first to buy a bottle."

Psycho rubbed his stomach. "I'll admit I've had cravings—red licorice and black olives."

The ballplayers looked at him as if he'd lost his mind. Psycho pulled a face and stepped into his jock.

Amid it all, Law sucked air. He'd heard enough. If he listened any longer, his ears would bleed. He looked at Brody, who'd gone as white as the locker room walls. They weren't in the same place as the married veterans. Brody ran free and Law didn't do serious.

The very *thought* of a wife and kids proved the best contraception. Law practiced safe sex. He knew Brody packed Trojans. The kid's wallet bulged with rubbers.

"Ladies, get your ovaries onto the field." Coach Jared Dyson looked pointedly at Psycho as he passed through the room. A barrel-chested man with a tough-eyed stare, he was all baseball. "Hurry the fuck up."

Law ran his hand through his hair and slapped on his baseball cap. He realized he was in need of a cut. His hair was almost long enough to tie back. Team owner Guy Powers never complained about the length of a player's hair, though. He was more concerned about production.

Law nodded to Brody. "I'm gone."

Brody beat him to the door. Both men jogged down the tunnel toward the dugout. The remaining players showed within minutes and started their warm-ups. All thoughts quickly shifted from baby-making to kicking Raptor ass.

One fifteen. Home field, packed house.

A local recording artist sang the national anthem.

The Rogues took the field.

Play for both teams ran clean and competent; neither made mistakes or errors. The only confrontation came during the seventh-inning stretch when the mascots faced off.

That's when Ottawa's Rappy—an enormous bird with a wide wingspan and large, yellow plastic feet— drew a line in the dirt near home plate and dared the Rogues' Rally Ball to cross it.

Rally was a big white baseball with red stitching. The costume's leg- and armholes showcased long red-and-blue-striped sleeves and matching tights. Rally Ball had rolled and belly-butted the bird. Rappy then wing-slapped Rally.

The Richmond fans roared, threatening to pluck feathers. The home plate umpire separated the mascots with a warning of ejection. Both moved to their respective dugouts. Rally Ball glared over his round shoulder and Rappy spiked his yellow middle finger.

Following the disruption, the Rogues came to bat. The players' appearances were punctuated by musical selections. The songs were cranked to the max as the batters moved from the on-deck circle to home plate.

Psycho took his walk to "Crazy Train" by Ozzy Osbourne.

"Rock You Like a Hurricane" by the Scorpions gave Romeo focus.

Van Halen's "Jump" made Chaser's heart pump.

Kason made his statement with "Who Let the Dogs

Out?" by Baha Men. The fans erupted with *woof, woof, woof.*

Psycho managed a single, but the other Rogues fanned air. Richmond again took the field. The game was now the pitcher's battleground.

Brek Stryker was on the mound for the Rogues. Diligent and precise, his ninety-six-mile-an-hour fastball dropped consecutive batters. Profanity and frustration accompanied each Raptor back to the dugout.

Overhead, summer heat stole into May, and the sun bleached the sky white. The players grew hot, sweaty, and irritable over their inability to score.

Psycho punched Romeo and Chaser in the biceps to motivate them. Romeo grunted and Chaser slugged him back. The men curled their lips and narrowed their eyes dangerously. They were mad at themselves for not bringing it. They began to battle harder.

Bottom of the eighth and the Rogues needed a rally. Brody hit fifth in the lineup, followed by first baseman Rhaden Dunn. Law batted seventh.

"Start us off," Law shouted to Brody as the shortstop strutted to the batter's box. "This Is Why I'm Hot" by MIMS blasted from the speakers.

Law pushed off the bench and moved to the railing for a better view. He stood to the left of Psycho, who chewed grape Dubble Bubble. Law was always amazed that Psycho's enormous bubbles didn't pop in his face.

The crowd surged, clapping and stomping. Cries of *Charge!* rocked James River Stadium. The players fed off the fans' energy. Law let the excitement slide under his skin. His heart beat faster; his breath came harsher.

At the plate, Brody batted left. Two practice swings, and then the pitcher laid a fastball over the middle of the plate. The umpire called it a strike, and Brody snarled his disagreement. Rolling his shoulders, he dug in deeper.

Next pitch and Brody knocked a second fastball foul. "Strike!" the umpire repeated.

The count was 0–2 and Brody locked his jaw. Tension set his shoulders. He crossed himself. Twice.

The pitcher delivered a curveball, and Brody crushed it. Law watched as the ball cleared the left-field wall. He pumped his arm. "Airmailed to Plain, West Virginia." Brody's hometown.

The fans jumped, hugged, and shouted their praise. Their applause popped like firecrackers.

Brody rounded the bases and headed home. He bumped knuckles with his teammates and exhaled his relief. The Rogues were up by one.

Rhaden Dunn now took his bat. "Welcome to the Jungle" by Guns N' Roses echoed as he dug in at home. A precise hitter, he kept the rally alive. He smacked a slider over the third baseman's head. His bat splintered, and he was slow out of the box. The base coach held him at first when he should have had a double. Rhaden cursed himself, angry at his lack of speed.

It was time for Law to prove his worth. No player wanted to be responsible for killing a rally. He didn't need the coach ripping him a new one.

He tightened the Velcro on his gloves and adjusted his batting helmet in the on-deck circle. "I Fought the Law" by the Bobby Fuller Four brought him good luck. It had played his first time at bat and followed him over the years. The Ottawa catcher eyed him through his mask, sizing Law up. Law stared him down.

Clarity braced his racing heart. He blotted out the noise and concentrated solely on the pitch. Time slowed as the pitcher went through his windup and powered the ball across the plate. Gripped by the moment, Law's entire body tensed as he connected with a changeup.

Long but not gone, the ball hit the right-field wall, then bounced back and over the outfielder's head. The Raptor recovered the ball and went for the out at second. His throw was on target but weak. Rhaden Dunn took third and Law landed a double. Risk Kincaid next hit a ground ball to the shortstop. He outran the throw to first.

The fans went wild. One run, no outs, and the bases were loaded. The crowd supported pitcher Brek Stryker even after his foul ball was caught by the Raptors' catcher.

One out, two to go, and the Rogues returned to the top of the order: their power hitters. Psycho's triple brought in three more runs. Romeo went down on strikes.

Kason's patience in waiting for the right pitch took him to a 3–2 count. One of the toughest bats in the league, Rhodes drilled a hanging fastball to left center.

Misjudged by the center fielder, the in-between hop escaped him. It was the shortstop who retrieved the ball and fired it home. The catcher mishandled it, and the Rogues added another run to their lead.

Brody again tried to contribute to the score. His rocket-shot to right field didn't clear the wall. The inning closed on his out. The score was now 5–0.

Law grabbed both his and Risk's gloves and went back on defense. The Rogues needed to hold on to their lead.

At the top of the ninth, Ottawa's bats turned hot. It was open season on stealing bases and there were now runners at first and third. The cleanup batter for the

Raptors crunched a curveball over Brody's head, which Kason caught and rapidly fired to Law.

The runner slid headfirst into the base just as Law went low for the tag. Law caught a flash of the hard brim of the batting helmet a split second before contact.

His brow suddenly felt shoved to the back of his head. Stars sparked behind his eyelids and his vision blurred. He blinked against the pain. Through it all, he clutched the baseball tight as he pressed his glove to the runner's shoulder.

"Out!" the umpire ruled.

Disregarding Law's injury, the runner shot to his feet and jogged to the visitors' dugout. Jeers rained down on the Raptor, followed by an uneasy silence as the crowd awaited news on Law's condition.

Distorted vision prevented Law from standing. He was surrounded by two Brody Joneses, two Risk Kincaids, and three Psycho McMillans, which was damn disconcerting. The image of the trainer wavered and the team physician faded to gray. Law closed his eyes against the headache splitting his skull in two.

"Locker room for X-rays," Doctor Provost ordered. James River Stadium had its own high-tech medical unit available for emergencies.

Law squinted against the sun. He blew off the support of the trainer and fought the earth's spin as he rose. He crossed the infield and entered the tunnel. Applause followed him all the way to the locker room.

Once seated on the examination table in the medical unit, he eased off his baseball cap and gingerly massaged his forehead. He felt both a dent and a goose egg. Fortunately, his vision had cleared. His headache, however, had worsened.

After his CT scan, the doctor pressed an ice pack to Law's head. "No skull fracture or brain injury," Provost pronounced. Law exhaled, relieved. Going down for the count was a player's nightmare.

"Take it easy on your day off," the doctor advised as he wrote a prescription for pain meds. "Ice your forehead, and if you have any problems, call my office."

Law took the script, but had no plans to fill it. He had a high tolerance for pain. Sliding off the exam table, he left the medical unit.

Ten minutes passed, and the team carried their win into the locker room. Concern edged their celebration as the players circled Law and took in his injury.

"Lumpy." Psycho tried to touch the bump on Law's forehead, but Law batted his hand away.

"The runner nearly poked your eyes out," Brody protested.

A half inch lower, and the brim could have blinded him. Law shrugged and assured them, "I'll be fine."

Romeo cut Law a look as he moved to his locker. "Make the most of it, bro. If I were you, I'd find a woman for some TLC."

Something to consider, after he met with Zen Driscoll. His little black book was loaded with the names of women who'd willingly tend his wound, then later be his lover. He had two nurses on speed booty call.

Law stripped, snagged a towel and his shaving kit, and took to the showers. No matter how many times a day he shaved, he still had shadow. He moved slowly, fighting his headache until it eased. Inside the shower stall, the hot water steamed like a sauna. He splayed his hands against the white tiled wall and hung his head against the pulsing spray, letting the water wash away his pain.

He had no idea how long he'd spent in the shower, but it must have been a good while. The Bat Pack and Brody Jones were now dressed and sat at a small round table playing cards. Risk Kincaid stood to the side, talking on his cell phone. Several other players milled around. An unusual sight, as the men always left the park quickly, especially following a win.

Romeo cut him a look and grunted, "Damn, you take long showers."

"Jacking off?" Psycho coughed into his hand.

"Hope you're feeling good enough to dress yourself," said Chaser. "If not, I call socks and shoes."

The fraternity of sportsmen. Law dried his hair with a towel as he took in the men. They'd been concerned over his head injury and hung out until he'd returned.

One corner of his mouth curved slightly. "I can manage my clothes," Law assured Chaser.

"What about driving?" The card game over, Brody folded his hand, pushing to his feet. "You need a ride? I've room in my Caravan."

Law doubted there was more than an inch of space in Brody's van. The kid had moved all his possessions to Richmond at the beginning of the season, yet hadn't fully unpacked the vehicle. Brody presently lived in a room above Duffy's Diner in north Richmond. He hadn't set up a permanent residence. He liked living his life on four wheels.

Law met each player's gaze. "I see only one of you—no more double vision." His reassurance released the men.

"Thanks," he added as they filed out.

Psycho turned, pulling a face. "Don't go all mushy on us."

Law appreciated the brotherhood. The Rogues looked out for and protected their own.

He kept his movements even and balanced as he dressed. Steady on his feet and close to feeling his normal self, he finally left the park. Driscoll Financial was his next stop.

A thirty-minute drive later, Law parked his silver Bugatti Veyron on Stonewall Jackson Parkway in the heart of the historic district. Against the soft burnished glow of the late-afternoon sun, the redbrick buildings rose solid and stoic, holding the past in the present.

He cut the engine, released his seat belt, then searched his front pants pocket for a roll of tropical-flavored Life Savers. He peeled back the wrapper and popped an orange one in his mouth. Orange was his favorite flavor. He had a sweet tooth and enjoyed several rolls of candy a day.

Exiting the vehicle, he stood on the sidewalk and took a moment to admire the Bugatti's sleek, racy lines. The car had been a gift to himself, bought with the bonus money from his latest contract, not from his inheritance.

Law never forgot who signed his paychecks. Without fan support, he wouldn't have a job. He took care of those who took care of him. He led a complicated life, balancing celebrity, sports, family wealth, and a personal need for solitude.

He followed in his grandfather's philanthropic footsteps, reaching out to the Richmond community whenever he could. He rang the bell for the Salvation Army at Christmas and volunteered for Special Olympics each summer.

In the evenings, he often sat at the veterans' center and listened to war stories. He donated generously to rehabilitation centers that provided ongoing therapy for those military men and women injured overseas. Team owner Guy Powers praised Law for being so visible around town. But Law didn't do it for good team publicity.

He'd been taught what was right and what was expected of him. Yet the city's warm reception never quite reached his heart. A limousine accident had broken up his family on his eighth birthday. His childhood had died with his parents. Since then he'd shared joys with his team, but never formed any rock-solid bonds with anyone.

Fortunately, sports and his grandfather had kept him alive. He'd never have survived without Randall and baseball.

He flexed his shoulders, rolling the memories back. He next checked his watch, a platinum Panerai that had once belonged to his father. He was fifteen minutes late to his appointment.

He locked the sports car and set the security alarm. Through the passenger window he caught sight of Wonder Woman's Lasso of Truth curled on the floor mat next to a box of athletic shoes and a six-pack of bottled water. He kept the lariat in the car in case his administrative assistant tracked down the owner of the costume. Law had every plan to see the Amazon Princess once again.

He turned and scanned the block before him, noting two familiar businesses. On the corner, a steady stream of customers entered Jacy's Java, a gourmet coffee shop owned by Risk Kincaid's wife. Law was a regular, favoring strong espressos and orange-cranberry muffins.

Two doors south, starting pitcher Brek Stryker's wife, Taylor, owned Thrill Seekers: hardcore adventure tours for the strong of heart. Extreme skiing at La Grave, France, had always appealed to Law. However, the no-risk clause in his major-league contract curbed his adrenaline rush.

He walked to the end of the block and entered Driscoll Financial. The short, dark-paneled hallway and hardwood floor led to a reception area. The room was decorated with style. An ornate gilded mirror reflected all visitors; the wingback chairs were covered in rich burgundy leather. Sconces provided subtle lighting. Scarlet impatiens bloomed in a brass urn. *Forbes, Fortune,* and *Newsweek* were tucked into the magazine rack. *The Wall Street Journal* was folded neatly on an antique tripod table.

Polished and professional, Law thought as he approached the receptionist. Zen Driscoll was thriving after his baseball career. Law was glad to see his former teammate doing so well.

"Mr. Lawless." Ellen French recognized him and smiled her welcome. "Follow me. Mr. Driscoll is expecting you."

She rose from behind her desk and directed Law toward the second door on the right. She knocked twice, then ushered him inside.

Law hadn't been in Zen's office since Zen and his wife, Stevie, had renovated the space. He took two steps over the threshold, turned in a full circle, and stared at the transformation.

He was swimming with goldfish.

Two of the walls had been gutted and now gargantuan Plexiglas aquariums ran the breadth and length of the newly plastered and painted drywall. Fluorescence streaked the water gold. Green gravel and turquoise rocks lined the bottom of each tank. The air pumps bubbled and orange slices bobbed on the surface. Heaters hummed as hundreds of goldfish explored dark caves, castles, and tall plastic plants.

"Black moors, bubble eyes, fantails, shubunkins, commons." Law recognized the different types of goldfish from his own childhood aquarium. "There's even a lionhead."

He was impressed. The tanks were mesmerizing. "Damn, dude, I didn't know you were into goldfish," he said to Zen.

"Not so much me as my daughter." Zen's voice held fatherly pride. "Ellie helped with the renovation, so my office ended up reflecting her fascination with the sea. At age six, she wanted to be a mermaid. At eight, a scuba diver. Now, turning ten, she's leaning toward marine biologist."

In the office of this three-time Gold Glover and All-Star favorite, there were no team photographs, signed baseballs, or trophies. Memories of the Rogues came second to the man's love for his daughter. Family came first. Zen was a damn good father.

"Who cleans the tanks?" Law had to ask.

"The owner of Tropical Fish Mart comes every Saturday morning," Zen informed him. "Ellie helps, too."

Law knew the girl's history. Four years earlier, Risk Kincaid had returned to his hometown of Frostproof, Florida, for a charity weekend of softball and golf. The scheduled bachelor auction was to raise money for parks and recreation.

Risk had brought Zen along for company. Once in

town, Risk had introduced Zen to Stephanie "Stevie" Cole, chairwoman of the fund-raising event. Risk had suggested Zen be auctioned along with himself and the Bat Pack. Zen's protests had been voted down.

The night of the auction, six-year-old Ellie Rosen had carted a wagonload of books to the high school football field and auction site. She lived with her grandmother, following her parents' demise in a car accident. Legally blind, her grandma couldn't share Ellie's love of books. Ellie needed someone to read to her and decided Zen looked smart enough to manage *Green Eggs and Ham.*

With the girl's milk money and a little help from Risk, Ellie had won an evening with Zen. The shortstop and little girl had bonded. Zen traveled to Frostpoof to visit Ellie on holidays and Ellie flew twice to Richmond to visit him and Stevie. Ellie had been the flower girl when Zen and Stevie wed.

The day Ellie's grandmother passed away, Ellie was suddenly alone in the world. There were no living relatives to put a roof over her head. Having considered starting a family, Zen and Stevie adopted Ellie. Both claimed bringing Ellie into their home was the best move they'd ever made.

Law had watched Ellie grow; she'd been raised by a village of Rogues. The ballplayers all claimed her as their niece. The team spoiled her rotten.

"Your daughter's ambitious," Law said.

"She's still an avid reader, a bit shy, and at times too serious," Zen stated. "Losing both her parents and her grandmother by age ten did a number on her. Stevie and I want Ellie to be a kid and not to worry about her future."

Law understood family loss.

He sympathized with the girl.

Zen rose from his chair and rounded his desk. "It's so great to see you, man." The men thumped backs and punched fists in greeting. They were dressed similarly: tailored shirts, sharply creased khakis, and Italian loafers. Zen had loosened his tie, and Law had undone the top two buttons on his white oxford. After years of sharing a locker room, it was easy for them to relax in each other's company.

"I watched the game from the conference room," Zen said. "Rogues looked strong. Nice win, but that was a nasty bump you got. Major sympathy face, pal."

Zen offered Law a chair patterned in navy, green, and gold paisley. They discussed the game before moving on to business. Afterward, Zen pressed the intercom button on his phone. "Ellen, please inform Catherine that Law has arrived."

A stunning blonde soon entered Zen's office. Law stared openly at Catherine in her cobalt-blue blazer and black pleated skirt. Tortoiseshell reading glasses were tucked into the small designer pocket above her left breast. The heels of her black ankle-strapped pumps clicked on the mahogany floor until she hit the Oriental runner. All sound was then absorbed.

She juggled files, a can of orange soda, a Ziploc packed with ice, and a delicate teacup. Her narrow shoulders were squared, yet the sway of her hips was supremely feminine.

Sexy hot genes and a cool demeanor, Law noted as she set the files and white china cup on Zen's desk. She turned with classic grace to face him, her expression concerned.

"James Lawless, meet Catherine May," Zen said. "Cat's my newest associate."

"A pleasure." She greeted Law, her voice low and

hoarse, as if she had a cold. She glanced at Zen, then back to Law. "I heard you like orange soda." She handed him the can and Ziploc. "The ice is for your forehead. Zen mentioned you'd been injured. I'm so sorry."

Sympathy face, and a woman wanted to nurture.

It worked for Law.

"Appreciated." He stood, and accepted the plastic bag. Barely two feet separated them, yet Catherine held her space. She wasn't intimidated by his closeness or his size. He offered his free hand, and she shook it. The lady was as soft as she looked, all silken skin with a light press to her palm. He liked her nails, a natural length with clear polish. He avoided women with acrylic claws. An aggressive lover had once scratched his scrotum. His pain had sent her packing.

Law shifted his stance and studied Cat further. He liked what he saw. Short hair feathered her oval face. Her gaze was deep green and intelligent. A beauty mark sexed up the corner of her right eye. Good genes had blessed her with high cheekbones and a sensual mouth.

Her fragrance was fresh and breezy, lavender and linen. A direct contrast to Wonder Woman's spicier scent.

Their gazes locked and remained on each other too long. Zen blurred in the background. Déjà vu. Law swore he knew her, yet they'd never met. He'd have re-membered Catherine May.

A sexual tug sent his blood south.

His groin tightened.

She took in his mouth and her pupils dilated.

Her lips parted and the lapels on her blazer flut-tered from her indrawn breath.

Air stuck in his lungs, too.

The pulse at the base of her throat quickened.

He could hear his own heartbeat in his ears.

The softening of her features hardened him.

He was about to pop a wheelie.

Zen Driscoll cleared his throat and Cat jumped back.

Law jammed his hands in his pockets to make a discreet adjustment.

Cat's blush belied her appearance of reserve.

His body's reaction stunned him. An odd betrayal, since all his thoughts beyond the game had centered on Wonder Woman. Yet his attraction to Cat hit pure and potent and confused the hell out of him. The two women were complete opposites.

Wonder Woman had dark hair and lush breasts. She'd teased, flirted, and haunted his thoughts. His initial impression of Catherine was one of beauty, brains, and business.

But once they'd checked each other out, he'd felt Cat's heat. Awareness pressed between them like two naked bodies. His feelings for Wonder Woman and Cat split him in half. He was at odds with himself, a first for Law.

"How long have you been with Driscoll Financial?" Law asked Cat. He hadn't seen her when he'd last visited Zen earlier in the year. She had to be a recent hire.

"Four months," Cat responded.

She'd joined the firm in February, Law calculated, around the time the Rogues had headed to Florida for spring training.

"Cat oversees new investment opportunities," Zen informed Law. "She does most of the legwork for the firm."

The lady had great legs, Law noted. The hem of her

skirt hit just above her knees, and she had trim ankles
and sleek calves. Her pumps accentuated her small feet.

Cat angled a chair toward the corner of Zen's desk
and took a seat. Law liked the sweet set of her shoulders and the smooth way she crossed her legs. She
slipped on her glasses, looking poised and professional. Then took a sip of her tea, the aroma man-
darin orange.

Law eased onto his chair, popped the tab on his
soda can and took a long sip. He pressed the Ziploc to
his brow. The ice cooled his libido as well as numbed
his forehead.

Cat opened several folders labeled HAUNT. She then
spread the documents across Zen's desk for everyone
to see.

She looked at Zen, who deferred to her. "Why don't
you run the meeting," her boss said.

And Cat proceeded to do so. She gave detailed accounts of the bank loan, real estate closing, and
profit/loss statements for the upcoming year. Law took
it all in between sips of his soda.

Cat edged the paperwork closer to him. "The cur-
rent owner of the club is ready to move on the deal.
Haunt should prove a solid investment. Once the papers
are filed with the bank and at the courthouse, the club
will be yours."

He reserved a moment to ensure the documents
were in order. All that was left was his signature. Cat
supplied him with a pen.

Their fingers brushed, and the hair rose on Law's
arms, all prickly and electric. The lady had buzzed him.
He was glad he'd worn long sleeves.

"Dan Hatton's pleased to sell you the club," Zen said
once the paperwork was signed. He rested his elbows

on the desktop and steepled his fingers. "Hatton liked the fact that you're single and a professional athlete. He felt your reputation would contribute to Haunt's continued success."

"The club fits my lifestyle right now."

Catherine May was not surprised by Law's response. She'd figured him a major player both on and off the field. His reputation preceded him. Law was known to be edgy, yet at ease in his own skin.

"You're still not following in your family's footsteps?" Zen asked Law.

Law shook his head. "My grandfather's cut me some slack." He looked at Cat, then touched on his background. "I was born to a family of hoteliers, but board meetings, renovations, and expansions bore me. I wasn't made to push papers. I like to push myself physically. Someday I'll take my place beside my grandfather, but not today or tomorrow."

He scratched his jaw. "I'd like to fatten my personal portfolio in the meantime. I saw right away that Haunt had great specs and potential. When I attended the club last night, I found the anonymity a turn-on."

A turn-on. Cat cast him a look from beneath her lashes. He'd been at the club the previous evening, and so had she. In a warehouse that size, they might have passed each other, but she wouldn't have recognized him in costume.

She could picture him as a pirate, medieval Highlander, or musketeer; any character with arrogance and swagger. The swipe of his sword would be long and phallic.

No matter his charade, there was something disconcerting about the lower half of his face—his mouth and whiskered jaw. The strength of his neck and width of his shoulders made her palms itch.

He was a good-looking man with his unruly dark hair, darker eyes, and that smug slash to his mouth. A two-inch scar stood out on his left cheekbone, stark white against his tan. Law combined angular features and *GQ* style. He'd date several women at a time and have many more calling and texting him. Men would imitate him and women would want to be intimate. He was that hot.

Zen leaned back in his chair and disclosed, "I sent Catherine to the club to research the crowd."

Law turned to her. "What's your take on the place?" he asked.

She sipped her tea, choosing her words carefully. She had no reason to mention her past boyfriends and their infidelities. Nor the way she'd walked the darker side of midnight and locked lips and hips with a superhero. She wished to erase the entire evening, yet the images had yet to fade.

The very thought of Captain America tightened her breasts and her nipples poked the satin cups of her bra. A sexual heat spread between her thighs. She pressed her legs so tightly together, she feared a muscle spasm.

She fanned her face with a file folder. "You don't need a PhD in partying to see the club's a success. Haunt was all heated pheromones and sexual intent. A costume and mask release inhibitions. I watched an underworld demon seduce an angel out of her wings."

"A fallen angel." Deep dimples came with his smile. "Santa and a Playboy Bunny hooked up in the parking lot. I saw a court jester getting into a cab with Cleopatra. A horny hula dancer put Humpty Dumpty back together again in the alley."

Law removed the ice-filled Ziploc from his forehead. He swiped his shirt cuff across the drops of condensation, then slowly massaged his brow. His head didn't hurt overly much, but he liked the concern in Catherine's eyes as she worried her lower lip.

Sympathy face. He had one bad-ass bruise.

And Law planned to use it to his advantage.

"How often would you return to Haunt?" he finally asked her. "Would you become a regular?"

Her eyes touched on his mouth, then lifted to meet his gaze. "The club was a novelty, but not a place I'd revisit." She gently rubbed her throat. "I shouted to be heard over the music and still haven't gotten my voice back."

"I'll do my best to convince you to attend Haunt's opening night under new ownership," said Law. "I'd planned to invite the Rogues, Zen, Stevie, and now you, Cat."

It would be one hell of a party, wild and crazy; free and easy. "I'll think about it." That gave her room to decline later.

Zen pointed his finger at Cat. "You'd need a different costume. You mentioned this morning your wig was too tight and the boots gave you blisters. You can exchange yours for something more comfortable. Pay for the lost lasso—"

"Lasso?" Law pierced her with a look that set off internal alarms. A muscle jerked in his jaw. His stare made her blink. "Your costume?" It was more demand than question and his voice held an intensity that shook her.

She felt the unsettling need to protect herself. "Annie Oakley," she lied. Cowgirls carried lassos. "Fortunately, I didn't lose my spurs."

Zen looked at her oddly, but didn't comment further. Law cocked his head, openly trying to picture her in the Wild West. He stared so long and hard he unnerved her. Apprehension hit low. Her stomach started to hurt. She couldn't tell whether he believed her—or not.

Long moments ticked by before he said, "Wonder Woman lost her Lasso of Truth. I found it on the dance floor after she'd left. Once I've learned her real name, I'll return it."

All breath escaped Cat. Panic pulsed and she nearly swallowed her tongue. "You met Wonder Woman?"

Law folded his arms over his chest, crossed one ankle over his knee, and sank deeper in his chair. "I collect vintage comic books, especially the superheroes. I couldn't resist the Amazon Princess."

A dozen men had hit on Cat the previous night: an astronaut had offered her the moon and a Neanderthal had clubbed her. A football player had made a forward pass and a policeman handcuffed her. Cupid had shot her in the ass with a rubber-tipped arrow. She'd ignored them all, up until the Avenger.

Her throat worked as he finished off his soda. "Your costume, Law?" she asked.

"Captain America."

Not what she wanted to hear.

James Lawless had humped her happy.

She'd run from him, believing she'd escaped into the night. Now, in the light of day, he sat beside her, sex in a white shirt and khakis. Temptation snared her as tightly as her lasso.

She fought his pull and swore to take the secret of her costume to the grave.

Chapter 2

James Lawless watched Catherine May's eyes widen.
She looked at him as if he had more than a bump on
his brow, almost as if he'd grown horns. Once he'd informed her that he'd attended Haunt as Captain America, she'd panicked, all round-eyed, parted lips, and
rapid breathing.

Cat clutched her teacup so tightly, Law swore it
would shatter. Her hands shook so badly on her next
sip, tea spilled on her skirt. She didn't even notice.

Something was definitely wrong.

Zen, too, had caught Cat's distress and covered for
her. He returned to the business at hand. "I've asked
Catherine to come up with a list of potential investments for Prosper, too. She's compiled a list of small
businesses, all promising high returns: Give the Dog a
Bone Day Spa, Satin Angels Lingerie, and A Likely
Story, an independent bookstore. Each of them could
prove worth your while."

The companies sounded perfect. Law was certain
the college could find students interested in managing

them. The future was about to prove brighter for three lucky applicants.

Law smiled at the mention of Satin Angels. "The Angels play in the Lingerie Football League." He'd attended several of their games.

Zen nodded. "They took first place last year. Six teams were involved. The players wore sexy nightwear and drew a huge crowd."

The game was a hot destination for Boys' Night Out. It was pure fantasy to watch a female quarterback in a black silk teddy toss a football for five yards. Applause had rocked the Richmond Arena. When the tight end in a soft-pink baby-doll had caught a pass, the men had raised the roof.

Law looked at Catherine, who sat straitlaced, her face inordinately pale. Her detachment bothered him. He tried to draw her back. "Have dinner with me," he suggested. "We can go over the numbers before my tour tomorrow."

Cat's pained expression indicated she'd rather eat dirt than dine with him. *What the hell?*

Zen glanced at Catherine. "Cat missed lunch today," he informed Law. "She'd forget dinner and work late if I didn't push her out the door."

Cat was a workaholic, whereas Wonder Woman liked to party. Law would locate the comic book heroine in due time. Tonight, he'd concentrate fully on Catherine and his future investments. The lady was damn easy on the eyes. A dinner meeting would serve them both well.

"Cat rode the bus to work this morning," Zen went on to say. "Her sister Sarah's SUV was in the shop and Catherine loaned Sarah her Volvo for the day."

"Sarah had a dozen family errands to run," Cat told Law. "She needed transportation more than I did."

"Have dinner with Law and he'll take you home."

Cat waved off Zen's suggestion. "I don't want to impose—"

"Not a problem," Law insisted.

She shifted on her chair. "I live quite a distance—"

"Out of state?" he pressed.

Her face closed as she rose and said, "I'll need to gather the business files." She cleared Zen's desk of the legal documents along with her teacup. Her fingers brushed Law's palm as he handed her the Ziploc full of melted ice. She zapped him once again. His sex stirred, way too visibly.

Catherine caught the play in his pants. Heat colored her cheeks.

Law folded his hands over his groin—too little, too late. He'd pitched his tent. Son of a bitch.

Her shoulders stiff, Cat sidestepped his chair and took her leave. The click of her heels was rapid on the hardwood floor.

Once she'd moved beyond earshot, Zen pursed his lips. "As a favor to me, don't use Cat for batting practice. She's bright, driven, and the perfect associate."

Law dated often and was sexually active, yet he'd never fallen in love. Women retreated fast when he couldn't commit. He'd been called a cold, unfeeling bastard more than once.

An overhand toss and Law landed his empty can of orange soda in Zen's wastebasket against the far wall. "I'll walk a straight line with Cat," he assured his friend. Wonder Woman was a whole different story. Once he found her, it would be lights-out and long nights of sex.

"Catherine's worked with several Rogues," Zen continued. "She has the ability to recognize opportunities before anyone else. Her honesty draws clients. Cat's known for keeping confidences and connecting prime properties with secure investors."

A half smile curved as Zen said, "She's beefed up Psycho's and Romeo's portfolios with strong stock options. Psycho's put his returns into Psycho Choppers, custom-built motorcycles. Romeo's bought into a bagel franchise."

The locker room had buzzed with the players' latest ventures. Law hadn't realized Catherine May had secured their futures after baseball. The lady had skills.

Zen ended their meeting with, "My wife admires Cat and I plan to make her a partner later this year. Keep it professional, Law."

"I've no plans—"

"You were a human tripod," Zen accused.

Shit. "She touched me," he said in his own defense.

"She took your Ziploc." Pause. "Don't take her heart."

"I've no intention—"

Lavender and lilac wafted toward them, indicating Catherine May had returned. Law pushed to his feet, turned, and found her standing in the doorway, her arms piled with files.

He crossed to her. "Let me take those for you."

"I'm capable—"

"I'm polite."

She relented. The transferring of files went poorly. He slipped his hand over the stack and his knuckles brushed the top of her breast. *Soft* crossed his mind as sparks shot between them. She immediately jumped back, leaving Law to juggle the stack. He barely kept the papers from spilling from the folders.

Damn. He looked at Cat; her expression was as flustered as it was frightened. He understood her embarrassment, but what scared her? She appeared to fear him, which was crazy. He wasn't Freddie Krueger.

"Ready to go?" he asked.

"As ready as I'll ever be," she said under her breath.

Outside on the sidewalk, late-afternoon shadows crept across his shoes and up his pant legs. Patterns of light decorated Cat's ankles and calves.

Cradling the files under one arm, Law reached into his pocket for his roll of Life Savers. He offered Cat tropical pineapple. Palm up, she allowed him to roll back the wrapper, then drop the candy onto the flat of her hand. There was no touching this time around.

He popped an orange candy into his mouth as they walked to his car. He pressed the button on his key-chain and opened the passenger door for Cat.

"Let me remove the items on the floor mat," he was quick to say. He settled the folders behind the seat in a small luggage compartment, then snagged the bottled water and athletic shoes. The Lasso of Truth was the last to go.

He caught Catherine's eye as he wound the lariat into a golden loop and slid it in the storage space. She'd bitten down on her bottom lip, raking its full-ness. Her breath rattled as though she was having a panic attack.

"The lasso belongs to Wonder Woman," he attempted to reassure her. "I'm not into whips, chains, handcuffs, or kink."

He sensed that she didn't believe him. He felt her shiver as she slid by. Once seated, she belted in. Law scratched his jaw. He didn't understand her unease. Most women would have laughed off his comment on the lasso, yet Cat kept one eye on the coil as if it were a snake ready to strike.

He rounded the hood and eased in beside her. "Restaurant of your choice?" he asked.

"Someplace quiet where we can spread out the files and talk."

He knew of such a place. His penthouse.

He started the Bugatti and power hummed, raw and untamed. He suddenly found himself as hyped as the engine and incredibly horny. He debated a midnight booty call. A quick text and a willing woman would warm his bed.

The thought died a quick death. Wonder Woman still claimed his brain. And charming Catherine May into trusting him was a priority tonight. Damn, she was distant. Cat needed to chill.

He eased the sports car into traffic and took the long way home through downtown Richmond instead of the interstate. It was the dinner hour and people were congregating at countless restaurants. Couples and groups entered sushi bars and steak houses. Some chose fast food.

Beside him, Cat breathed easier. She'd settled deep into the gray leather seat, her gaze on the city lights and activities. Her profile was lovely, classic, and calm. Wisps of her blond hair curved against her cheekbone and chin. Her hands were folded in her lap, her fingers no longer fidgety. She'd crossed her legs, the hem of her skirt inching up just a little.

The digital clock showed six thirty as he pulled into the underground parking lot of the Richmond Grace, the oldest hotel in the city. There had been renovations over the years, yet the setting still embodied a feeling of pedigree and opulence. Old Hollywood, European royals, and world leaders had passed through its revolving doors. It was *the* place to stay, and reservations were often taken for a week or a month.

Heir to the Grace hotel chain, Law reserved by the year. He had a penthouse suite that encompassed an entire floor. His grandfather resided there, too, in a suite in a separate wing. Heritage allowed Law to live a quiet, private life away from the ballpark. He valued the luxury and escape.

While Randall Burton Lawless would have preferred that his grandson take a more active role in the family hotel business, Law was a physical animal. His high energy and God-given talent for baseball had landed him in professional sports. He'd never regretted his career choice.

To please Randall, Law familiarized himself with the hotels during the off-season. In exchange, his grandfather watched all his games. Randall was a man who understood the value of details. He could discuss any given play with the insight and wisdom of a seasoned veteran. Randall could have been a sportscaster.

No more than a few seconds passed before a valet runner claimed his Bugatti at the guard gate. "No zero-to-sixty on the ramp, Jay," Law reminded the young man.

Jay nodded, shamefaced. "Never again, sir."

Two nights earlier, security cameras had caught the teenager hauling ass on the inclines. Personnel had been ready to fire the kid when Law requested that Jay be given a second chance. The teen was grateful.

Law waited while Jay assisted Catherine from the passenger side. She was all soft scent and fluid grace. Her hair was glossy, her figure gorgeous. Jay had the balls to wink at Law. Law let it pass.

Cat looked around, as surprised as she was anxious. "We're at your hotel."

"Not *my* hotel, but my grandfather's."

"It's all in the family."

"My penthouse is private, quiet—"

"How private?" Her hesitancy was evident.

She didn't want to be alone with him. "We're not on a date, Cat. My administrative assistant will be in his office and a server from the restaurant will remain throughout our meal."

A relieved sigh escaped her as she stepped back, putting six feet between them. Law folded down the passenger seat and retrieved the files. "This way." He motioned for her to follow him.

Catherine May wet her lips nervously. She was set to follow him when her knees locked. She was so stressed and tense that her body froze. How foolish she must look as a human statue while Law proceeded toward a bank of elevators.

James Lawless had appeal, she had to admit. He was tall and solidly built, and she appreciated him even more as a man than as a comic book hero. In retreat, his dark hair hit below his white collar and his tailored shirt stretched starched and taut over wide shoulders. Even after two hours in Zen's office, the creases on his khakis remained knife sharp. He moved with arrogance and pure athletic strut. The man had a really tight ass.

Suddenly realizing he'd lost her, Law returned. He raised an eyebrow, his expression concerned. "Problem?" he asked.

The dilemma lay with her, not him. Law wasn't aware that she'd attended Haunt as Wonder Woman. The fact that they'd rubbed together and caught fire was her secret. She tightened her resolve. She needed his business more than his pleasure.

"My foot fell asleep," she lied, stomping her left one for good measure.

His gaze swept her, checking her out as only a man can a woman, with heat and deep regard. His eyes fixed on her black, strappy pumps. "Still prickly?" he asked.

Her entire body tingled. "Much better now."

She kept pace with him back to the elevators. He punched a code into a wall pad and the double doors parted. She stepped into his world.

Ascending to his penthouse, she took in the polished brass railing that divided the burgundy satin wallpaper from the lower cherrywood paneling. Two leafy potted plants adorned the corners of the lift. An ornate oval mirror on her right cast back Law's reflection. He watched her as she now watched him. Her heart quickened, and she was the first to look away.

The elevator deposited them in an entry hall on the twenty-first floor. The doors glided open and an eighty-pound white boxer barked his welcome.

"Bouncer." Law set the files on a sleek ebony bench, then hunkered down. He was immediately bowled over by the dog. Law rocked back on his heels to keep his balance.

Cat looked on as the energetic and muscular boxer butted his big head against Law's jaw. To Catherine's surprise, the dog started to *bounce*. Slightly bowlegged with springy knees, the dog bobbed like a hydraulic lowrider.

"Cat, meet Bouncer," Law said, introducing them.

Bouncer came to her. He had a prominent underbite, and one tip of his ear bent slightly. Paws planted wide, he gave her his tough-guy stance.

Cat patted his head, and the dog sniffed her knee. She scratched his ear, and he stuck his head under her skirt. The tiny spikes on his collar snagged her panty hose, sending a runner straight to her crotch.

Law was quick to grab the dog's collar. "Be a gentleman." Bouncer dropped onto his haunches. "Sorry about your nylons," he said. "A new pair will come out of Bouncer's allowance."

Cat ran her hands down the black pleats in her skirt. The hole in her panty hose circled her knee. "I'm fine," she managed. "No need to deprive Bouncer of his pocket money."

Law looked down at the boxer. "Bouncer was a rescue dog. I adopted him at Dog Days of Summer, an event sponsored by Brek Stryker."

"I like his bounce," Cat said.

"His documentation showed abuse and neglect." Law rubbed the dog's shoulders. "His previous owners kept him in a cage so tiny, Bouncer barely had enough room to turn around. Bowed knees and hip dysplasia nearly crippled him."

Animal cruelty hurt Cat's heart.

"Poor guy had to have three major orthopedic surgeries to get back to health," said Law. "His birthday's tomorrow. I intended to take him to Give the Dog a Bone. If Bouncer stamps his approval on the spa, I'll consider the investment." He smiled.

Catherine would make sure the boxer got an extra piece of organic cake, a party hat, and a private hydrant to lift his leg on.

"You're home early, sir." A stocky bald man in a navy business suit walked toward them. His lavender tie was brightly decorated with yellow, white, and red balloons.

"Catherine May, this is my administrative assistant, Walter Hastings," Law said.

"A pleasure to meet you," said Walter, his tone formal. Cat shook the man's hand.

"A moment of your time?" Walter requested of Law. "A friend just called to say her date cancelled for a wedding and she asked if I could go with her. I know this is all very last-minute, but would it inconvenience you if I left early this evening?"

"No problem," Law said. "Have a good time."

Cat's stomach sank and she was suddenly short of breath. Walter's early departure would leave Law and her alone until the server arrived with their dinner. She'd have preferred that he stay.

Walter appeared pleased. "Thank you, sir. Before I go, I should brief you on a few things."

"Would you like some privacy?" she asked, uncertain whether she should remain or move down the foyer while the men conversed.

"Stay," Law insisted. "Walter's news isn't top secret and won't detonate as soon as he delivers it."

His reference to *Mission: Impossible* drew a smile to Cat's face. Out of courtesy, she took a step back. Bouncer came to stand beside her. He again sniffed her knee, but didn't rocket up her skirt. She scratched his ear.

Law winked, and his warmth touched her.

The man was physically charged.

Walter cleared his throat before beginning. "Your grandfather and I caught the game. Randall was concerned about your injury. He wished to call the family doctor, but I assured him the team physician was competent. Would you like ice, perhaps an aspirin?" Pause. "Whiskey?"

Cat listened as Law refused all three. "I'm fine. My headache's gone and my vision's cleared." He looked down at Bouncer. "Has he had his walk?"

Walter nodded. "The hotel dog walker took him to Lockland Park. Apparently Bouncer has several play-mates there. According to Alice, he's smitten with a champagne French poodle named Peek-a-Boo Pom-Pom."

Law cut Bouncer a look. "A poodle, huh?"

"Pom-Pom's a registered purebred and impeccably groomed," Walter went on to say. "She's a bit standoff-ish with Bouncer."

"You'll win her over, big guy." Law voiced his confi-dence in the boxer. "We're headed to a doggy day spa tomorrow. A bath, a little T-bone cologne, and Pom-Pom will be chasing your tail."

Bouncer barked as if he understood every word.

Cat silently wished the boxer luck in his courtship.

"Your mail is laid out on your desk," Walter added. "Revelle Sullivan from player promotions called. You have a commercial shoot tomorrow at four at Mazzo Jacuzzis. She suggested you buy a Speedo."

Cat's eyes went wide. She'd rubbed against Law at Haunt. A Speedo would be too small, too tight, for this man. He'd poke out.

"No Speedo," Law said. "I'm going with black board-shorts."

Catherine was aware of Revelle and her affiliation with the Rogues. Zen Driscoll spoke highly of her. Game's On connected players with lucrative ad cam-paigns. Whether promoting car dealerships, dog bis-cuits, or organic cereal, the players built their names within the community as well as worldwide.

Cat was inordinately relieved that Law's commercial

would capture no more than his chest. His very broad, solid chest.

"I signed with Mazzo Jacuzzis for two television commercials," Law explained to her. "The owner, Harold Mazzo, wanted more than the typical ad of a man with blond arm candy, sipping a can of beer. I've tested the Hotsy Twelve, and the heat, blast of the jets, and swirling water revive every muscle after nine innings of play. I had one installed in my personal gym. It's an honest endorsement."

"One final notation," Walter wrapped up. "Revelle sent an e-mail reminder about the Chalk Walk and Great St. James Canoe Race. I posted the dates on your calendar."

Again, Law included Cat. "If you're not familiar with the events, they're both awesome. In late July, the Chalk Walk brings ballplayers together with the community. Fans pay big money to produce colorful chalk pictures alongside their favorite Rogue on the sidewalk in downtown Richmond. We draw on the same block as Driscoll Financial. Viewers donate a few dollars to vote for their favorite drawing. All proceeds go to cancer research."

Law grinned, his dimples deep. "Last year, Psycho McMillan won first prize. He was paired with a college art student. The girl had drawn an intricate Civil War battlefield: officers on horseback, bayonets and cannon fire, fallen soldiers. Psycho managed to color between the lines."

Cat had met Psycho. Macho, handsome, arrogant. He lived to win, whether the competition was chalk drawings or the World Series.

"The Great St. James Canoe Race is a wild time," Law continued. "It's in early September, and the Rogues paddle the river for Homes of Hope, houses built for single mothers. Both events are for great causes. I participate as often as I can."

Walter looked at the boxer. "Shall I schedule a dog walker this evening, sir?"

"Bouncer and I need some guy time," Law stated. "We'll take a jog around the park before bed."

"Be sure to take security."

"I've got Bouncer."

"It will be late and dark when you jog. Randall prefers Maxim and Lynx to be at your side."

Law shook his head. His grandfather would always see him as a kid, no matter his age or accomplishments. He could live with that. The hotel kept six bodyguards on retainer. Many of their high-profile vacationers requested protection.

"Fine," Law agreed.

"Will you require dinner service?" Walter asked finally.

Law deferred to Cat. "Most nights when the Rogues play at home, I have my meals sent up from Beauvais, the hotel restaurant. Chef Amaury prepares both French and American cuisine. My dining room table is long, so you can spread out the file folders. We'll keep it all business."

"Works for me," Cat agreed.

"Shall I place your orders before I depart?" offered Walter, as he shifted his stance, straightening his tie.

"Catherine will need a menu—"

"I'll let you order for me tonight," she assured Law. Walter appeared antsy to leave and Cat didn't want to hold him up further. This was Law's family hotel. He would know the best items on the menu.

"Very well, sir." Walter turned to leave. "Have a good evening."

"Walter—"

The assistant paused with one foot out the door.

"Any word on the lost lasso?"

"I contacted twelve costume shops today," Walter responded. "Unfortunately, no one had rented a Wonder Woman outfit. I'll begin calling again in the morning." With a nod of his head he was gone.

Cat's heart seized. Her disguise had been rented outside the city limits. She'd have to swear the shop owner to secrecy until she could retrieve the Lasso of Truth and return the costume in one piece.

Silence collected, then lengthened between them, broken only by the click of Bouncer's nails on the foyer's onyx marble tiles as the big dog made two circles, then lay down.

"Your assistant appears very dedicated in his search for the owner of the lasso," she finally managed.

Law shoved his hands in his pockets and leaned his shoulder against the wall—a man very low-key and comfortable in his skin. "We've worked together for eight years now. He knows what's important to me and makes it a top priority."

"I'm sure you'll find your Wonder Woman." Somehow she managed to keep her voice even.

"She's not mine," Law confessed. "Just someone I met in costume and would like to meet in person."

Cat purposely changed the subject. "Walter works from your penthouse?" she asked.

Law nodded. "His office is next to mine." He shot her a self-deprecating grin and ruefully admitted, "Early in my baseball career, I employed young, unqualified women. I doubt many knew the alphabet and none could type. They were desk dressing, nothing more. Time and again I missed phone messages, interviews, and business appointments. It was my fault for hiring them, but damn frustrating nonetheless.

"My grandfather finally suggested that I hire a male administrator. Walter's a confirmed bachelor and old enough to be my father. He's a great adviser and organizer. He keeps my life on the straight and narrow."

"Not an easy task." Had she said that aloud? Her cheeks heated.

One corner of his mouth lifted. "I've never been easy to manage, but I have matured over the years."

Matured? She didn't believe him for a second. The man had purchased Haunt, a playground for adult anonymity. Costumes were a sexual stimulus and hormones ran wild. Pleasures stirred the night. He'd have his choice of sexual partners.

Law absently rubbed his forehead, wincing just a little. Pushing off the wall, he offered, "Would you like a cocktail before dinner?"

"I'm not much of a drinker."

"Perhaps a coffee liqueur after our meal, then." He took her arm and drew her down the hallway.

His effect on her was immediate. The warm wrap of his hand above her elbow detonated goose bumps all over her body. Heat flushed her chest and her breathing deepened. Her panties dampened. There was no keeping her cool around this man. She broke contact the second they entered the living room.

Law's penthouse was not what she'd expected. A trio of superheroes protected his space. Batman, Superman, and Aquaman stood larger-than-life and authentically costumed. They looked so real, Cat expected them to greet her.

Tentatively, she touched Batman's hand. "Molded fiberglass?" she asked.

Law nodded. "The statues are very lightweight and easily moved. Tonight they guard the living room, tomorrow Walter will carry them down the hall to his office. He's a fan of comic book characters, too. It's quiet in the penthouse most days. He says the heroes keep him company."

Little boys still lived inside Law and Walter. Cat had grown up with four brothers, all comic book fans. It appeared men secretly wanted superpowers to fight evil. Or perhaps they just liked the masks and capes.

Of the three heroes, she favored Aquaman, ruler of the seas and Atlantis. Cat wasn't much of a swimmer, but she admired his ability to breathe underwater and telepathically communicate with marine life. Who wouldn't admire a hero who could propel himself through the water at high speeds and swim *up* Niagara Falls?

She crossed her arms over her chest and stepped deeper into the room. Known for its Golden Age ambience, the Richmond Grace was decorated with antique furniture, original oil paintings, chandeliers, and Persian rugs.

Law's space, however, was ultramodern, tasteful, and distinctly male. The black marble tiles now glimmered with an inlay of pearl-and-teal abalone shell. He'd updated the living room with black leather sofas, geometric tables, and soft lighting. Clusters of spiral bamboo in enormous tangerine glass vases tapered toward the vaulted ceiling.

A wet bar banked French doors that opened onto a wide balcony. A lover's terrace, Cat thought, where a flowering trellis and thick hedges kept sexual secrets.

On the far wall, two hundred, possibly more, professionally preserved and framed comic books drew her attention. She crossed the room to take them all in. Each one appeared to be in mint condition.

Small platinum plaques at the base of each frame designated the date and issue of each comic. Installed within the wall and attached to each plaque, high-tech sensors alerted hotel security to theft or vandalism. The comic books were to be seen and not touched.

"My brothers loved *The Flash*." She stared at an original 1940 issue.

"I bought that one at auction," Law said as he dropped into a deeply cushioned armchair. Bouncer sprawled at his feet.

Cat wasn't a collector, but she understood the value of each purchase. "Have you always liked comics?" she asked.

"I was born with a comic in my hand." His smile was rueful. "Superheroes inspire me."

She lifted her gaze to a 1962 *Spider-Man* and a 1974 *Wolverine.* She stood on tiptoe to view a comic book separated from the rest, one tucked into the top corner. "Clone Man," drew her smile, and Law's sudden frown.

A local comic strip illustrator for the *Richmond Times-Dispatch* had syndicated "Clone Man" in a twelve-comic series. In the 1980s, a restaurant had opened in the superhero's honor for birthday parties and special occasions, only to later close its doors when kids turned from reading to video games.

"I was lucky enough to attend a Clone Man party."

The memory warmed Cat's heart. "My parents didn't have a lot of money. My brothers, sisters, and I all wanted a Clone Man bash. We collectively agreed to celebrate one big birthday in the summer so my parents could get a group rate and cut the cost of individual parties. We had a blast."

She studied the comic more closely. Dressed in black with a red sparkler helmet and purple cape, Clone Man was a cosmic magician. Thick smoke and his house of mirrors helped him fight crime. His reflection multiplied into a magical army. The bad guys always thought themselves surrounded and outnumbered.

"Did you ever celebrate a birthday at Clone Man?" Catherine knew Law was from Richmond. "You'd have loved it. Our combined birthdays brought my family closer together. We shared, laughed, and my brothers bought Clone Man helmets in the gift shop. My sister and I got a fistful of sparklers and a flexible, wavy mirror that cloned our images. That was one of the best nights of my childhood."

It had been one of the very worst for James Lawless.

Damn, he didn't want this. Didn't need this. Not here. Not now. And not with a woman he'd just met.

A stillness settled over him and tension knotted his neck. Memories hit hard—haunting, vivid, and all too real. He pressed his fist to the hollow spot in his chest. He couldn't catch his breath.

Never in a million years had he expected Cat to recognize the superhero. Most people overlooked Clone Man. Law had purposely hung the framed comic high and nearly out of sight. Its value was minimal to most collectors. Viewers blew by the comic book without interest. Not so with Cat. She'd shared a family celebration far happier than his own.

He was the last man to exchange secrets or confidences, yet Cat's story broke the seal on his past and he slowly bled out.

"Law?" Catherine's voice sounded distant and tinny. He could still see her, but her image was small, as if she stood at the end of a tunnel.

Alarmed, she crossed to him, her fingers fisted in her pleated skirt. She took a chair at right angles to his own. She said nothing, allowing him time and space to pull himself together.

"I'm sorry." Her voice was no more than a whisper. "Whatever I said, did—"

"It wasn't you, it was me." His throat closed. "You shared a great family moment, yet your memories of Clone Man are so different from mine. I've never had anyone look at my collection and immediately pick him out of the crowd. You caught me off guard."

"There's no need to explain." She was giving him an out.

He had no choice. Time folded back, returning him to an event that had shaped his life. Pain gripped tight and his words rose from a dark place inside him. "November sixteenth, twenty-four years ago, I spent my eighth birthday at Clone Man. I'd invited five friends, and my parents and grandfather, Randall, chaperoned our group.

"The party was great and Clone Man did some amazing magic tricks. We were all mesmerized. My parents bought us the latest issue of his comic book in the gift shop as we left. I had something to read on the way home.

"It had snowed all day and ice had accumulated on

the roads." His voice deepened. "Our limousine driver, Carl, had been with the family for forty years. He was cautious on the drive back to the hotel."

Law's jaw worked. "I remember the passenger windows were frosty and the heater hummed. I was seated in the back between my mom and dad, and my friends and Randall were in the front two rows. My grandfather had classic nineteen-thirties carriage lighting installed in the limousine, which gave me enough light to see my Clone Man comic. I began to read out loud. I hadn't finished the first page when headlights hit our windows." He swallowed hard. "Big, blazing, killer headlights."

He blinked, the memory blinding. "It all happened so damn fast. I remember both my parents holding on to me for dear life before I blacked out. I later learned that the driver of an eighteen-wheeler had crossed the median and run into the limo head-on. The limousine slammed into the guardrail, which gave way on impact. We rolled down a ravine."

Law bent forward and drew air deeply into his lungs. "I was knocked unconscious and lost three days of my life. I awoke in the hospital with a broken arm, two fractured ankles, and fifty stitches in my cheek." His words were as scarred as his face. "My grandfather was standing by my bedside, clutching my Clone Man comic in his hand. He wore a neck brace and his face was so badly bruised I barely recognized him. His jaw and chin still bear the scars.

"My very staid and solemn grandfather cried as he told me what had happened. I'd never seen him so sad. We were the only two survivors. Randall was already sixty-two. His wife had just passed away from breast cancer the year prior, and he was still mourning her loss. We needed each other. He brought me to the hotel and raised me."

Law exhaled his pain. "In my eight-year-old mind, I wished with all my heart that I'd been a superhero, that I could've prevented the crash and saved everyone's life. A childish notion, perhaps, but one I held on to for many years."

"Your thoughts were courageous." Cat's words were soothing, a balm to his soul.

He ran one hand down his face. "When family and friends die, those . . ."

". . . left behind question why they survived," she finished for him.

Cat understood. He watched her watch him, and an invisible bond stretched and strengthened, only to snap back, unable to fully form between them. She had peaceful eyes, he noted. Her hand now rested on his forearm, her gentle squeeze supportive. The softness in her expression would ease his sorrow should he seek her solace.

Indecision scraped hard. Cat's recognition of Clone Man had gutted him. He should have stuck to business. He'd never done vulnerable or needy. He refused to do weak. An unguarded moment didn't bind them forever.

In the end, his heart shut down. His feelings went from nice and relaxed to awkward and tense. His insides tightened. He loved sports and sex, and held great respect and fondness for his grandfather. Beyond Randall, he felt nothing for anyone. He had no desire to fix himself. Caring and sharing belonged to men who needed to tap into their feminine side.

Law pushed to his feet and Bouncer stood, too,

always his ally. Law needed to get back on solid ground. "I'm a big boy now." His tone was harsher than he'd intended.

He momentarily wondered if he'd ever been a kid. After the accident, he'd refused to be a burden on his grandfather. He'd grown up fast, maturity and cynicism his closest friends.

"Comics aren't just a hobby," he said. "They're an investment."

Confusion darkened Catherine's green gaze. He'd taken her from confidante to someone he distrusted in thirty seconds flat. Yet her eventual acceptance of his retreat came as easily as her offer of compassion. She rolled with his flow and didn't require an explanation.

"My father saved stamps and collected old coins," she told him. "Two of my brothers horded baseball cards and my sister bought Beanie Babies. Legs the frog and Squealer the pig were handed down to her daughter.

"I've investment clients who showcase vintage guns, steam trains, and amass oil paintings by numerous masters, art never displayed in a museum. Their hobbies remain time insured, just like your comic books."

Once again, Cat seemed to understand. Law went from being angry that she got him to appreciating her support. His throat dry, he crossed to the bar and poured a Tasmanian Rain over ice. Bouncer tracked him, and Law treated him to an ice cube. Law then offered Cat a choice of bottled waters. "Bling, Veen, Equa, what I'm having?"

She went with, "Tap water, no ice."

One corner of his mouth tipped. "No melted glacial ice or water from an aquifer banked by rose quartz?"

"I'm fine with the faucet."

He actually grinned. "You can't tell the difference between bottled and tap, can you?"

She shrugged. "I don't need water in a fancy frosted bottle or one with Swarovski crystals to quench my thirst." She met his gaze as he came to her with a tall glass of tap water. "My yearly bill for drinking water is less than a case of Bling."

"You're a conservative woman," he said.

She cut her glance to the wall of framed comics. "You're a man of means."

"There's a private auction early next week." He surprised himself by sharing the information with Cat. He'd yet to mention it to his grandfather. "I've got my eye on Superman Action Comics Number One, June 1938. There are fewer than one hundred copies in existence."

"Superman ushered in the Golden Age of Comic Books and began the superhero genre," recited Cat. She blushed a moment later and confessed, "I watch *Jeopardy!*"

"Superheroes draw the highest market value," Law added. "Superman is the holy grail."

"Good luck with your auction."

"Do you have a favorite comic?" he asked.

She eased off her chair, the curve of her bottom imprinted on the leather. Catherine May had a very nice ass. She crossed the room and scanned the wall, a woman of grace and sweet hip action.

"I'm a big fan of Howard the Duck," she admitted. "I always found humor in the misadventures of an ill-tempered, talking duck accidentally beamed to Earth by physicist Dr. Jenning."

Law's grandfather favored Howard as well. Interesting.

Cat looked over her shoulder. "Who do you admire most?"

Law didn't miss a beat. "Captain America."

Cat stiffened perceptibly. "You wore his costume to Haunt."

At the memory of the club, his thoughts shifted to Wonder Woman, only to slide back to Cat. She wasn't disapproving of the place, but neither was she in full support. Something about Haunt bothered her. The corners of her eyes pinched with each mention. He'd figure it out, given time.

He'd invited her to a business dinner. They needed to discuss his investments. "Let's order our meal," he suggested.

"I'll have whatever you're having."

The hotel phone sat on an end table beside the leather chair he'd vacated. He picked up the receiver and punched two numbers into the pad. Chef Amaury answered on the second ring and personally took Law's order.

"*Gelée de langoustine, crème d'avocat et crevettes,*" he said. "*Une poêlée de filet de saumon avec du riz sauvage et légumes frais, et gâteau au citron avec le sucre glacis.*" And for Bouncer: "*De boeuf et* kibble *pour mon chien. Merci, et bonsoir.*"

He hung up and turned to Catherine. She looked pale around the lips. "You speak French?"

"German and Italian, too."

"What did you just order?"

He envisioned her thoughts of snails and frog legs and smiled. "I promise your dinner won't crawl or hop across your plate."

Chapter 3

Catherine May's cheeks reddened. James Lawless confused the hell out of her. The man collected comic books and was built like a superhero. He drank designer bottled water and spoke three foreign languages. He played baseball as if his life depended on it. But where was the emotion?

He'd trusted her enough to share a tragic event in his childhood. But as soon as things started getting deep, he'd abruptly severed their connection and escaped within himself. She needed to back off.

It was probably for the best, anyway. After coming completely undone on the dance floor at Haunt, she knew any further involvement would totally mess with her head. If Law could detach and move on, so could she.

She wound her way around the U-shaped sectional sofa and set her water glass on the bar. A short while later an intercom buzzed, announcing room service was on its way up.

Law opened the door to the wait captain and a

second formal server dressed in the hotel's traditional maroon uniform. The server pushed the dinner cart into the foyer, then proceeded down the hallway to the dining room. Law scooped up the stack of file folders as Catherine looked on. She wondered if all his meals were taken so grandly or if he ever made a peanut butter and jelly sandwich for the fun of it.

Law's dining room was formidable. Alabaster wall sconces cast soft lighting on family photographs. The framed pictures showed a happier time in Law's life. Catherine scanned a few of the photos and Law gave her the locations of the shots.

"My grandfather and I traveled holidays and summers after the limo accident," he relayed. "Randall believed life was an education. We cruised Croatia's Dalmatian Coast and later vacationed in Tucker's Town, Bermuda."

He ran one finger around a photo of a luxury cruiser in an oval frame. "Randall named his yacht *Grace* after his late wife. When my grandparents first married, Randall honored Grace by naming his hotel chain after her. Richmond Grace, London Grace, Tokyo Grace, the entire hotel chain evokes her memory."

Catherine found that very romantic. The exotic locations in the photos jumped out at her: Montego Bay, Monaco, Fiji—all billionaire playgrounds. Law's family name entitled him to confidentiality, privacy, and elite status.

Cat's own father had worked two jobs to keep food on their table and a roof over their heads. A long weekend at Virginia Beach had been their biggest family outing. Unable to afford the price of a hotel, they'd camped out. The tents had been crowded, the nightly campfire cozy.

She had two weeks of vacation coming this July. Her only criteria were to travel out of state and be pampered at a spa.

Beside her now, the wait captain slid back her chair, one tufted in black and silver. The table sat twenty, a glossy jet black that reflected her image. She ran her fingertips along the sleek edge.

"African blackwood." Law set down the files, then took his seat at the head of the table. "The wood is prized and primarily used for classic woodwind instruments. I'd admired the blackwood while in Escourt, South Africa. Shortly after my return to the States, the table arrived as a gift from the locals in appreciation of Dig a Ditch."

Cat was familiar with the foundation. Zen Driscoll kept a brochure visible to visitors, and everyone in the office supported the cause. She'd read that Law had spent three off-seasons in the underbelly of third-world poverty. The farmers had been destitute and water shortages had claimed crops. Law had dug irrigation ditches alongside the South Africans.

Their survival had inspired Dig a Ditch. Contributions provided machinery and pipe, and hundreds of volunteers had joined the effort. Many had technical skills; all had big hearts. Law still held a seat on the board of directors, but he'd never taken a bow for the achievement. He claimed it was a group effort.

Catherine admired his modesty. He did what needed to be done without a lot of fanfare.

Once they were comfortably seated, the wait captain discreetly took his position by the door. The server then produced a short, linen tablecloth and triangular-folded napkins. Silverware and wineglasses followed. The covered dishes now lined an antique buffet with warming pans beneath the main entrées.

Catherine wondered about Law's lifestyle. "Have you always lived at the hotel?" she asked.

He nodded. "My grandfather's presence motivates staff and ensures the highest quality of service. Both my parents worked alongside Randall. Hotels and hospitality were in their blood. Penthouse suites provided security and direct access to their corporate world."

"You're very self-contained," she noted. "You have room service, housekeeping, and maintenance at the press of your phone pad."

"My life can be hectic," he stated. "Living here simplifies things. This is what I've always known. There's no reason to change."

Catherine couldn't imagine the permanence of his penthouse. His life might be simplified, but he'd never enjoy the little experiences that touched her life. Washing dishes, doing laundry, and vacuuming all took up precious time. There was, however, something soothing about ironing a blouse and cleaning windows. She gained a sense of accomplishment, even with the smallest tasks. Self-sufficiency provided an independence she valued above all else.

Law's personal life was so different from her own. They connected best on business. She slipped her napkin onto her lap, then withdrew her glasses from the breast pocket on her blazer. The top file folder was in reach, and she flipped it open. Spreadsheets fanned across the table.

Law's deep chuckle drew her gaze. "I bet myself that

I could hold your attention through the main entrée before you turned to business. I lost."

"What did you lose?" Cat asked.

"My self-esteem."

She couldn't help smiling. He knew as well as she did that his self-worth wasn't the least bit deflated. She'd have dinner with him, but wouldn't feed him ego munchies.

The wait captain poured their white wine. "Montra-chet 1979, compliments of Chef Amaury."

The server also took that moment to entice her with the appetizer, a work of art on a fine china plate, which looked too good to eat. "*Gelée de langoustine, crème d'avocat et crevettes,* or mashed avocado in a savory shellfish jelly with shrimp mousse and a marinated prawn."

She savored every bite.

Catherine May was having a culinary orgasm. The sexy slits of her eyes followed by the flick of her tongue as she licked the last of the shellfish jelly from her fork left Law as stiff as a table leg. Wood was not welcome while dining. It distracted from the meal.

Cat caught him looking at her, and she quickly set her fork aside. "The appetizer was delicious."

"The main entrée will make you moan."

"What about dessert?"

"You'll be reaching for a cigarette."

"I have a pack of matches in my purse."

The lady had a sense of humor, Law thought, as the server cleared their first course, then produced the entrée. Cat's eyes went wide in appreciation of Amaury's culinary skills. The French chef would have bowed and kissed her hand.

"Seared salmon, wild rice, and fresh vegetables."

Her relief was evident. "I like fish, but I was afraid it might come with a heavy sauce."

"Amaury creates numerous salmon dishes; some are served with a raspberry brandy sauce and others with dill and butter. I prefer the lighter version." Law cut the salmon with his fork. The fish was perfectly cooked.

Once again, he took inordinate satisfaction in watching Cat eat. Her manners were impeccable, her expression intense. Law could imagine her in bed, when food took second place to physical pleasure.

He liked a woman who could do justice to a meal; someone who knew she wouldn't gain five pounds in the process. So many of his dates were on diets, some as thin as the asparagus on his plate. They'd pick at their meal, eating little.

He'd witnessed starvation in South Africa and hated when food went to waste. Cat was secure in her body. She had a great figure, which he attributed to a high metabolism. Zen claimed she was a workaholic.

"Tell me more about your family," he initiated when the server removed the dishes of the main course.

She took a sip of her white wine and half sighed, half smiled at him. "I'd rather discuss Give the Dog a Bone."

With the mention of *dog* and *bone*, Bouncer trotted into the dining room. He looked from Law to the server, and his tongue made a full swipe of his muzzle. The boy was hungry.

"Beef and kibble?" asked Law, and the boxer started to bounce. Law nodded to the server, and the man set a big bowl of Bouncer-chow at the corner of the antique buffet. The dog dug in.

"*Et gâteau au citron avec le sucre glacis.*" A few minutes

later, the server brought their meal to a close with dessert. "Petite iced lemon cakes."

Cat's restraint in turning to the subject of the doggy spa instead of tasting dessert impressed Law. She'd gone all business even though an internationally famous confection beckoned. He teased her by sampling his own cake, taking slow, small bites and looking blissful. She looked ready to lick his lips.

Catherine gave him the rundown on Give the Dog a Bone for fifteen minutes, ending with, "The owners have wanted to retire for some time. The canine spa is marginally profitable now and income could increase under new ownership."

Her gaze shifted from the spreadsheets to the lemon cakes and Law heard her swallow. "The spa has special events throughout the year," she concluded. "The Bone Hunt at Easter is a big draw, as is Rudolph the Red Dog Reindeer. Dogs wear reindeer ears and a harness and hook up to Santa's sleigh for holiday photos."

Her overview completed, Cat took her first bite of cake. Law swore her eyes glazed with the sweetness. The hotel pastry chef had won more awards and trophies than the Richmond Rogues. Cat didn't say another word until she'd finished her dessert.

"Noir de Noir?" The server offered them a French blend of espresso.

They both accepted. Between sips, Catherine laid out the financial reports on Satin Angels and A Likely Story. Law already knew his way around vinyl catsuits and lace-up bustiers, so Cat concentrated on the bookstore.

"Do you read?" The question slipped out, and she blushed.

"Books, not comics?" he baited. Her color deepened and he let her off the hook. "My library's stocked with biographies and psychological thrillers."

"Your personal library is no doubt larger than A Likely Story," she returned. "The independent bookstore is housed on the first floor of a Victorian house. Small and quaint, it can't compete with the major chains. It's a pet project of mine to find the perfect owner."

Law already had that owner in mind. Her name was Margaret Whittaker. At fifty-two, Margaret had gotten pink-slipped from her previous position in publishing. She'd been an editor at Parker Press for twenty years, only to be replaced by a younger woman with a new vision.

Margaret lived and died books. Depressed and down to her last dime, she'd signed up for several business classes. The professor had brought her to Law's attention as a prime candidate to be a store owner should an opportunity arise. The time was now.

"That's all for tonight." Catherine pushed the papers back into their proper folders and stacked them neatly. She glanced at her watch. "Thank you for dinner. It was amazing. But I should be heading home."

"Do you turn into a pumpkin at nine?" he asked.

"I have a family obligation," was all she'd give him.

He knew he couldn't press her to stay longer. She'd already pushed back her chair and now stood, one hand on her abdomen, a woman well fed.

Law allowed her to escape, just this once. Catherine was smart and savvy and he liked her company. He was surprised that two hours had passed without a thought of Wonder Woman.

Trained in rapid departures, the wait captain and server had the dining room cleared and cleaned in under a minute. Dishes were reloaded on the cart and the two men hit the door seconds before Law and Catherine.

Law carried the files as they caught the elevator and descended to the parking garage. He'd promised Bouncer a late-evening run in the park. The boxer would hound Law if deprived of their usual outing. Law needed to jog off his horniness after he took Cat home.

They picked up his Bugatti and instead of punching in Cat's address on his GPS, Law asked her for directions. She'd gone quiet on him and he liked to hear her talk. Her voice had a soothing, stroking quality like a mental massage. Following her instructions, he soon discovered she lived west of the city, close to an hour's drive.

The suburb, a division of moderately priced homes, hugged the county line. Cat directed him to a cul-de-sac of six houses with postage-stamp yards. Night became day as strings of white sparkling lights lined driveways, hung in trees, and wrapped mailboxes and lampposts, illuminating the crescent curve of the street. Open garage doors and porch lights cast additional lighting.

An enormous barbecue bumped the curb, all rusty and rickety and bent in the middle. Several redwood picnic tables lined the sidewalk. People shouted and dogs barked.

"A neighborhood block party?" He put the car in park.

She shook her head. "My family."

Holy crap. Cat had to be joking. He counted thirty people, only to lose track as the group took note of his Bugatti.

Cat eased out and faced an onslaught of questions. Law sensed the family's closeness and protectiveness as well as a healthy dose of curiosity toward him.

Two young boys pressed their noses to the driver window, their breath fogging the glass. He saw a teenager drop to the ground and slide under the car like a mechanic. Law quickly cut the engine.

Cat cracked the passenger door and asked, "Care to celebrate my nephew's C in algebra?"

All this commotion for a C? Law clutched the steering wheel, his knuckles now white. Crowds seldom bothered him. Rogues fans surrounded him hundreds deep after a game, requesting an autograph. Amid the stadium fanfare, he'd managed to keep his distance. Yet there was something about Cat's relatives, gathered close, all expectant and welcoming, that suddenly suffocated him. He'd always avoided family gatherings. They were too damn personal.

Cat eyed him with understanding. "Too much?" she asked. "We tend to overwhelm."

Law worked to control his breathing, which was as rapid as the beating of his heart. He'd look the fool if he started the engine and hit reverse.

"You don't have to stay." She stretched out her hand, pressing her thumb and forefinger together as if passing him something. Something invisible. "Here's an escape card," she explained. "Use it anytime."

He brushed his fingers against hers as he accepted the invisible pass. Her energy buzzed him. "This works like the Get Out of Jail Free card in Monopoly?"

"Exactly," she said. "Although meeting my family isn't a jail sentence."

"How many relatives do you have?"

"Forty-two show up for special occasions."

"All for a C in algebra?" He couldn't believe it. He'd dated numerous women over the years and never met their families. He now faced a village.

Cat lowered her voice. "My nephew Mike hates school. Last year he cut classes and ran with a rough crowd. He had to repeat the tenth grade. His parents enrolled him in vocational school, where he now takes auto mechanics and works on cars. He's the one under your Bugatti."

Law glanced out his window and saw the toes of the kid's Converse sneakers pointing at the sky. He hoped the boy didn't have a wrench in his pocket. The sports car needed every titanium spring and bolt.

"Five minutes." Law sucked it up and agreed to stay.

Cat pulled back, set two fingers to her lips, and whistled like a man, so freakin' loud she brought the crowd to silence. The lady had lip power. Even the teenager under the car crawled out to listen.

"This is James Lawless," she informed everyone. "He's a Richmond Rogue and a friend of Zen Driscoll's. He's now a client of mine. We worked late and he drove me home. We've had dinner, but he'll join you for a beer. He's got to get home to walk his dog."

Her family accepted his short stay with agreeable nods and eager smiles. Everyone took one giant step back. Law counted to ten and swung his door wide.

"What kind of dog?" A little girl with blond pigtails hopped like a pogo stick.

Cat answered for him. "A big white boxer named Bouncer."

"I have a cocker spaniel named Cookie," the girl told Law as he dipped his shoulder and slid from the vehicle.

His foot had barely hit the pavement when young Mike the mechanic hit Law with, "Dude, pop the hood."

An easy enough request, so Law obliged. The teenager wore a gray T-shirt scripted with DIPSTICK. He rubbed his palms on his torn blue jeans before diving shoulder-deep into the engine. "Bugatti Veyron is the fastest street-legal car in the world." Mike's muffled voice traveled to Law and all those gathered behind him.

Cat's family hovered, as fixated on the boy as on Law's car. Law realized the village was extremely proud of Mike. Their support came in the form of additional questions and lots of praise.

"Speed?" from an elderly man on Mike's right.

The kid looked up and grinned. "Zero to one hundred in two-point-five seconds," he said admiringly. "There's four banks of four-turbo cylinders and a second key required for the Bugatti to reach maximum racing mode. The belly of the beast has a seven-gear ratio and all-wheel drive. The car is so aerodynamic, give it wings, and the fucker could fly."

Mike's curse was overlooked as the village nodded in unison. Law caught tears in the eyes of a woman he determined was Mike's mother. Several older men slapped Mike on the back. The kid knew his cars, Law realized. He could easily be a candidate for Prosper someday.

"How about that beer?" Cat found her way to his

side. "Paul," she called to a tall man with curly blond hair. "Corona longneck for Law."

Paul circumvented the crowd and returned with an iced bottle. No one rushed Law; all eyes remained on Mike and his ongoing discussion of the sports car.

Law found his way to the least populated driveway. Once there, he drew a deep breath. He scanned the yard and bushes, and soon found a pair of beady eyes on him. A black fox? He looked closer. No, a puppy. Its muzzle punched the air and its hackles rose. There was growling.

"That's Foxie So Fine," Cat said as she came to stand beside him. "She's a six-month-old schipperke." Hearing her name, the tailless dog with the foxlike face trotted out. Her ears twitched, alert and curious, and her little black eyes stared a hole in Law.

Cat lifted the dog against her chest. Foxie licked her chin. "She likes to hide in the hedges."

"She was lying in wait."

"Foxie doesn't bite. Much."

Law reached out to pet the pup, only to have her chomp down on his little finger. He felt no pain, but the schipperke wouldn't release him.

"Foxie likes you." Cat seemed surprised. "She's claiming you as one of her humans."

"How many humans does she own?" He tried to ease his finger from Foxie's mouth, but the pup held fast.

"She's my girl, although she favors men," Cat said. "Foxie adores my dad, my nephew Mike, and now you."

"When will she give me back?" Law asked.

"Say 'I'm yours.'"

"You're kidding me, right?" Law was certain Foxie's spiky teeth had now broken skin.

"Say it or stay attached."

Law's jaw worked. He felt damn silly responding to a dog's whim. He swore Cat was playing him. "I'm yours," he finally managed. Foxie unlatched.

"She's small and it's dark," said Cat. "I'm going to put her inside."

She left Law rubbing his little finger.

Eventually, a woman crossed the street to meet him. She introduced herself as Cavanaugh May, Cat's mother. Cavanaugh was as beautiful as her daughter. She could've easily been taken for Cat's older sister. Law's throat closed as he wondered what his own mother would have looked like at Cavanaugh's age, had she survived the limo accident.

"That's quite a bump on your forehead." Cavanaugh brushed her fingers across his brow, a motherly touch.

"Kiss his boo-boo, Grandma," said the little girl who owned the cocker spaniel.

"Not necessary." Law stiffened, suddenly feeling eight and very much alone. Once, at age six, his mother had kissed his forehead when he'd banged his brow on the monkey bars; and again at seven, when he'd slid headfirst into a tree while tobogganing. He didn't need another woman mothering him. "I'll be fine," he assured the young girl.

Cavanaugh studied him for a long moment, as a mother would her child. But Law wasn't her child.

Most mothers were mind readers. Law didn't need her inside his head.

"Make the introductions," Cavanaugh said to Cat on her daughter's return. "Let the family meet James."

Catherine took Law by the arm and made the rounds. Law met everyone from the two twin toddlers,

Amelia and Angela, to their great-grandmother, Eloise.
A woman whose name escaped Law asked him to hold
her infant son for just a second while she dashed to the
bathroom. That second stretched to several minutes.
The blanketed bundle squirmed and grunted. Law was
relieved when the mother returned.

Between names, Law took long pulls on his beer. He
didn't want to be rude, but the welcoming crush from
the village felt like an enormous hug. Law didn't do
hugs. The May family took caring and sharing to a
whole new level.

Their warmth skated along his skin and sought an
opening to his heart. His chest compressed and closed
off his windpipe. He battled for breath.

Throughout his visit, no one asked him about baseball or the Richmond Grace. They treated him like a
regular guy. All conversation centered on Mike and his
C in algebra. The boy was the hero of the night.

The focus on Mike drew memories of Law's own
parents as they'd fostered his education and love of
sports. He might have been born into money, but he
hadn't been spoiled. He'd had chores and earned an
allowance, which his dad presented at Sunday dinner.

His father would make a big deal over Law's accomplishments, however small. Law could still hear the
pride in his father's voice and feel the weight of his
dad's hand on his shoulder—

The sudden pressure on his bicep jerked him back
to the village. A big man with a hard face and direct
stare offered Law a three-fingered handshake. "My
father, Roger," Cat said, introducing the two men.

"Table-saw accident." Roger flexed his hand. "I've
been a carpenter for thirty-seven years."

"Last month, a nail gun misfired and four framing nails shot through Granddad's wrist. He got stitches," a wide-eyed young boy told Law. "He lived to tell about it."

"Impressive," Law managed. These days, he had no such shared family experiences. A dull ache struck, intense and unexpected, and he was suddenly winded.

"Roger fell off a ladder last week." Cavanaugh eyed her husband with concern. "I'm pushing the old man to retire—"

"I still have houses to build," Roger stated.

"Dad built all the homes on the cul-de-sac," one of Cat's brothers—Danny, if Law remembered correctly—supplied. "A house for each of his kids. He wants to keep our family close."

Close felt claustrophobic to Law. He fingered the invisible escape card. He'd give himself one more minute, then split. *Sixty, fifty-nine, fifty-eight.*

"Let's grab you a hamburger." Roger nodded toward the barbecue. "One with the works."

"Another beer?" Danny asked as he took Law's empty.

"You must try the potato salad and baked beans," Cavanaugh insisted. "They're old family recipes."

"Some other time," was all Law could manage.

Catherine May sensed Law's withdrawal. His vibe was polite but restrained, his gaze now shuttered. He'd met every one of her forty-two relatives and now needed his space.

She loved her family and the way they came together as a unit. She also understood that en masse they could shell shock an outsider. James Lawless had outstayed his intended time.

Cat made a show of looking at her watch. "Sorry, but Law has to leave."

Her mother looked disappointed. "Enjoy the rest of your evening," she bade him.

"Stop back again," her father invited.

Law nodded, unable to speak.

Cat walked him back to his car. Mike dragged himself from under the hood and rolled his shoulders. "A wet dream on wheels," he said as he lowered the hood. "Ever drive it full out?"

Law shook his head. "I'd need a racetrack."

Mike's older sister, Mari, jogged over. "Time for dessert. Grandma made your favorite: root-beer-float cake."

"Lame cake," Mike scoffed in front of Law. "I'm not eight anymore."

Cat caught the look on Law's face. Eight was the age he'd lost his parents. His gaze held shadows as he said, "I had Orange Crush cake with raisins at every birthday."

"Shit, man, for real?" Mike stared hard.

Law nodded. "For real."

Cat watched her brother's kids walk away. They bumped shoulders and tried to trip each other all the way to their driveway. Cat was amazed neither took a nosedive.

"How often do you celebrate?" Law found his voice.

"Several times a week," she answered. "When Cassie was potty trained at eighteen months, she was rewarded with Gerber sweet potatoes while the rest of us grilled hot dogs and made s'mores. We splurged on pork chops when my sister Sarah passed her dental hygienist exam. The coals in the barbecue never cool."

Law went quiet as he passed her the invisible escape card. "I appreciate the out."

"You were never fully in."

"I'll meet you at Driscoll Financial tomorrow at ten. I'm taking Bouncer to Give the Dog a Bone. You should bring Foxie, too." Keying the engine, he made a U-turn. The taillights on his sports car were soon lost to the night.

"Law is one fine-looking man." Cat's sister Sarah joined her at the curb.

"He's one hell of a ballplayer." Cat's brother Danny crossed the street with long strides. He held a paper plate with a huge piece of cake. "Had it not been Mike's night, I would have asked for an autograph."

"He has commitment issues," Cat's mom noted as she crossed to her children. "He's the Tin Man."

Law had a heart, Cat knew, yet tragedy had broken him at a young age. He'd closed off the world that had hurt him. She'd hoped her family's warmth might have touched him, yet he'd gone stiff and on guard and never fully relaxed.

"He needs a haircut," Roger May stated as he wrapped his arms around his wife's shoulders.

"I like it long," Cat said without thinking. Her cheeks heated, and she was glad they stood in shadow.

"Sure he's only a client?" her sister pressed.

A flash of Law as Captain America zapped Cat. He had a superhero body and was Rogue hot. The combo fluttered her tummy. "We're all business," she tried to convince both her sister and herself.

Darkness soon snuck across the yards as the families unplugged their outdoor lighting. It was time to call it a night. Cat tracked down Mike, gave him a hug, then headed home. Her house sat on the southern tip of the cul-de-sac, a three-bedroom with wide window seats in the living room, a small gourmet kitchen, and a short back porch with red patio furniture, where she could unwind and watch the sun set.

The fact that her entire house could fit in Law's living room hit her hard.

She also realized that the four tires on his Bugatti cost more than her Volvo.

Their dinner tonight equaled a month's worth of her groceries.

A single vintage Superman comic cost more than she'd make in a lifetime. Perhaps *two* lifetimes.

At the end of the day, she felt no envy or want, only empathy for Law. She had family, and that was priceless.

Chapter 4

Driscoll Financial
Seven AM

Catherine May arrived at the office just as Merry Maids were about to depart. The cleaning team was making a final sweep. Cat didn't expect any of the financiers to show until closer to nine. Zen had left a message on her cell phone. He planned to take Ellie to school, as her science fair project was too big for her to carry on the school bus. The young girl had studied the saltwater ecosystem of peppermint shrimp. Zen didn't want the aquarium sloshing onto the other bus riders.

Cat's first stop was her office. She released a wiggly Foxie from her shoulder-bag mesh carrier. The puppy liked to hide and took refuge under Cat's desk.

She next prepared a pot of rain-forest-nut coffee in her personal Keurig and left it to brew. Returning to the hallway, she heard the front door open and close with a quiet click. It wasn't unusual for clients to drop by early; this man, however, was far earlier than most.

The muted hall sconces left him in shadow until he reached reception. In the harsher light, Cat took him in. She'd seen him before, but only from a distance. The man had been speaking to Zen at the time. A comfortable conversation during which Zen had smiled a lot and the older man had nodded often, as if in approval.

As he now neared Cat, she guessed him to be in his late seventies, perhaps early eighties. His hair was more silver than white and his brown eyes were sharp. His persona was as tailored as his black suit. His walking cane was dapper. He looked regal and rich, a man who could loan King Midas gold. He was that mesmerizing.

"I'm Catherine May," she said.

"I know." The man eyed her speculatively.

That he knew her and she didn't know him was a bit disconcerting. Cat waited for him to continue.

"My name is Rand." Even his voice had polish.

"Did you have an appointment?" She couldn't imagine Zen missing a meeting with this man. He appeared too important.

"I never schedule time. I simply show," he informed her. There was no conceit to his words, merely fact. "I've known Zen for years and consider him family. He's a brilliant financier. Those he employs are at the top of their game. You specialize in asset acquisition. Zen claims you 'have edge.'"

"I'm a woman working in a man's world," she said frankly. "I push twice as hard to prove myself."

"You're very young."

"Age doesn't always bring wisdom."

"You're also quite beautiful and could talk an investor into buying the Golden Gate Bridge."

"Are you in the market for a bridge?"

One corner of his mouth lifted slightly. "I'm in the market for information." He shifted his stance, and Cat caught him leaning more heavily on his cane. He appeared to have a bad knee. "Might we meet for a few moments now?"

"My office is on your left," she offered. "The coffee is hot and the chairs are comfortable."

He nodded, then motioned for her to precede him, a man of gentle manners. Two steps inside, and her schipperke darted out and attacked Rand's cane. The pup believed it to be a large stick. Foxie's sharp little teeth clamped onto the base, and she snarled in her attempt to drag the cane backward.

Not a good first impression. Cat's cheeks heated as she scooped up her dog. Canine pinpricks marred the wood. Very expensive wood. "I'm so sorry," Cat apologized. "I'll pay for a new cane."

"The cane is antique," Rand told her. "The craftsmanship comes from the Italian masters collection. The handle is a horse's head of finely tooled silver; the bottom has a hand-applied horn tip." He pursed his lips, calculating. "You owe me five thousand dollars."

"I'll write you a check."

"No damage done, my dear," he said easily. "The cane now has character."

The man's face had character, too, Cat noted. Crow's-feet fanned at the corners of his eyes and deepened at his mouth. He had a notable scar along his jaw and a shorter one under his chin. He had a tan, but didn't look weathered. He had very few wrinkles. He was quite handsome for his age. He reminded her of someone, but she couldn't place the face. The shared resemblance would come to her.

Clutching Foxie close, Cat returned to her desk and

gently placed the pup in her carrier. The schipperke started scratching at the mesh as if attempting a prison break. Cat quieted her with a dog biscuit.

"Foxie's not usually in the office," Cat explained. "She's taking part in my ten o'clock business meeting. She's only here for a few hours."

A potentially destructive few hours, Cat realized. Foxie had chewed one rubber edge off the floor mat under her chair. The pup never swallowed the items she chewed; she spit it out, all over the carpet.

"Please have a seat." Cat offered Rand any one of the three gray leather chairs before her desk.

He took the one in the middle, facing her straight on.

"Coffee?" she asked.

"Black, please."

She poured a cup and allowed him time to settle in. She took her own seat behind her desk, a horseshoe-shaped workstation built by her carpenter father. The oak had been sanded but left in its natural state. A sheet of pale cranberry glass had been cut for the desktop. The glass cast a rosy glow onto the file folders, calculator, calendar, and note cubes.

Rand took one sip of his coffee and got down to his first order of business. "I expect client confidentiality. Our exchange doesn't leave this room."

Cat nodded, curious now. Zen Driscoll allowed absolute discretion, as long as nothing illegal went down.

"I require the financial status of the Rogues organization," he next stated. "I sit on the board of directors of several banks in the city, but have no connection to Richmond First, the institution that holds Guy Powers's note."

The Rogues. Baseball. He'd gotten her attention.

She sat a little straighter, her thoughts fully on the team. "I have several contacts at the bank," she assured him. "Is the organization in trouble?"

"Serious trouble, if my sources are correct," he said. "I don't want speculation, I want documentation. Contact me with facts and figures only. We'll proceed from there."

"Give me a day or two. I'll see what I can discover," said Cat. "Once I have the particulars, how shall I reach you?"

He drew back his suit jacket and slipped a business card from the satin inside pocket. He set the card on the corner of her desk, facedown. "My private number. You're officially on retainer."

Cat let the card lie. "Were you a sportsman, Rand?" She wondered as to his interest in the professional baseball team.

Again, the curve at the corner of his mouth. "I enjoyed lawn tennis as a boy and the occasional game of croquet."

"May I ask what your primary interest in the Rogues is?"

"Baseball is the all-American pastime."

He'd avoided her question nicely.

Cat let it pass.

"Thank you for your time, Catherine." Rand took a final sip of coffee and rose from his chair. "Tell Zen you've got my situation under control. He need not worry."

Rand moved unsteadily toward the door, his knee once again giving him trouble. "Two knee replacements and I'm still wobbly."

Cat caught his sigh. She offered her arm and he took it. "Are you driving? Shall I call a cab?" she asked.

He shook his head. "My chauffeur is waiting."

They walked down the hallway together, slowing at the door. He released her arm and took a step back. "I trust few people, Catherine May, but there's something about you I like. It's not the fact you earned a perfect score on your SATs in mathematics or that you have a master's degree in economics from Cornell. You have a strong sense of family and solid values. We'll make a good team."

He'd run a background check. "At age twelve, I broke my ankle twice in one year learning to Rollerblade. I've read *Wuthering Heights* ten times. I'm allergic to eggplant." She looked down at her black tank dress and mauve shrug. "I dress conservatively. I have a dental appointment tomorrow at—"

"Six." A final lip twitch. "I know."

Cat held the door for Rand and watched as he hobbled onto the sidewalk. The sunrise cast gold onto his stretch limousine—a lot of vehicle for one man. The driver stood by the curb and was quick to reach his boss. The passenger door opened and closed without a sound.

Catherine leaned against the outside wall and watched the limo pull away. The license plate read RG-1.

A most interesting morning.

She returned to her office and set Foxie free. The schipperke scampered beneath the desk once again. Cat relaxed on her chair and mentally rewound her time with Rand. Their meeting had been short and to the point. The man was a time manager; obviously, he made every second of each day count. They'd made a connection, and she believed him a good man.

Her heart sank at the prospect of the Richmond

Rogues facing bankruptcy, but due to the floundering economy, large corporations were failing all over the country. It was a buyers' market for those who could afford the bailouts. Rand looked like a man with a very large vault.

He also had a strong forehead, sharp brown eyes, and scars. The scars could mean nothing or they could mean a great deal. Surely he couldn't be . . .

Cat reached across her desk and lifted his business card. The cream-colored vellum was high quality, the lettering in bold black script. The three lines stopped her heart.

RANDALL BURTON LAWLESS
PRESIDENT & CEO OF GRACE HOTELS WORLDWIDE
804-555-1111

Her stomach clenched. She'd just done business with James Lawless's grandfather. A man whose financiers had financiers. And he'd said he trusted her. She'd hit high finance, but confidentiality forbade her from telling a soul.

James Lawless and Bouncer swung by James River Stadium on their way to Driscoll Financial. He'd hoped to meet with his grandfather that morning, but Randall's secretary had been quick to inform Law that his employer had left the hotel on personal business. Law would have to catch up with him later in the day.

He'd spent a restless night, his bedsheets twisted around him like a lover. He now had two hours to kill before he met with Catherine May. The previous evening hadn't gone well. Their talk had been all business until Clone Man forced open a window to his past. Cat had caught him at his lowest. That bothered him most. Life after loss sucked. Grief was best left buried. He didn't need her sympathy.

Law parked in the players' lot and lifted Bouncer from the backseat of the black Mercedes GL, one of the hotel's sport utility vehicles. He attached a short lead to the boxer's collar. Dogs weren't allowed at the park, but his teammates snuck in their pets on their days off when they came to work out. Psycho McMillan's Newfoundlands often greeted the Rogues at the door. The dogs were as big as ponies, woolly and drooling.

Law had no plans to lift weights or hit the batting cages. He came for the fraternity. There were times his penthouse felt too large for one person, so he scaled down his day at the stadium. All the players had home gyms, yet no matter the hour, there was always at least one Rogue pumping iron or watching game footage in preparation for his next time at bat.

Law found shortstop Brody Jones, center fielder Risk Kincaid, and first baseman Rhaden Dunn in their workout gear, slumped on benches, all pumped and sweaty. Towels wrapped their necks and water bottles were sucked dry as they took a break, shooting the breeze.

"Bouncer," the men called to the boxer. The big dog nearly wriggled out of his fur in his excitement. Law unclipped his lead and the dog made the rounds, lapping up the attention.

Brody eyed Law. "Scary face, man." The bruising on Law's forehead had spread, now circling both his eyes and inching down his nose. "You wouldn't need a mask for Haunt. You could go as a prizefighter."

Hitting the nightclub was not on Law's agenda. Finding Wonder Woman was, however, and he hoped by the end of the day that Walter would discover her identity. He wanted to meet the real woman.

"Team updates?" Law asked, once Bouncer had returned to his side. The workout room belonged solely to the players. It was a place where truth and fact squelched rumors and speculation within the organization. The coaches and trainers never entered without knocking. Team owner Guy Powers came to the lower level only following a World Series win. He'd been to the locker room four times in the last twelve years.

Risk cut Rhaden a look. "Tell him," he said.

Rhaden appeared uneasy. He was married to Powers's niece, Revelle Sullivan-Dunn, who operated Games' On, the player promotions network. Rhaden was able to inform the team of any major administrative changes long before the memo filtered down from the top.

The first baseman wiped his face and neck with his towel and set his jaw. "Revelle had lunch with one of the comptrollers. Word has leaked out that Powers is late paying his corporate note. Revelle was stunned. According to insider reports, the Rogues were forced to borrow twenty-five million from Major League Baseball two years ago because of a cash shortfall, a loan that MLB tried to keep secret. That came after the club had already exhausted a line of credit with MLB for tens of millions of dollars."

"Powers borrowed heavily to keep the Rogues afloat

as well as to buy real estate," Risk said. "Those loans have all come due."

Law was aware of Powers's investments. The team owner had purchased ten blocks of surrounding properties near the stadium. Last summer, Law had bid against Powers for a family grocery store and lost. The store would have been perfect for one of his business students. Instead, the grocery had been leveled and replaced by a high-rise.

"What about his ex-wife?" Law asked. Corbin Lily owned the Louisville Colonels. Corbin and Guy had a history. They were National League rivals, but still respected each other. Corbin had bailed out Guy on more than one occasion.

"Corbin's stretched thin, too," Rhaden relayed. "She's renovated her stadium and hit salary cap, only to have her revenues drop."

A sinking feeling gripped Law. "What are Powers's options?"

Rhaden didn't look happy. "Speculation only, but come midseason trades in July, he could clear house of all free agents."

Law swore beneath his breath. "That sucks."

Rhaden's jaw worked. "There's also the possibility he could trade the Bat Pack for cash and future considerations."

Law tensed. Psycho, Romeo, and Chaser anchored the Rogues. They were part of the Core Four, which included Risk Kincaid. They'd played fifteen years together and made up the cornerstones of the franchise. It would kill team morale if the power hitters were released. The ticket holders would rise up in protest. The fans would picket the park.

"If Powers sells the team, I'm leaning toward retirement," Risk stated. "I have two good years left, but I won't leave Richmond."

The other players agreed.

"What's the time frame on all this?" asked Law. "Any prospects on new ownership?"

Rhaden shrugged. "Revelle's not certain. Powers was granted an extension. The full banknote is due August first. But Guy wants to act sooner. If he doesn't make the deadline, shit will hit the fan. It's rumored he wants out now."

Rhaden scruffed his knuckles along his jaw. "Investors Gerald Addison and Blaine Sutter have approached Powers over the years, offering on the franchise."

"They own Techno-Air Dynamics," Law said. The CEOs had held their yearly conference at the Dallas Grace over the Christmas holidays. His grandfather had flown down to oversee the event. It had been all wine, dine, and wealth. And major New Year bonuses. "Dynamics builds both commercial and military planes."

"Baseball would be a hobby for them, then," Rhaden said with disgust. "Powers at least played minor league ball. An owner who's never bled the sport can't really comprehend the game."

"How many players are aware of the situation?" Law hoped the problems within the franchise hadn't been aired. He'd have Zen Driscoll work behind the scenes and research outside interest.

"Only us, for now," Rhaden told him. "We play two series out of town next week. There's no need to rile Psycho until we have a few more facts."

Risk agreed. "Psycho would tell Powers where to stick a bat. We don't need the drama just yet."

Law glanced at his watch. "I've got an appointment. I'm gone."

"Where are you headed?" asked Risk.

"I've got a business meeting with Catherine May."

Risk grinned. "Zen struck gold when he hired her. Cat thinks like a man."

Law believed Catherine could play in the big leagues. He hadn't, however, fully separated his personal and professional feelings for the woman. She had him swinging like a pendulum.

Her compassion was genuine and a little too comforting. He didn't want her understanding. Her sympathy unmanned him.

Life was best lived through sports and sex.

He refused emotional intimacy.

Driscoll Financial. Nine forty-five, and Catherine May was leaning against the counter in the break room. She polished off a cranberry-cinnamon muffin from a breakfast tray delivered from Jacy's Java, the gourmet coffee shop on the corner. Jacy was one fine baker.

The abrupt slam of the front door drew Cat's attention down the hallway, where she caught sight of James Lawless and Bouncer. The boxer trailed Law and was obviously well trained. Although Bouncer sniffed every corner, he never lifted his leg to mark his territory.

She wished Foxie So Fine were equally well mannered. Cat had cleaned up twice after the puppy. Fortunately, the accidents hadn't left a stain. Foxie was presently in her office, chewing on a pink Nylabone.

One look at Law, and Cat's insides warmed. He stood at the receptionist's desk and Cat took a moment to admire him. She liked to look at the man from a distance. Up close, the image of Wonder Woman dry humping Captain America came into play. That affected her greatly.

There'd be no repeat of that performance, ever.

Law made clothes look good. His broad shoulders filled out a lavender button-down shirt, and charcoal gray slacks showcased his athletic ass and long legs. A plum-and-gold-checked tie hung loosely about his neck; the Windsor knot rode the third button. She guessed his burgundy loafers to be a size twelve, maybe larger.

Law's stance was stiff, his expression aggressive. His black hair was brushed off his forehead, his profile shaded with bruises. There was a darkness to his mood, as if life didn't sit well.

"You're early," Cat heard Zen Driscoll say from his office doorway. The boxer bounced at seeing Zen, and Zen scratched the dog's ears. "Your boy's put on a few pounds since I last saw him. Bouncer's looking solid."

"He eats well at the hotel."

"Catherine's here, but she has several phone calls to clear before you head out," Zen informed Law.

"Got a minute, yourself?" Law asked Zen.

"Fifteen to be exact, before my first appointment. Come in, have a seat." Zen stepped back, allowing Law and Bouncer to pass ahead of him. He then pulled the door shut, but the lock didn't fully click.

Cat tucked a stack of file folders under her arm and left the break room. Eavesdropping wasn't her style, but she had to walk past Zen's office to reach her own. Her boss had just arrived and she hadn't yet mentioned Randall Lawless. Rand was still her secret.

From behind the door, the men's conversation was

muffled and broken. What she was able to hear left Cat numb.

". . . check this out for me?" from Law.

"I can or Catherine . . ." Zen said.

". . . you or another man, starting today," Law insisted.

"Cat's perfectly capable . . ."

"Old boys' club . . . my choice."

Cat's ears burned. For whatever reason, Law preferred to work with a man. She hadn't a clue why he'd made this decision. She'd done a tremendous job with Haunt, then gone on to line up a small investment tour.

Somewhere between meeting her family and the crack of dawn, he'd suddenly found her lacking.

Old boys' club, indeed. Chauvinist. A woman could research facts as fast as any man. Law hadn't given her a chance. She could outperform any financier in the office, even Zen, on a good day. Randall Burton Lawless trusted her. His grandson, however, didn't.

Defeat smacked hard, and hurt followed. Her hands began to shake. She nearly dropped her file folders. She moved blindly down the hallway, self-pity in each step.

By the time she reached her office, logic set her straight. There was no room for emotion. The investor was all-important to the firm, and she owed Zen her loyalty. If Law wanted to work with a man, she'd bow out gracefully and assign a male associate for today's tour.

She scanned the hallway to see who was available. Justin Strumm's door stood ajar. Justin was old-school, a senior financial adviser who saw today and not tomorrow, and always played it safe. His clients made money, but their investments climbed over decades. Cat, on the other hand, made money for her investors the day they signed with her.

Pressed for time, Cat walked right in. She found Justin of the Jungle, as she privately referred to him, watering his plants. All had animal names: the elephant's ear, monkey flower, and zebra plant. The man had a green thumb and always wore earth-brown suits.

"Can I help you, Catherine?" His smile was patient as he set the watering can on one corner of his desk. Justin openly disapproved of her futurist advice. He often felt she'd gone rogue.

Cat had never lost a client's money. Her gut instinct continually proved true. She forced a smile. "My schedule is jammed today," she said quickly. "I've set up an investment tour for James Lawless—"

"The ballplayer?"

"One and the same." She set the file folders on his desk, sighing for effect in an attempt to appear overworked. "Here are the specs. I need someone to take Law around and close the deals."

Justin fanned through the top folder. "You're very thorough."

She did her best, always.

"We split the commissions?" he asked. "Say sixty-forty?"

"Fine," she agreed. Anything so she could get going.

He pursed his lips. "My day is fairly free. I don't have a client meeting until two o'clock. I'll do you this favor, but you owe me."

Owe him? She'd just given him three significant deals. Unless he screwed up royally, the closings would go smoothly. Justin's commission would allow him to buy the cottage he'd been renting on Cape Cod every summer.

Cat's own commission would go into savings. Her account had matured slowly. She'd yet to decide her own investments because she'd been too wrapped up in her clients to look out for herself. Law had freed up her morning; she had time now.

"I hate to rush, but I have a commitment outside the office." She moved toward the door.

"A word of advice, Catherine," Justin said as she was leaving. "Keep a closer eye on your calendar. It's very unprofessional to overbook clients. Your reputation is on the line. Zen would not be happy."

In this case, Zen would be relieved and Law would be pleased. They now had a man to do a woman's job. She prayed Justin could pull it off. The man could be pretentious.

Quiet yet quick, she cut back to her office. Zen's door remained closed. She secured Foxie in the mesh dog carrier, snatched her purse, then left by the rear exit. The alley wound toward Jacy's Java. Law had cut her off at the knees and Cat needed a strong cup of coffee to boost her esteem.

Jacy's Java was a coffee shop unto itself. Center fielder Risk Kincaid's wife owned the place and operated it with sparkle and finesse. Catherine passed through the red double doors and smiled. Jacy kept her customers amused by changing the eclectic décor often. The most recent shift was from retro to the Roaring Twenties.

Cat took her place in line, then looked around. The 1920s memorabilia took her back in time. Enormous movie theater posters plastered the walls. *The Lost World* hung near the door, the first film version of dinosaurs inhabiting a land that time forgot. Next to it, *The Jazz Singer* featured Al Jolson as Jack Robin. Jack had defied his father to pursue his musical dream. *The Mark of Zorro* was her favorite. There was something about a man in a mask . . .

Captain America wore a mask.

He was a hero best forgotten.

Before her now, a vintage roadside billboard for Burma-Shave, a brushless shaving cream, fronted the counter where the baristas took the customers' orders. The slogan "A beard that's rough and overgrown is better than a chaperone" would have made motorists smile.

Business was booming, and Jacy Kincaid took orders along with her staff. She was easy to spot in her orange, fringed flapper dress and sequined headband with a pink feather. Jacy noticed Cat and waved. "What's your pleasure?" she asked.

Catherine scanned the gourmet coffees listed on a chalkboard above the sliding-glass pastry case. The names all reflected the Jazz Age. She debated between the Spirit of St. Louis, a raspberry-mocha latte, and the Great Gatsby, a double shot of espresso. Frustration forced her into the espresso power boost. "The Gatsby and a cream-cheese muffin." It was a two-muffin day.

Jacy looked at the dog carrier when she rang up Cat's sale. "I don't usually allow pets. Health department rules," she stated. "Take a back table and"—she peeked through the mesh—"no barking."

Foxie held her bark.

Once served, Cat sought a place to sit. Jacy's offered customers unusual seating. There were speakeasy bar stools and tall tables as well as car couches. Parked throughout the shop, seating from original vintage cars offered a new coffee experience. A six-seat cable car accommodated groups.

Car couches from an authentic Packard and a Cadillac touring car were available, as well as the rumble seat from a Ford Roadster. Cat chose the Roadster. The Ford had been cut in half, and only the rear end remained. The exterior gray metal gleamed, as polished as the chrome. The steel license frame held a Michigan plate. Kerosene tail lamps bracketed the back. Steel-welded spoke wheels were anchored to flower-etched linoleum.

Jacy had told Cat the linoleum had come from a farmhouse in central Ohio. Original heel scuffs and tack marks carried the past into the present.

Cat climbed onto the dark-red leather seat, finding it well-worn but comfortable. She placed Foxie's carrier on the floorboard, then set her white mug and muffin on a rectangular coffee table. The photograph on the mug advertised Holcomb's Haberdashery, a store offering the finest in men's flannel suits. Her muffin rattled on a blue plastic plate, and Cat quickly peeled back the festive confetti-printed wrapper.

No one chose to join her on the rumble seat, so Cat took the time to recoup and reevaluate. Her heart remained heavy. Law hadn't given her a chance. She'd given him her best, but apparently that wasn't good enough.

The old boys' club. Elite athletes had a bond. Their sense of brotherhood lasted a lifetime. If Law chose Zen over her, so be it. She had other clients, including Randall Burton Lawless.

The thought of the older man drew her smile as she sipped her espresso, strong, hot, restorative. A bite of muffin, and she moaned. There were magic ingredients in Jacy's recipes. Cat soon felt herself again.

Wide windows allowed her to catch the action on the street. Things started jumping when James Lawless left Driscoll Financial with Bouncer at his side. Law's strides were athletic, long, and purposeful. The sun glistened all around him, marking him a golden boy. Justin Strumm lagged behind, appearing rushed and harried.

"You're staring a hole through my window." Jacy Kincaid crossed the shop to chat with Cat. She leaned an elbow on the window frame of the Roadster and winked. "Bouncer's one fine-looking dog, don't you agree?" she asked, tongue in cheek.

"If you're into muscle and attitude."

"The total package can frustrate a woman."

"Frustrate and hurt," Cat admitted.

Jacy's eyes widened. "What's Law done?"

Cat seldom shared confidences outside her family, but Jacy was here now, and she was known to keep a secret. "He wants to work with Zen or another male associate over me."

Jacy looked confused. "Zen, I can understand. Ballplayers are often as close as brothers. But another male associate? Totally insane. You're the whiz kid at the firm. Zen talks you up every chance he gets."

Cat was as puzzled as Jacy. "I officially met Law yesterday, and we got along well. This morning, he dumped me. I heard Law request a new associate from behind Zen's office door."

"You were spying?" asked Jacy.

"Walking by. Their conversation slipped through

the cracks." She worked her bottom lip. "I played my hand first. I gave him Justin Strumm."

"Justin?" Jacy covered her mouth, fighting a grin. "The man's inflated with his own importance. He and Law will butt heads."

"I hadn't meant for there to be conflict," Cat said. "Justin gets along well with older clients. He was the only one in the office not in a meeting."

Jacy scrunched her nose. "Law's an enigma," she confided. "He's gorgeous, generous, and women love him. The man's got edge."

Edge? Cat blinked. Randall had used the same word to describe her. Maybe she and Law were more alike than either of them thought.

"Law gets down and dirty playing ball, then slips into a tux for social galas," Jacy continued. "He doesn't get serious or share confidences. Most people like to talk about themselves, whereas Law is very private. According to Risk, Law's past is totally off-limits."

Cat took a sip of her espresso. Their discussion of Clone Man had opened Law's childhood wounds. The tragedy remained as raw and painful for the man as it had for the eight-year-old boy. Cat wondered if he'd ever fully coped with the loss of his parents and friends. Or if the pain was so deep it suffocated him. She felt compassion for the man. She also knew he'd never accept her sympathy.

Turning back to the window, she saw Law loading Bouncer into a Mercedes GL. The insignia on the front plate read RG-3. Richmond Grace. The SUV belonged to the hotel.

Law lifted the big dog as if he weighed no more than a Chihuahua. The boxer bounced on the backseat, excited to go for a ride. Law soon settled behind the wheel, and Justin retreated half a block and got into a second vehicle.

"They're taking separate cars?" Jacy questioned.

"They should be riding together," Cat said. "Dialogue is important. Otherwise Justin won't close the deals."

"It appears Law would rather talk to Bouncer," Jacy observed.

The men pulled their vehicles into traffic. Justin drove a Toyota Corolla and tried to stay on the SUV's bumper, only to have two cars cut him off. Justin stopped for a yellow light at the corner, and Law continued on.

Justin hit the gas pedal the moment the light turned green. Catherine had never seen a Corolla take the busy corner on two wheels.

Jacy squeezed Cat's shoulder. "Law's going to realize that choosing a man over you was a big mistake. And by then you'll be busy with other investors."

Jacy soon headed back to the counter. A steady stream of customers were in need of their midmorning caffeine fix.

Cat finished off her muffin and settled deeper in the rumble seat. She'd give herself ten more minutes, then head back to the office. It was time she faced Zen. She'd disappointed him and needed to make amends. She was more than a little irritated with Law for putting her in this position. They'd had no formal closure.

Vintage magazines, newspapers, and journals cluttered the coffee table. She selected *Woman's Home Companion*. The laminated vintage pages of the magazine dealt with family meals. Cat took a quiet moment to read the recipes for chicken à la king and Minute Tapioca.

Her contentment lasted only so long. It broke when the Mercedes returned. Catherine strained her neck, but there was no sign of the Corolla. Law parallel parked, then hopped out. Bouncer followed. She wondered what Law might have forgotten in Zen's office.

He wasn't after file folders, she soon realized. The man was after coffee. Cat dipped her head and fought for control as Law and his boxer strolled into Jacy's Java. Cat swore the dog had the athletic strut of his owner. Given Bouncer's underbite, the dog's jaw appeared as locked as Law's own. The man looked ticked.

Cat was in no mood for a confrontation, but neither did she have a means of escape. She'd only draw attention to herself if she tried to leave. Law was too close to the front door for her to make a clean exit.

"My coffee shop has gone to the dogs," she heard Jacy say as Law neared the counter. "I adore Bouncer, but he can't stay. Coffee to go?"

Law ordered the Gambler, a black coffee. To-go cup in hand, he turned and scanned the crowd. Foxie took that moment to bark, and Law located Cat. The 1920s recording of "When My Baby Smiles at Me" played softly in the background. A corner of Law's mouth curved, but he wasn't glad to see her. The man was all snarl.

Jacy Kincaid looked from Law to Cat, then raised her voice. "Take it outside, you two. No dogs and no arguing in Java."

Catherine's cheeks heated. She never drew attention to herself, yet all the customers now tracked Law and Bouncer as they crossed to her seat. The boxer stopped to sniff the base of a classic Wrigley gum vending machine, then moved on to the back tire on the Roadster.

Law stared down at her. His heat and intensity collected like fire. Her heart squeezed at the sight of his severely bruised face. He was a wounded warrior. He leaned in, lowering his voice. "The coffee shop was your *commitment* outside the office? You chose an espresso over me?"

She hadn't written off their meeting. He'd been the one to sign off on her. "Where's Justin?" She hoped Law hadn't ditched her associate as rudely as he'd dumped her. James Lawless wasn't her favorite ballplayer at the moment.

"Justin doesn't like dogs and refused to ride with me," Law informed her. "Bouncer was offended, so we took two vehicles. Once we arrived at Give the Dog a Bone, the owners' Pomeranian growled at Justin and the man split."

"He deserted you?" Just rewards, thought Catherine.

"He's not a dog person."

Foxie yipped, wanting attention. Bouncer nosed the mesh dog carrier. Foxie snapped, and the boxer drew back. "Don't let her latch on to your muzzle, big guy," Law told his dog. "You'll have to say 'I'm yours.'"

"Bouncer couldn't commit." Cat spoke without thinking. Her reference wasn't lost on Law. It was he who didn't like to commit.

Law went very still.

And Cat's heart slowed.

Time suddenly blurred, and they were the only two people in the coffee shop. The exact same sensation had encircled them at Haunt, then again in Zen

Driscoll's office on their first meeting. They tuned out life to be alone.

"I commit to what's important." Law's words rose raw in his throat. "I take care of my grandfather and Bouncer first, winning baseball games ranks second, and the sexual needs of a woman come third. I do my best to consider other people's feelings and often put them ahead of my own."

The caffeinated boost from the espresso made Cat bold. "Your consideration overwhelms." She kept her voice even. "However, you should have come to me before going to Zen when problems arose between us. I would have tried to fix them."

His gaze narrowed. "What problems? I want to work with you."

"Old boys' club," she said slowly, distinctly.

"That conversation was between Zen, me, and the four walls," he said stiffly.

"The door had ears."

"You eavesdropped?" His expression was pained.

"I passed by Zen's office to get to my own."

"How much did you hear?"

"Enough to know that you no longer wish to work with me."

Law exhaled through his teeth, a low hiss. "You didn't listen long enough, sweetheart. Catching part of the conversation gave you the wrong impression. You're my financial adviser. Zen's doing me a personal favor."

Catherine wondered if Law had voiced the same concern as his grandfather had earlier that morning. Both men had interest in the Rogues. Whispered speculation about the team would cause conjecture.

Quickly, she put everything in perspective. Perhaps

she'd jumped the gun and misjudged him. The fact that he didn't fully trust her bothered her most. She'd get through the tour, then assess their working relationship. She'd take one business at a time.

Shouldering Foxie's carrier, she pushed herself off the rumble seat. "It's Bouncer's birthday. Let's celebrate."

A smattering of applause returned Catherine to reality. She blinked, looked around, and found numerous customers watching Law and her as intently as they would a soap opera. Cat hated public displays.

Could the day get any more embarrassing?

Apparently it could, and Law was the instigator. "I want to replace the pair of panty hose that got ripped last night." His deep voice resonated through the coffee shop. "Satin Angels has great thigh-highs and garters."

The coffee regulars choked and chuckled, some nearly spewing their lattes.

Jacy Kincaid grinned, then waved them off.

Cat wished the linoleum would swallow her whole.

Chapter 5

James Lawless and Catherine May crossed the street to his Mercedes GL. Once again, he hefted Bouncer into the back of the vehicle. "After his surgeries, I don't want him straining his legs," Law told Cat. "He's strong, but I don't take any chances."

Foxie So Fine yipped and whined until Cat placed the schipperke on the seat next to the boxer. Bouncer hugged the door, and the black, foxlike dog remained in her carrier. She was still too close for the big dog's comfort. Foxie barked at Bouncer all the way to the canine spa.

Give the Dog a Bone sprawled on ten acres. Oak trees arched over the entrance road. Law stopped at the guard gate, filled out the visitation forms, and supplied shot records on both dogs. He then pulled ahead.

Fences stretched the length of the driveway leading to the main three-story building, designed as a dog house. Canine trails wound throughout the property and, off to the left, two greyhounds outran a staff member.

Law parked the SUV. He next collected Bouncer and hooked him on a lead. He lifted Foxie's carrier from the backseat. "I've got them both," he said.

The schipperke's excitement rose in shrill yips. The boxer sniffed the air, absorbing every scent. They entered the spa through a bright blue door.

A plump apricot Pomeranian with orange bows at her ears greeted them as if she owned the place. Her owners, Sam and Jane Carter, soon followed. The husband's hands were arthritic and his wife looked frail. Cat had met and chatted with the couple the previous week. She acquainted Law with the Carters and apologized for running late.

"Happy birthday, Bouncer." Jane bent to pet the boxer. "We have three great hours planned in your honor."

The schipperke barked, wanting a piece of the action. "Foxie is Bouncer's party guest," explained Law.

"This is Precious." Sam nodded to the Pomeranian. "She's a party crasher. If treats are being served, she's there."

"Let the fun begin," said Jane. She handed Law a birthday card in the shape of a boxer. Inside, Jane had printed out the canine events.

"I worked out an agenda," said Jane. "The pool is temporarily closed for cleaning. Dogs love to swim, and on your next visit, Bouncer can play Barco Polo. There's always a lifeguard on duty."

The boxer had never dog-paddled, Law realized. Water sports would strengthen his back legs.

"You're welcome to attend each session or you

can sit and enjoy the view from the back verandah," Jane suggested. "There's an obstacle course where dogs test their agility. A German shepherd and a black Lab are running the course now. Our dog walker has the greyhounds, Sammy and Sinatra, out for a stroll."

Law had seen the greyhounds earlier. They'd been racing as if on the trail of an invisible bunny. The dog walker had been left in the dust.

"We'll tag along," Law said, motioning to Cat.

"This way, please." Jane led them down a hallway of dark brown, nonskid industrial tiles. Bone-shaped benches lined the walls. Photographs of the Westminster winners as well as visiting spa pets showcased every breed.

Cat breathed deeply. The cinnamon-scented air was as warm and calming as a tranquilizer. The Every Dog Has His Day grooming station was their first stop. The owners faded left, choosing not to hover as Law observed their staff at work.

Decorated in red-hydrant wallpaper, the room held a wide-screen television, playing *101 Dalmatians*. Once released from her carrier, Foxie ran around the room twice before settling down. Bouncer stood and took it all in, until Foxie clamped on to his muzzle.

Cat looked at Law. "Foxie likes your dog."

The big dog's eyes were wide and a little wild. "Bouncer calls her Jaws," Law supplied with a smile, "but not to her face."

"I'm yours," Cat said on the boxer's behalf. The schipperke was slow to release Bouncer, nipping him twice more.

Cat went on to introduce Law to Lily and Craig, the spa groomers. Craig bathed the big and medium breeds and Lily handled the miniatures. The dogs were treated to HydroSurge baths. "The session provides sore-muscle therapy," Craig explained. "Turns an older dog into a puppy again."

Following the whirlpool, the groomers moved the dogs to large bathtubs and scrubbed them down with tearless citrus-and-vanilla shampoo. Law and Cat stood off to the side throughout the session.

The dogs were dried off with fluffy towels, followed by a blow-dry. They were treated as well as any customer at a beauty salon.

"It's on to the Rubdown Club." Cat drew Law left, into a room painted with canine cartoon characters. Huckleberry Hound, Pluto, Underdog, and Snoopy caught her eye.

"There's Astro from *The Jetsons* and Scooby-Doo, too." Law looked over the artistry. "Mighty Manfred the Wonder Dog was Tom Terrific's sidekick. My grandfather liked Terrytoons."

They took a seat near the back window and looked on as a male masseur alternately gave Bouncer and Foxie a twenty-minute canine massage. Foxie was a little wiggly, but Bouncer immediately rolled over, his tongue lolling out his mouth.

"I could use a massage, too." Law ran his hand inside the collar of his shirt. "My injury at second base left a crick in my neck. I've got a pinched nerve in my shoulder."

"Sorry, I don't do people, only their pets," the masseur said as he eased Bouncer off the table.

Both dogs lay down, relaxed and ready for a nap. The masseur dimmed the lights on his departure. "There's a twenty-minute break before the dog walker arrives. See Spot Run offers scenic trails through the woods."

Law rolled his shoulders and looked at Bouncer.

The boxer was now snoring. "My boy's not in jogging mode."

Cat noted that Foxie was chasing rabbits in her sleep. She also caught Law wincing when he twisted his head from side to side. He had a full business day ahead of him, and he appeared to be hurting. She debated touching him . . .

His bruised face drew her sympathy. "I'll give you a short massage," she offered.

Cat was about to touch him. Law had hinted for her attention, but hadn't expected her to agree. He had access to a masseuse at James River Stadium as well as one at the hotel. Yet a back rub from Cat held far more appeal.

She rose and moved to stand behind him.

He sat up straighter on the bench.

She released a soft breath.

The sound raised more than his blood pressure.

His dick misbehaved.

The deep press of her fingers at the base of his skull made his shoulders slump. Her touch evoked pleasure. He swallowed his moan, afraid it would sound too sexual.

Slowly, expertly, she expanded the circles up and down his neck. She then widened her massage to include his shoulders. She leaned closer, and her breasts brushed his back. She didn't seem to notice, her attention solely on his muscles.

Her scent was lavender and linen, suggestive of sun-dried cotton bedding. Such sheets would tuck in lovers.

His shoulders loosened and his groin tightened. For a slender woman, Cat had strength in her hands. She kneaded, rubbed, and manipulated his muscles with ease. Her efforts affected him far more than Svana, the hotel's Icelandic masseuse. Svana's soothing hands had aroused many men, yet the six-foot blonde never turned Law on.

Cat's touch affected him greatly. He rocked his hips back and exhaled gradually. Bench sex crossed his mind. A slight twist to his right, and Cat could ride his thighs. She'd be on top and in control. Fuckin' A.

He shook himself. A most inappropriate thought at an inopportune moment. Cat deserved his respect. She was more than a quickie at a canine spa. It was too damn public.

He got a grip on his thoughts.

Behind him, Cat flexed her hands, releasing his shoulders. Law was afraid to shift on the bench. He didn't want to shoot her a visual.

She stepped back and asked, "Better?"

"Much better, thanks," he replied.

His shoulders felt relaxed. His groin, however, was anything but.

The dog walker saved Law's ass. The young man knocked twice, then entered and introduced himself as Chad. He gave them a rundown on the wooded trails. Chad chatted with Cat for several minutes, which took her focus off Law. He was slow to pull himself together. He didn't want to hit the trails as a walking erection.

After a discreet adjustment, he stood. Bouncer and Foxie had wakened and were set to go. Foxie again latched on to the boxer's muzzle. This time it was Law who spoke for his dog. "I'm yours," he said. The schipperke backed off.

Law couldn't remember the last time he'd walked

through the woods—if he'd ever taken such a stroll. Chad moved the dogs forward, throwing sticks, jogging, and playing hide-and-seek behind the trees. Foxie and Bouncer were panting after the first mile. They had two to go.

Law fixed his gaze on Cat. Sunlight scattered through the branches and a breeze shook the occasional leaf from the trees. Her cheeks were flushed, her gaze downcast, as she picked her way along the dirt path lined with mulch and wildflowers.

She wore black ballerina flats that looked too delicate for the woods. Her small smile indicated she was happy.

Law enjoyed looking at her. She had both softness and strength; she was blond and gorgeous. Their attraction tugged at his senses, tangible and warming. He found himself more interested in spending time with her than in touring the potential investment properties. At least the businesses brought them together.

He liked Cat. He felt as if he'd known her longer than a day. She was a triple threat: friend, financial adviser, and eventual lover. He knew he'd take her to bed. *When* was the question.

She'd want more intimacy than he was able to give. They would make love, but there'd be boundaries. Lines she couldn't cross. Closeness was beyond him.

It was best to return to business.

He blew out a short breath and second-guessed himself. Maybe he should have trusted Cat to get information on the ball club. Guy Powers's financial situation seemed precarious at best. But Law had known Zen

Driscoll longer than Catherine. Zen was as close as a brother.

He knew Zen could dig deeper than most to discover the financial state of the team. Zen had been a Rogue, while Cat was a stranger to sports. The old boys' club would talk more freely to Zen than they would to an outsider, no matter her beauty.

He slowed his pace and looked on as Chad and the dogs bounded full speed ahead. Bouncer and Foxie rejoiced in their freedom, the boxer slightly in the lead. Law was surprised at how gentle Bouncer was with the schipperke, as she continued to attack his muzzle. The big dog stood patiently until she unclamped. Bouncer tolerated Foxie's mouthing, treating it more like a game than an annoyance.

Cat followed Law's gaze. "They seem to like each other."

"Bouncer's easygoing."

"Foxie doesn't have many friends."

"Could be because she bites."

"They're sweet bites," corrected Cat. "Sadly, my niece's cocker spaniel is afraid of Foxie. My parents' dachshund can't run away fast enough. Griffin's short little legs can't outdistance Foxie. She's just a puppy and wants to play."

"She lacks social skills."

"Bouncer likes her."

"My boy has dubious taste in female dogs," Law said as he leaned back against a wooden fence. He spread his arms along the top rail, hooking his left heel over the bottom rung. "Yesterday Bouncer drooled over a French poodle; today he's chasing fox-face."

"Who do you chase, James Lawless?" Catherine's

curiosity got the better of her. Heat rose in her cheeks
and she worked her bottom lip. She'd crossed the line
between professional and personal, and immediately
wished she could pull back.

He answered before she could apologize. "I don't
chase, but I let women catch me." His grin shot a
dimple deep into his cheek. "I was born with average
looks—"

Cat rolled her eyes. The man was a heartbreaker.

"—a talent for sports—"

He was a two-time Gold Glover and voted by fans to
the All-Star game three years running.

"—I draw a decent paycheck."

Law was the highest paid second baseman in Major
League Baseball. What he didn't earn from sports, he
drew from the Grace hotel chain. He was loaded.

He ran his knuckles over his eleven o'clock shadow.

Cat found she liked a man with stubble.

His hair hung below his collar in the back.

The unconventional length was more masculine
than a shorter cut. Law looked like a rogue.

"I'm lucky to have my grandfather and Bouncer as
my family." His words made her blink. She'd been
openly staring at him.

"I consider my assistant, Walter, a cousin, of sorts,"
he added. "The man breathes business, and when I
can't keep him busy, he works in the administrative
offices at the Richmond Grace. He's formal, but good
with people. My grandfather approves of him. Randall offered Walter a permanent position with the
hotel chain should he leave my employ."

"Has Walter located Wonder Woman?" She hated to
ask, but the question nagged her constantly.

Law shook his head. "Not yet. It's as if the Amazon

Princess vanished into thin air." He raised one hand to shade his eyes against the sun. "Every man has a fantasy. As long as it doesn't interfere with his reality, there's no harm done."

No harm. Cinderella had lost her glass slipper, and Cat had dropped her Lasso of Truth. Prince Charming had found Cindy, yet if Cat had her way, Captain America would never locate Wonder Woman.

She didn't want to think what would happen if Law discovered her comic book identity. He'd want more than a thank-you for the return of her gold lariat.

She'd already ground against his groin for a major orgasm at Haunt. Lying naked with this man would brand her for life. He'd leave a sexual tattoo on her body.

"Who chases you, Catherine May?" Law asked.

She'd had two boyfriends in the past year, both lost to Haunt. They'd taken pleasure in anonymity and played nightly, the last she'd heard. "No one's after me at the moment," she told him. "I'm caught up in my work. I love my job."

Law pinned his gaze on her. "You're the type of woman who needs a man to remind her that she's a woman."

Zen had called her a workaholic. She put in long hours at the financial firm. Success motivated her to work even harder. A fold-out bed, and she could live in her office. She had her own coffeemaker. Jacy's Java delivered breakfast every morning.

"I like my life," she told him. "I leave work early for family celebrations. They keep me grounded. My mom watches Foxie most days. After visiting Give the Dog a Bone, I might enroll Foxie in canine day care. The facility seems well managed. The staff pampers the dogs. Pets can even attend yoga sessions, which provide calmness. Yoga is an indirect way to teach obedience and focus."

"I once dated a yoga instructor and have tried a few poses," he said. "I can't picture your pup doing Surya Namaskar."

She raised a brow and he explained. "That's Hindi for the sun salutation. Foxie's more prone to the corpse position."

"She can do more than lie down," Cat said, defending her pet. "Puppies can be positioned."

"So can yoga teachers."

The *Kama Sutra* crossed Cat's mind. She ducked her head, not wanting Law to read her. His chuckle indicated he knew the direction of her thoughts. She hated when they both had sex on the brain at the same time.

"It's time for the Hard Bark Café." The dog walker had circled back to them. Foxie and Bouncer approached more slowly. They both looked worn-out.

Cat scooped up Foxie and cuddled her close. "Eat?" she asked the pup, and the schipperke perked up. The boxer started to bounce.

They returned to the main doghouse. Sherry, the hostess at the café, settled everyone into a chow-down room. Short benches for the owners bracketed two sides of the low table. The dogs sat on thick plaid cushions. The Bone Appetite menu was displayed on a plastic stand.

Sherry offered everyone party hats, which Bouncer shook off his head three times. He preferred a blue bandanna of distinction around his neck. As his guest, Foxie was fitted with a glitzy rhinestone tiara and collar. The Pomeranian, Precious, walked in with the spa owners, Sam and Jane, and the atmosphere grew festive.

Unaffected by how silly she might look, Cat put on a yellow-and-orange polka-dot hat. The thin rubber strap was short and snapped under her chin.

Seated beside her, Law reached over and traced his finger under the band. His touch was gentle, soothing, and lasted seconds too long.

Cat eased back and Law leaned closer. He cupped her jaw. The edges of time blurred as the curve of his knuckles nuzzled the soft spot beneath her chin. Raising his hand ever so slightly, he brushed his thumb near the corner of her mouth. Sketching higher, he stroked her cheekbone.

He held her gaze.

And her pulse quickened.

A minuscule space separated them.

They shared the same air.

Her mouth parted, and his warm breath slipped between her lips like a tongue. She felt kissed.

His expression was as intense as it was thoughtful.

"The red mark's gone," he finally said.

Bouncer barked, startling Cat. She nearly fell off the bench. Goose bumps scattered down her spine as she clutched the table for dear life. The chin band shouldn't have drawn his touch; it was no more than a slight snap against her skin. Law's concern surprised her.

Her focus again on the party, Cat read along with Sherry as the hostess ran down the dogs' menu. "Bouncer's Pawty Package includes all natural yappetizers. The pups will start with a selection of peanut butter Woofers, cheesy Bark 'n Fetch Bones, and chipped beef treats. The paw print cake is the highlight of the celebration."

Sherry wrapped slobber bibs around the pets' necks, then proceeded with the feast. A photographer passed through their private dining room, snapping shots. He caught Bouncer with peanut butter on his nose and Foxie with her cheeks puffed like a chipmunk. The Pomeranian, Precious, ate all the chipped beef treats.

The photographer motioned Law and Cat together for a shot. Law's arm was around her before she could resist. He pulled her so close, her cheek rested on his shoulder. She hoped the point on her party hat wouldn't poke out his eye.

As the dogs continued to chow down, the pet owners enjoyed an assortment of vanilla and strawberry pup cakes, baked by Betty Crocker. Following the party, the dogs spent thirty minutes in the Chew Toy Room.

Catherine glanced at her watch. They'd spent more time at the spa than she'd intended. It was time to move on. Two other businesses remained on their tour.

Sam and Jane Carter walked them to their SUV. Jane handed Law an UltiMutt gift basket. Cat scanned the goodies: Greenies, pepperoni sticks, and Bark-B-Que chews, along with an enrollment form for the Bone-of-the-Month Club.

Law was generous with his praise of the spa. Bouncer barked his agreement. The boxer looked content but dead on his paws. Foxie still had energy to spare. She refused her mesh carrier, preferring to snuggle beside Bouncer on the backseat. Cat's last look at the two found Foxie latched on to the boxer's muzzle.

"The hotel is closer than your house, and I need to grab my boardshorts, towel, and a change of clothes," Law said as he started the engine. "Let's leave the dogs with Walter. You can pick up Foxie after Mazzo Jacuzzis."

Her stomach squeezed. "I hadn't planned to attend your commercial shoot." Although seeing Law in his swim trunks held great appeal.

"Turnabout is fair play," he said. "I'm touring with you now. Later you can sit in on the promotional spot."

"The tour is business," she reminded him. "The canine spa, lingerie shop, and bookstore are all potential investments."

He cut her a look. "If I buy all three businesses, will you come to the shoot?"

She gave him her full attention. In profile, his dark hair couldn't hide the smug curve of his mouth. "Are you serious?" she asked. "You haven't even been to Satin Angels and A Likely Story yet."

"These walk-throughs are pretty much pro forma," he told her. "You're thorough, Cat. The numbers are solid and I'm fully aware what I'm buying."

"This is too easy," slipped out.

"You'd prefer me difficult?"

"I'm not complaining," she said with a smile. "Each acquisition fits your requirements for Prosper. They're great opportunities for the right small-business owner."

"That's my plan."

Ten miles down the road, Law took a left onto a ramp that merged with the interstate. Traffic was light for a Friday. He checked the rearview mirror often, his gaze flicking to the dogs, assuring their safety.

He parked in the gated garage at the Richmond Grace. While Cat waited in the SUV, he led Bouncer up to his penthouse, carrying Foxie. Cat noticed the puppy had clamped on to Law's forearm. Her schipperke had claimed him once again.

Fifteen minutes later, he returned, a navy nylon duffel in tow. He tossed the bag onto the backseat.

Once behind the wheel, he assured her, "Walter makes a great dog sitter. He took to Foxie immediately."

"Did she claim him?"

Law shook his head. "She allowed Walter to hold her for all of five seconds, then wiggled down. The last I saw her, she was sniffing out the kitchen. She'll get an afternoon snack."

"Foxie will look for a place to hide."

"Then Walter will spend the day seeking her out."

"Your assistant won't get much work done."

Law started the SUV and drove out of the garage. "He's already answered my mail, paid my bills, and laid out my schedule for the next three months. He's put in hours on the phone, calling every costume shop in the city, but has yet to locate Wonder Woman. He's frustrated," Law said as he drove to Satin Angels, which was located in the Westwood Mall. "The man needs a break."

"Maybe the costume was homemade." Cat sought to throw him offtrack. "Or maybe Wonder Woman's from out of town."

"All possibilities," he agreed. "No matter her situation, I will return her Lasso of Truth."

The man was determined.

Cat was even more so. James Lawless would never locate his fantasy woman.

She kept silent for the remainder of the drive.

Westwood Mall stood four stories high, a massive

octagon of glass and shiny steel beams. The stores inside were boutique and high-end. Two supervised playgrounds allowed children to work off steam while their parents shopped. Three movie theaters offered family entertainment.

Law and Cat took the escalator to the second floor. Once there, Satin Angels attracted customers to a corner boutique. The lingerie shop gave Victoria's Secret a run for its money.

French sexiness flirted with innocence in the display window. Against a backdrop of virgin-white sheets, a fuchsia brocade bustier with turquoise garter straps straddled a pair of black silk boxers.

The display was hot, arousing, and quickened Cat's pulse. She'd been in the shop several times over the years, but never accompanied by a man. Entering with Law gave a whole new meaning to temptation and seduction.

The manager, Romely Evans, greeted them at the door. The brunette looked sleek and peek-a-boo provocative in a cutout vinyl catsuit in vivid citrus green. She was the perfect advertisement for playful, flirty, and bedroom naughty.

Catherine introduced Law. Romely didn't shake his hand; instead she skillfully took him by the arm and turned him into the store—his new tour guide. Which was fine by Cat.

While Romely walked Law through the floor plan and inventory, Cat took a moment to look around. Designer fashion seduced in silk and satin, Swiss lace, and glittering gemstones. There were no terry cloth robes or bunny slippers in the shop. The sexy cover-ups were pure eye candy, see-through and meant to entice.

She noted the hosiery, from fishnets to classic black

with rhinestones decorating the back seam. A woman would pull on the stockings and her man would roll them down. The pleasure would be twofold.

"See something you like?" Law came to stand behind her—very close behind her. She was both surprised and relieved he'd returned to her so quickly. Romely seemed more his type, sexy and forward. Willing.

Cat felt small, vulnerable, and unable to breathe with Law at her back. His body heat was tangible, his maleness raw, uncut, carnal. She dipped her head, fighting for nonchalance. "The lingerie is gorgeous, but I've—"

"No one to appreciate it?" His words were as soft as his breath against her neck.

"I could wear it for my own pleasure." Frugal was Cat's middle name. She shopped sales. "Have you looked at the prices?" she asked. "You'd have to wear the same baby-doll every night for a year to justify the cost."

The huskiness of his laugh resonated through her body. "Sometimes it's good to splurge and feel spoiled, sweetheart."

Cat hadn't felt pampered for a long, long time.

"I'm going to buy you something sexy." Law's tone brooked no argument. "You can choose or I'll make the selection."

"There's no reason for you—"

"A man never justifies his gift."

She turned slowly and found herself flush against his big, hard body. *Close* became a new dimension. A breath of air separated them.

Neither stepped back.

Time hazed, and they were suddenly as alone as two people could be, and so into each other nothing else mattered. Attraction laced them as tightly as a strapless corset. Neither could fight it.

"Your favorite color?" he asked.

"Basic black."

He shook his head. "You're not a spinster."

"I like cotton and flannel."

"Fabrics for sleep, not for sex."

"I need six hours of sleep to function."

"Sex invigorates. Plus you wake up happy."

"You weren't smiling this morning." Cat recalled the hard set of his jaw, the tenseness in his shoulders.

"I slept alone."

There'd been more to his angst than he was willing to admit. Catherine didn't push him further.

Law let his gaze drift over her. "You'd look hot in—"

"A peach teddy or maybe a red chemise and matching thong?" Romely Evans's suggestions broke their private moment. She swiveled the hangers for Law's inspection.

"Too flashy," he said. "Cat would look best in teal-green satin, a long nightgown that strokes between her thighs when she walks."

Cat's eyes widened.

Romely sighed, a near-orgasmic moan.

And James Lawless smiled to himself.

He loved to touch. A hot woman in cool satin did it for him. He loved to watch his lovers prepare for bed. He appreciated the tease and anticipation. Ribboned corsets were easy to untie; tiny hooks and eyes frustrated a man. Naked was the goal. The friction of skin on skin climactic.

He wanted Catherine May. If he could have her sexually and without sentiment, he'd go for it. Yet she was a woman who'd mark a man's heart. Once bedded, she'd linger on his sheets and invade his dreams. He wouldn't be able to shake her.

A little flirting went a long way. He'd embrace her with satin. He'd purchase a nightgown so sensual that whenever she slipped it on she'd think of him. That should make for a few sleepless nights.

Romely returned with a long satin nightgown, so sleek and fluid it took on a life of its own. Law knew immediately the gown was meant for Cat. He could picture her in it. From the wispy lace straps and the modest lace inset to the thigh-high slits, the fabric would slide over Catherine's body like a man's hands.

The teal was close to the color of her eyes.

Cat looked awed. "It's beautiful."

"Would you like to try it on?" offered Romely.

She would, but she wouldn't. Law could see Cat's mental debate. He watched as she fingered the price tag, paled, and became all business.

"Mr. Lawless is here to tour the shop, Romely," Catherine reminded the manager. "Thank you, but there'll be no fashion show."

"Pity," Romely whispered as she passed Cat. "One look at you in this gown and he'd be a goner."

Not necessarily a goner, she thought. Law saw her as the type of female who wore long gowns. Such lingerie was sensual, but not strip-down sexy. She bet the women he bedded came to him in skimpy corsets with hot-pink G-strings, or wrapped in short silk robes covering nothing but skin.

"Anything further?" Romely asked on her return.

"Catherine needs panty hose," Law said. "A pair got ripped last night."

Cat wanted to swat him. He made the incident sound as if they couldn't keep their hands off each other and had torn off their clothes, hungry and wild.

Romely's raised brow indicated she thought so, too. "Crotchless?" she asked.

Law smiled, flashing dimples.

Cat contemplated the hosiery display. Innocent or wicked? Should she choose good girl over bad?

Her Wonder Woman alter ego would have gone with rhinestone-seamed thigh-highs and a silver thong with garter straps.

Cat went with practical. "Size small, sheer taupe, seamless toe," she said to Romely.

The manager's expression called Catherine boring. She collected the proper color and size, then gave Cat a last piece of advice. "Slitted is far more fun."

Cat wandered the store as Law took his sweet time at the cashier's counter. She couldn't tell if he was hitting on Romely or if the manager saw him as fair game. Either way, Cat remained patient while he wrapped up the sale and met her at the exit.

He passed her the gold gift bag tied with multicolored ribbons. "Your panty hose." His gaze was warm, his grin easy.

"Thank you." She appreciated his gesture. "We've one last stop before your commercial shoot. A Likely Story is in a Victorian house on the outskirts of town."

The bookstore welcomed its customers onto a wide verandah with a long row of white wicker rockers.

Confederate jasmine scented the air, the white blossoms bursting on privacy hedges.

The store's recent face-lift included a fresh coat of gray paint. The shutters were a bottle green.

The owner, Luella Fern, bore the frail air of a tragic heroine from a Jane Austen novel. Her hair was pale blond and styled to take ten years off her age. She wore a brown shirtwaist, accented by a pearl choker.

Cat noticed Law took great care when shaking Luella's blue-veined hand. He didn't want to squeeze her fingers too tight. The lady looked as if she could be easily broken.

"Feel free to look around," Luella told them once they'd entered the foyer. "The bookstore's on the lower level and I live upstairs. There are a few customers in the Tea Room, and I need to check on them." She hurried off.

Rooms opened off a hallway of dark hardwood floors. New and used books were displayed on shelves as well as mobile carts. Heavy velvet curtains were pulled back to allow streams of sunlight through the sheers.

Cat followed Law through the converted living room into the drawing room and on into the library. He moved on, and she remained.

The spacious Victorian house offered hardback and paperback best sellers as well as gilt-edged, leather-bound classics. Vintage magazines were stacked in large wooden bins. The sign tacked to the side read YOUR CHOICE, $1.00.

The container smelled musty and a spiderweb festooned one corner. Cat dove in anyway, feeling like a kid at Christmas.

An 1895 volume of *Puck*, one of Joseph Keppler's

Victorian USA lithographs, caught her eye. Issued weekly for a dime, the humor magazine depicted colorful cartoon characters and political satire. There were water stains on the back pages, yet Cat recognized something old, rare, and valuable when she saw it. She set the copy of *Puck* aside and dug deeper into the bin.

She scanned both a *New Yorker* and *Life* magazine from the late 1930s. An assortment of vintage comics were buried at the very bottom. She retrieved all seven. *Annie Oakley* and *Millie the Model* made her smile. *Firehair* brought romance to the pioneer West.

Several of the pages on *Blue Bolt* were dog-eared. The cover on *Human Torch* had faded. Someone had drawn mustaches and devil horns in Magic Marker on a 1965 *X-Men*, a classic devalued.

Catherine stared in disbelief at the final comic in the stack: *Captain America #1*. She had no idea of its worth, but she knew the boy in Law would totally freak. She stood still, clutching the comic close until he returned to the library.

Crossing the room, he soon nudged her with his elbow. "I'm ready to go. This place has potential and personality. Let's close the deal."

Catherine nodded, barely able to breathe. She wanted to jump up and down and wave the comic in his face. Instead she played him, just a little.

The recent panty hose incident was still fresh in her mind. She hadn't fully forgiven him for allowing people to think he'd ripped the stockings off her.

She nodded toward the bin. "Can I borrow a dollar? I left my purse in the SUV and I have something I'd like to buy."

No hesitation on his part. Out came his wallet and a

George Washington changed hands. He looked at her curiously. "What did you find?"

A drum roll would've been nice, but the wild beat of her heart sufficed. Ever so slowly, she turned the vintage comic toward him. She wished she'd had a camera to capture his expression.

He blinked, his jaw dropped, and it took a full minute for his shock to wear off. When she handed him the comic, he was a kid again.

His elation zapped her. The room was electrified.

Law handled the comic with the care given a newborn. He was soon deep into the issue and evaluating the comic cover to cover. "This is the find of a lifetime," he said. "An unrestored copy in near-mint condition."

After several minutes, he carefully closed the comic. "This issue depicted a believable villain in Adolf Hitler, and Captain America gave evil a well-deserved punch in the face. The menacing Red Skull makes his first appearance as does Bucky Barnes, Cap's sidekick."

Catherine clasped her hands. "I'm so glad you're pleased."

"Pleased?" His voice was deep, husky. "I'm out of my head, sweetheart."

His gratitude came with a spontaneous hug. He held her lightly, yet with enough strength that she couldn't pull free.

His appreciative kiss surprised them both.

Against him, Cat flushed with his warmth. The muscles in his back contracted as her curves brushed the hard planes of his body.

She inhaled, and he exhaled.

They breathed breast to chest.

Memories struck where their hip bones bumped.

His body was solid, strong, unforgettable.

Seconds ticked, expectant and significant.

Daunting for him.

Damning for her.

His angular features shifted from enthusiastic boy to mature man. He looked at her as if he was trying to place her but couldn't. He grew confused.

She couldn't take her eyes off him, this nonconformist with his long hair and inky brown eyes. His jaw worked, the scar on his cheek prominent.

He had that male x factor that turned women on with no more than a look. He was staring at her now.

She inhaled the cedar-and-lime scent of his soap, the starch in his cotton shirt, and all that was James Lawless. His strength was indefinable, his body inescapable.

He was momentarily hers.

The walls, bookshelves, wooden bins, and Captain America lost clarity as Law bent for a second kiss.

The man was a master. The initial slant of his lips, the light flick of his tongue made a woman want more.

Much, much more.

He coupled with her mouth with the fierceness she'd experienced at Haunt.

She kissed him back with the desire of Wonder Woman.

It was Law who broke their kiss.

Law whose eyes honed in on her mouth.

His breathing was raw, his recognition sharp. "I know your kiss."

Startled, she stepped back and hit her hip on the corner of the wooden bin. She rubbed the soon-to-be bruise.

"You couldn't possibly." There was no way she was

acknowledging what had happened at Haunt. "We met yesterday at Driscoll Financial."

"Kisses are like fingerprints—no two are alike."

He was scaring her now. "There have to be similarities."

He shook his head. "You could blindfold me and have every past lover kiss me. I'd recognize each one, as far back as sixth grade."

Panic squeezed Cat hard. The floor seemed to shift, and she clutched the wooden bin for balance. A lick to her lips found them warm and swollen. She tasted him on her tongue. "You're mistaken. Perhaps in sleep—"

"You're more than a wet dream," he said, cutting her off. "Lips don't lie, sweetheart. I've kissed you."

Chapter 6

Law couldn't take his eyes off Cat. He kept staring at her mouth—so soft, sweet, and responsive. She'd kissed him with want and need, then grown fearful.

Her nerves now ruled her. She'd backed into the wooden bin, then gone on to take out a table. If she wasn't careful, she'd soon be walking into walls.

She glanced around for the nearest exit, only to realize she'd have to pass him to reach the door. Her sigh was audible.

Cat was hiding something.

He was damn curious.

"The comic." She handed back the dollar she'd crushed in her hand when they'd kissed. "You'll need to pay Luella."

Law allowed her the change of subject, for now, anyway. He pocketed the wrinkly, somewhat sweaty bill. "I'll owe her six figures once the comic is appraised."

"Luella's in the Tea Room." Cat directed him down the hall, then took off ahead of him.

Law was slow to follow. He watched her retreat.

She couldn't walk fast enough.

Déjà vu. The sensation was sketchy and just beyond his grasp. He couldn't put his finger on Cat's pretty pulse, yet her heartbeat was a part of him. Of that he was certain.

He'd kissed her.

It was all about the when and where.

That would follow.

The Tea Room had cleared out. Only Luella Fern sat at a round parlor table, catching her breath. She welcomed them with peach lemonade, water biscuits with cream cheese, and ladyfingers with raspberry preserves. She looked at his comic book and asked, "You like Captain America?"

"He was a childhood hero," Law admitted as he took a seat across from her. "This is a first edition and quite valuable."

Luella's surprise crinkled the corners of her eyes. "My nephew tossed the comic in the bin years ago. I'd forgotten it was there."

Law was grateful Cat had unearthed it.

The older lady bit daintily into a water biscuit. "It's worth more than a dollar?"

"Much more," said Law. "The sale of your bookstore will make for a nice retirement in Richmond. The price of this comic would buy a beachfront condo in Florida."

Luella smiled at him. "I do like warm weather. I have a sister in Vero Beach."

Law would make sure she was set for life.

He looked at Catherine, who sat next to him, perched on a parlor chair, ready to bolt. She worried her bottom lip with her teeth, again and again. Law wanted to kiss her still. He knew the more he kissed her, the quicker he'd know who she was to him.

"Catherine will draw up the papers and deliver a check for the shop," Law told Luella. "Once I have an expert opinion on Captain America, I'll send additional payment."

Luella patted his hand. "You're a good and honest young man," she praised him. "Anyone else would have bought the comic for a dollar and never shared its true value." She smiled at him. "My long-deceased husband was a Baltimore Orioles fan. I also enjoy baseball. After today, I'll be cheering for the Rogues."

Law pulled out his wallet and extracted his business card. "If you ever want to catch a game, call my assistant, Walter Hastings. He's good for tickets."

A glance at his watch, and Law realized he was running late for his commercial shoot. He'd promised Harold Mazzo that he'd arrive by three fifteen for the four o'clock shot. It was already three forty. Law hated to be late.

He pushed to his feet, only to have Luella wave him back down. Rising herself, she moved to an antique desk and slipped a manila envelope from the drawer. "For your comic," she said.

Law was appreciative. Captain America might have been buried at the bottom of the bin for several years, but the fewer fingerprints on the cover the better.

Every time he looked at Cat, his palms began to sweat.

She turned him on without trying.

Standing now, he again shook Luella's hand with

great care. She walked them to the door, quite chatty as she planned her move to Florida.

Once outside, Cat took to the stairs and sidewalk as if her panties were on fire. He wondered if she wore a thong. After their trip to Satin Angels, his bet was cotton bikini.

Law caught up with her at the curb. He purposely took his time unlocking her door. He leaned in, brushing against her twice. She jumped both times, barely able to catch her breath.

The lady was fidgety.

His own dick twitched.

He took her by the shoulder, then turned her toward him before she could climb into the SUV. He had her backed against the front seat. Mere inches separated them.

Her hands fluttered, landing on his forearms. She squeezed so hard, she pinched him. Law stayed close. "We have another two hours together," he reminded her. "I don't know what's wound you so tight, but you need to exhale, woman."

"I'm not wound," she said to his tie.

"You're as tight as a clock about to cuckoo."

The release of her breath warmed the cotton of his shirt between the third and fourth buttons. She was still squirmy, so he moved even closer.

He tipped up her chin, forcing her to look at him. "I have a theory about kissing," he shared. "It defines a person. A man prefers passion over passive. You"— he ran his thumb across her lower lip—"gave me tongue in the library."

Her cheeks flushed. "We were caught up in the excitement of Captain America. That's all."

"If Cap does it for you, I'll have a comic around all the time," he said. "I know we've kissed before, Catherine. Time will tell me when and where, and then we'll return—"

She'd never go back to Haunt. "You're fantasizing," she rushed to say. "Get real, Law. If we'd kissed, I'd admit it. Nothing's gone down between us."

Lady had the jitters. She'd also lied like Pinocchio. She was hiding her past from him. He'd be digging deep to discover her secret.

He cupped her chin with one hand and held her steady. Her eyes went wide as he lowered his mouth to hers. A hovering kiss with more breath than lip. A tease, a taunt, a tickle of warning, and he let her go.

She dove onto the passenger seat and her black tank dress twisted high on her thighs. Her mauve shrug slipped off her shoulders, baring her collarbone. She looked disheveled, uneasy, and ready to hop from the vehicle at the first stop sign.

He planned to press the security locks.

Law saw what Cat didn't. Their attraction was just heating up. He had her right where he wanted her, about to jump out of her skin and into him. He'd catch her.

Cat felt caught. Law had rubbed against their past and was close to recognizing her. She should have done a happy dance at finding Captain America but never locked lips. His hug and kiss had been spontaneous and explosive. She hadn't expected the gesture to mean so much, yet the soft coax of his lips sparked a dangerous French kiss. One reminiscent of Haunt.

On the outside, she held it together.

Inside, her nerves were frayed.

She was a total basket case.

In two hours, they'd part ways. She'd collect herself then. A hot bath would help; a pint of Ben and Jerry's Cherry Garcia and life would return to normal.

Tomorrow, Law would travel with the team to Atlanta for a three-game series, then it was on to Miami. He'd be gone for ten days. And she'd reclaim her peace.

Cat adjusted her seat belt three times on the way to the commercial shoot. The strap went from too binding to too loose, then wrapped her waist instead of her hips. She broke two fingernails fiddling with the metal buckle.

Housed in a large warehouse, Mazzo Jacuzzis was the hot spot for gurgling bubbles and jets of water. Inside, steam hung in the air like the Amazon jungle. The mist dampened Cat's skin.

Harold Mazzo immediately attached himself to Law, who went to Harold's private office to change clothes. He returned to cameras, lights, and two women with bottles of baby oil. The oil was meant to add dimension to his chest, which was already so cut and ripped he looked like a superhero.

The brunettes rubbed the clear moisturizer on his upper body until he glistened.

A hint of jealousy pinched Cat when one of the assistants poured oil on her palm, then slipped her hand beneath the waistband of his boardshorts. The outline of her fingers didn't go deep, but the fact she was *inside* his swim trunks bothered Cat. The shoot was from the waist up. He didn't need his sex oiled.

A warning look from Law, and the woman removed her hand. She didn't seem fazed by his rejection. She moved to his pecs.

Law took direction from the producer, and Cat stood back and admired the Rogue. A stylist had brushed back his hair, only to grimace over Law's bruised face.

Harold felt the discoloring made the commercial realistic.

Law's body had dynamic proportions. Wide shoulders, thick chest, tapered waist, and one wickedly tight ass. His legs were long, lean, and perfectly sinewed.

His black boardshorts rode low on his hips.

A tattoo was visible at his groin. BASEBALL IS A GAME OF INCHES.

Cat heard the feminine whispers, and one woman giggled. She wasn't the only one who'd read his tat.

From what Catherine had sensed when she'd rubbed against him at Haunt, Law had more than his fair share of inches.

The ballplayer was a producer's dream. Each shot went smoothly without retakes. Law sat in the Hotsy Twelve, a black marble Jacuzzi shaped like a diamond. He threw back his head, stretched his arms along the edge, and narrowed his gaze. His nostrils flared, and he marginally parted his lips, just enough to exhale.

Seduced by steam and swirling water, Law relaxed to the point of appearing asleep. The rapid click of the camera told Cat the photographer was capturing Law as a raw, yet vulnerable man. James Lawless played hard and rejuvenated with hydrotherapy.

Law delivered his lines without mistakes. He sold the Jacuzzi as both healer and fantasy. He was so convincing, Cat was ready to write a check. Customers would be knocking down the doors once the commercial aired.

Water sluiced off Law as he rose like a Jacuzzi god

from the depths of the black marble diamond. Women surrounded him with towels and several patted him down. One assistant dried his inner thigh, her hand sliding balls high.

Law eased back a step.

This was a different side of Law than Cat had seen before. The man fed off female attention. He flirted, teased, and signed autographs, a single ballplayer in the spotlight. He shone. She felt like a dull bulb.

Ten minutes, he mouthed to Cat, as the Jacuzzi groupies walked him back to Harold's office. The women had helping hands, Cat noted. She wondered if he'd dress himself or if he'd need assistance.

Twenty minutes later he finally showed. His hair remained damp, his change of clothes fresh as if taken out of the closet. He now wore a black polo, jeans, and athletic shoes. Sporty and good-looking, he was ready for a casual evening. Every woman in the shop wished he was taking her home. And to bed.

Every woman but Cat.

He came to her then, placed his hand on the back of her neck, and gently rubbed. To those looking on, there was a familiarity, an intimacy to his gesture, as though he stroked her often. Resisting would prove more embarrassing than the massage.

Harold Mazzo strolled over, and the two men wrapped up their business. Throughout their talk, Law worked her neck, relaxing her, turning her on. Her breasts felt heavy, her stomach light. Her panties were damp. She was so aroused she couldn't think straight.

He knew she'd gone hot for him. The look in his eyes told her so. His expression was way too pleased.

Whatever his reasons, he was after her. The prospect scared her to death.

"Better, babe?" He bent down and kissed her forehead.

She managed a nod.

Law left Harold with a handshake and an agreement to do a second commercial once baseball season ended. They both hoped it would be after a World Series win.

Law had plenty to say on their ride back to the hotel to pick up Foxie. The conversation centered on hedge funds, money market accounts, and acquiring additional businesses.

"While I'm away, see if there's a local furniture company, paint shop, and toy store for sale," he requested.

She made a mental note. "Done."

"Prosper is expanding nicely." He sounded pleased. "I'm putting a new manager in place at Haunt. The staff's going to throw a killer party.

"Since you closed the deal," he continued, "it would mean a lot if you'd make an appearance, however short. You can invite your family, any relatives over eighteen."

Cat shuddered. The idea of her parents at Haunt left her queasy. How could she invite them to a club where she'd dry humped a superhero? It just didn't seem right.

"My family barbecues most Friday nights." If no one had a reason to celebrate, Cat would create one.

She'd do anything to avoid Haunt.

Law shrugged. "If you change your mind, Walter can direct you to any costume shop in the city. The Rogues will attend as superheroes, to distinguish them from the other guests. The players have agreed to sign autographs."

He appraised her from the corner of his eye. "You'd make a great mermaid."

Cat wasn't much of a swimmer, and the body-hugging gold netting and foam fin at the bottom would make it difficult to walk.

"You'd also look good in an Elizabethan costume," he suggested as he passed through the guard gate and parked the Mercedes in one of the prime spots.

In a packed club, Cat would suffocate in the long-sleeved velvet gown with the high, frilled collar.

He cut the engine, resting his wrists against the steering wheel. "Maybe a gingerbread woman?"

She'd seen the costume at Masquerade. The brown cookie jumpsuit covered a person head to toe. It had a large, round, foam mask for the head and cartoon-hand gloves. The decorative polyester with the faux raisin eyes, red gumdrop mouth, and white piping down the sides looked good enough to eat.

"A chipmunk," he tossed out. "Puffy cheeks, furry fabric body, and a bushy tail would be cute on you."

Cute? Every costume he'd suggested had her fully covered, all sweaty, itchy, and uncomfortable. He'd not mentioned flirty, sexy, or even eye-catching.

He could imagine her as a chipmunk.

She saw him as a horse's ass.

James Lawless reached across Cat to open her door. The brush of his shoulder against her chest froze her to the seat. High, round, and soft, her breasts teased his bicep. He could lean against her all day.

"Let's get the dogs," he said, exiting the vehicle.

Cat followed more slowly. She buttoned the mauve

shrug in a protective gesture, then tugged down her tank dress until the hem hit her knees. She looked ruffled.

As they entered the hotel elevator, she stood with her nose to the elevator door, as far from him as was humanly possible.

Law smiled all the way to his penthouse suite.

He'd challenged her to attend Haunt. He'd purposely conned her into believing he saw her as no more than a decorative cookie, even a chipmunk. Whatever she wore, she'd look hot. The costume wouldn't wear Cat, she'd wear the costume.

He wondered if the Amazon Princess would show on opening night. He'd soon set Walter to work on promotion, and Haunt would be splashed throughout the media. The club's new manager, Adrian Austin, was psyched and prepped to run the business.

Law had met Adrian in passing, a forty-year-old African American wired for a second chance. The professor from the local business college believed in Adrian. The graduate had recovered from his dealings with a brother-in-law who'd embezzled from a family bistro and left it bankrupt.

Adrian was driven and innovative. Pride and purpose ran in his blood. He deserved a second chance.

Security stood outside Law's penthouse. Two plainclothesmen, arms crossed over their chests, looked apprehensive over their assignment.

"Walter Hastings placed us in the hallway," the taller of the two explained. "We're on the lookout for a black fox."

"Fox? Or *Foxie?*" Cat was quick to ask.

"Walter talked so fast, it was hard to tell," said the guard. "We've been here for an hour. No fox."

Law frowned. Nothing rattled Walter.

He found his assistant in the foyer, pale and unstrung. The man had ditched his suit coat and tie and now crawled on all fours, searching under tables and around corners.

"Problem, Walter?" he asked.

"A most disturbing occurrence, sir," Walter confessed, still on his hands and knees. "I've lost Foxie."

Catherine's intake of breath indicated her concern. "When did you last see her?" she asked.

"We were playing catch," Walter stated. "Bouncer tired early, but Foxie chased and chased some more. I rolled the ball down the hallway, it bounced off the baseboards, and shot into Law's bedroom. Foxie ran after it, but never came back. When I went to the room and looked around, I found the ball on the floor near the foot of the bed, but there was no sign of her. I've called and called," Walter stressed. "Not a peep."

"No one's come or gone?" asked Law. "Maid or food service?" A cracked door, and the schipperke could've slipped out.

"Bouncer left with the dog walker a bit ago. I watched them leave. It was just the two of them. Other than that, it's been quiet," Walter assured him.

"Then she has to be here." Law offered Walter a hand up. Walter stood, his palms red, the knees on his pants wrinkled.

"Let's start in your bedroom." Catherine moved down the hall ahead of the men. "Foxie likes to hide."

"End of the hall, on the left," Law directed her.

"Sir?" Walter asked. "Are you sure?"

Law understood his question. His penthouse had

five bedrooms and whenever he brought a woman home, they made love in a guest room. Catherine May would be the first female to enter his sanctuary.

"We need to find Cat's dog," Law assured Walter. "If Foxie was last seen running into my bedroom, we start looking for her there."

"As you wish," Walter conceded.

Cat was first to cross the threshold, and she stopped cold. Her eyes went wide, her lips parted, and she breathed, "Oh . . . my."

Law saw the room through her eyes. A masculine Mediterranean space designed to his specifications. The room took him back to the last European vacation he'd spent with his parents. He'd been seven, and they'd stayed at the Athens Grace. His bedroom was done in Grecian décor.

A platform ultra-king-size bed with four columned posts was centered on the far wall. It was topped by a top-of-the-line Swedish mattress. He slept between midnight-blue silk sheets, warmed by a navy suede comforter. His pillows were orthopedic foam for solid head support. He couldn't afford to wake up with a crick in his neck. Playing second base took a lot of twisting and swiveling.

On restless nights, he wanted food, movies, and music at a finger's touch. His custom-made headboard arched like a bridge. The base supported a compact refrigerator and the lower drawers held snacks. Discreet lighting ran across the arch. A sixty-inch plasma TV popped up from the footboard.

Two navy leather chairs flanked wide windows that offered a panoramic view of Richmond. Late-afternoon shadows fell over the city, burnishing the sunlight to gold.

Cat took it all in, yet didn't pause in her purpose. She crouched down, clutched the hem of her dress in one hand, then called for Foxie. Law hit the floor, too, as did Walter.

Bouncer returned from his walk and joined in the hunt. His nose down, he zigzagged across the carpet, trailing Foxie like a bloodhound.

Catherine looked hot crawling on his carpet. Law would've suffered rug burn to have sex with the woman. Doggy-style seemed an inappropriate thought.

On all fours near the curtains, Cat twisted around so quickly that her bottom brushed his chin. The urge to bite her ass was strong. Cat blushed so red, Law was afraid her head would explode.

She apologized and rapidly crawled off in the direction of his walk-in closet. The door stood ajar.

"The light switch?" Cat scrambled to her feet, then ran one hand along the inner wall.

"To the right," said Law.

Anxiety had her accidentally pressing more than one switch. The closet was illuminated as paneled lights shone bright on a revolving clothes rack she'd set in motion. Shirts, suits, and slacks rotated past her.

His Windbreakers flew by, followed by Wonder Woman's lasso. Law had hung the golden lariat out of sight until he located the heroine. The sight of it seemed to disturb Cat. She'd gone pale on him. Her reaction to the rope was unnatural.

Law came to stand beside her. Bouncer leaned against Law's thigh. The big dog seldom barked, but today he let out a howl that could be heard at the reception desk of the hotel.

A random glance at his shoe rack caught movement

in a leather boot. There was wiggling, fur, and a serious yawn from Foxie as she rolled from the footwear.

Law was the first to grab her, surprising himself that he'd worried over the pup. The schipperke looked up at him with fox-bright eyes before she clamped down on his wrist, gentle this time.

"I'm yours," he said, and Foxie licked his hand.

Cat reached for the puppy. "I'll take her now."

A mother and child reunion, Law thought. Foxie was as much a part of Catherine's family as Bouncer was his. The boxer often seemed more personable and genuine than many of the people who crossed Law's path. Fans and groupies saw him as an elite athlete, and they wanted to swing from his star.

Cat moved toward the door, only to slow near an ornate curio cabinet containing family heirlooms and photographs. She studied the foremost picture in a platinum frame.

Law held his breath. The picture captured his parents on their wedding day. A highly personal photo, seen only by Walter and his grandfather. Yet Catherine May viewed it now.

His father looked clean-cut and polished in his black tuxedo. His mother was soft and lovely in a lace wedding gown. A great love shone in their eyes as they embraced each other and a golden future. The photograph was one of Law's favorites, and one he never shared with anyone. Ever.

Cat shifted her gaze from the photo to Law, her smile tentative. "You have your mother's hair and eyes and your father's . . . mouth."

The lady was right. Law favored both sides of the family. Her mention of his mouth hung between them. He hadn't forgotten their kiss. Apparently neither had she.

The memory seemed to make Cat uneasy. "It's time for me to head back to the office," she finally said. "I need to consult with Zen before he leaves for the day."

Had she not had a meeting, Law would have asked her to dinner. They'd spent the entire day together, yet he hadn't tired of her company. Unusual for him.

He followed Cat back to the foyer. Walter trailed Law. Bouncer dogged Walter.

"Allow me a second chance to watch Foxie," Walter implored at the door. "She won't escape me twice."

Cat smiled as she eased the schipperke into her carrier. "A playdate with Bouncer might be fun."

"I'm on the road for ten days," Law reminded her. "But you can drop off Foxie anytime."

She nodded, noncommittal. "We appreciate the invite."

An invitation did not guarantee Cat's appearance, whether for pet playtime or for the opening of Haunt. He debated asking her on an official date, but decided against it.

He respected Catherine and would never make her feel second-best. Only a jerk would take one woman to a club, only to spend the evening looking for another. He'd be busy trying to find Wonder Woman.

Should she show, Law planned to return her Lasso of Truth. She'd given herself over to him once. He'd go for twice.

Never in his life had he dated two women at the same time. Yet both Wonder Woman and Catherine May did it for him.

They took the elevator to the car park and climbed back in the SUV. Cat's cell phone rang as they drove to

Driscoll Financial. She answered, and Law caught one end of the conversation.

"A definite reason to celebrate, Mom," Cat said, a smile in her voice. "Dad brought you roses? He waltzed you around the kitchen? The man hasn't danced in years."

A short pause, listening on Cat's part and eavesdropping on Law's. "I need to meet with Zen, and afterward I have a dentist appointment. I'll be home by seven, no later than seven thirty. Fire up the barbecue. I'm in the mood for ribs. I'll stop by the grocery and pick up sodas." Her face softened. "Love you back, Mom." And Cat disconnected.

"Good news, I gather?" Law hinted.

She nodded, her eyes bright, her sigh one of total relief. "My dad works hard, and construction's been slow. He refuses money from his kids. Today the carpenter gods smiled on him. Warren-Waite contracted him to build and install all the cabinets in their latest parade of homes. That's ten houses and a year's worth of work. It's party time on Larkspar Lane."

The village would assemble and Roger May would be king. Law felt oddly hollow. He rubbed his chest, figuring he was hungry. The pup cakes and raspberry ladyfingers hadn't stayed with him. He'd fill the emptiness with dinner at Duffy's Diner.

He'd planned to locate Brody Jones and make sure the shortstop was packed and ready to travel tomorrow. The kid had party genes, and a good night's sleep was preferable to a hangover. The upcoming series would be tough. The Braves and Marlins wanted to drop the Rogues in the standings.

Catherine May was amazed that James Lawless found a parking place directly in front of Driscoll Financial.

It was Friday night, and people swarmed the sidewalks the way cars jammed the street. Families and couples converged on restaurants and clubs. Jacy's Java remained open to the caffeine crowd.

Beside her, Law let the engine idle. He appeared anxious to leave. Cat quickly realized he had places to go, people to see, women to bed.

She debated inviting him to her family's celebration, only to quickly dismiss the thought. The Mays overwhelmed outsiders, and Law was a solitary man.

She unfastened her seat belt and pushed open the door before Law could lean across and assist her. She couldn't handle more touching.

Hefting the mesh dog carrier from the floor mat, she hooked it over her shoulder. Once on the sidewalk, she turned and said, "Congratulations. You're three investments richer than you were this morning."

"All thanks to you, sweetheart." His dark gaze met hers, held, then shifted to her lips. Law was relentless. He had a way of looking at her mouth that left her feeling kissed. Cat licked her lips, expecting to taste him on her tongue.

Law's smile hit her belly low. Her pulse jumped and her stomach fluttered. His dimples deepened when she stepped back, nearly tripping over her own feet to escape his stare. She hated the fact that her nipples puckered and heat probed between her thighs.

He was fully aware that he turned her on.

He appeared to enjoy her sexual squirm.

"'Night, Catherine." His tone was a verbal caress.

Her knees turned to jelly. She slammed the door

of the SUV so hard the entire side shook. She then escaped into the building.

Five thirty, and the firm was quiet. Only Zen remained. She knocked on his door and entered his office. He looked up from his desk and removed his wire-rim glasses. "I hear your day was successful," he said.

She blinked. "How did you know?"

"Law texted me."

"When?" She'd just left the man.

"A second ago."

The man had fast fingers. "Are you headed out, or do you have a minute?" she asked her boss.

"I'm here until seven," he returned. "Ellie's at ballet, and after dance class, I'm taking my wife and daughter out to dinner at CJ Sam's."

The restaurant was kid-friendly and popular with families. Catherine had taken her nieces and nephews to lunch there several times. The atmosphere was relaxed, fun, and appealed to time-starved parents and juvenile taste buds.

Cat gently lowered Foxie's carrier onto the floor and took a seat across from Zen. The schipperke remained surprisingly quiet. She'd had an active day.

So had Zen, judging by his desktop, still piled with files, stock reports, and three financial newspapers. The man was swamped.

"What's on your mind, Cat?" he asked.

"Confidentiality," she began. "Randall Burton Lawless put me on retainer this morning."

"Impressive." Zen didn't appear overly surprised. "Rand asked about you last week. He'd heard you were working with his grandson—"

"And wanted to be sure I was reputable," she finished for him.

He nodded. "That sums it up. Randall is very protective of Law."

"Which I understand," Cat acknowledged. "Randall's wealth couldn't prevent tragedy. Law lost his parents and suffered greatly at an early age."

Zen narrowed his gaze on her. "Who told you about the accident?" he asked, as if the information was top secret.

"Law spoke about it last night."

"He's not one to discuss his past."

"Clone Man turned back time." She related the events of the previous evening.

Zen took it all in, his expression solemn. "You now know Law better than many of his teammates," he said. "He's one of my closest friends. He's opened up to you. Don't shut him down."

"We're all business." She refused to admit to their dirty dancing at Haunt or their deep kisses at the bookstore. The two incidents crossed the professional line.

Zen picked up his pen and rolled it between his palms. His expression was thoughtful. "I need you to be straight with me, Cat. You lied to Law this morning. You told him you attended Haunt as a cowgirl, not as Wonder Woman. Your reason?"

Cat's blush was immediate. "Anonymity, and I was foolish."

Zen understood. "Your costume let you play outside your comfort zone."

"Way outside."

He zeroed in. "You met Captain America?"

They'd met, kissed, rubbed, and she'd run. "Our paths crossed."

Intrigued, Zen put the puzzle together, faster than most. "By night, in a dark warehouse, with loud music, a black wig, a mask, and a sexy costume you were unrecognizable. By day, Law hasn't pegged you as Wonder Woman."

"I'd prefer to keep it that way."

Zen nodded. "I sent you to the club on business. Your secret's safe with me."

"Speaking of secrets," she said, shifting subjects, "Randall Lawless requested I deal solely with him." She grinned at Zen. "Rand said that you need not get involved."

"The man has faith in you."

"His grandson doesn't." Cat relayed what she'd overheard that morning outside his office. "There's no need for an explanation," she assured Zen. "I have a gut feeling whatever goes down with the Rogues will greatly affect both men."

"You're intuitive, Catherine," Zen praised. "Don't lose that edge."

She pushed to her feet. "We're good then?"

"We're fine." Zen smiled at her. "I'm very glad you're with my firm."

"I won't let you down."

"I know."

Chapter 7

"You're a dumb-ass, Brody." James Lawless caught up with his teammate at Duffy's Diner, sulking over his plate of cold mac 'n cheese. "Stop staring at the waitress like you've just seen a ghost."

"I damn sure have."

"What?" Law asked, not understanding.

"I'm engaged to her." It was hard for Brody to say.

Brody Jones ignored the stunned look on his teammate's face. Ignored it good. No doubt that was the last thing Law had expected to hear when his buddy sat down next to him in the booth with the bright red leather and shiny black tabletop. The slick '50s burger joint with its hand-mixed shakes and deep-fried onion rings was *his* diner. He was so fuckin' ticked he couldn't force down a bite of food.

All because of Mary Blanchard. She'd shown up, looking like homemade apple pie with a sweet caramel glaze. He'd avoided such pie for a very long time now. Memories of apple pie belonged in Plain, West Virginia, not in Richmond. Shit.

Law stared hard at Brody from across the table.

"I don't believe you. She's cute, but definitely not your type."

"She damn sure isn't. That's the problem."

Brody continued to track the brunette with the big blue eyes as if she were in the crosshairs of his rifle. He couldn't help it. He was one angry son of a bitch, and given the tension in his body, he was about to put his fist through a wall.

He would have if Law hadn't decided to park his ass across from him.

"Has she seen you?" Law asked.

"Not yet. I ordered and was served before she started her shift. She's working the table section; we're in the back booth."

"You're hard to miss, Brody."

"She hasn't looked beyond her station."

"Drink your ice water." Law pushed the glass toward him.

"I need more than that to cool me down."

"Talk to me," Law pressed. "Why are you so damn angry?"

"I told her not to come to Richmond," Brody growled. "She didn't fuckin' listen to me."

How could he explain to Law that the pink-cheeked waitress with the baby-doll eyes had once been his high school sweetheart? Later, his fiancée.

"Mary's a nice girl," he told Law. Too damn nice. Brody wasn't looking for sweet and smiling or a continued engagement. He'd just never gotten around to telling her that.

How could he? She hadn't let him. She'd been quick in telling his mom and the entire town that they were getting married. Word had spread over Plain like a town banner.

He'd given her a ring soon after making it with her in the backseat of his van on graduation night. He'd left Plain two weeks later on an athletic scholarship to the University of Michigan.

Mary had hugged him and cried soft tears, already missing him before he'd even gotten past her driveway. She'd made him promise to visit often.

Sucked in by sex, he'd agreed.

Yet once he'd hit the city limits, he'd never looked back. He'd made a whopper of a mistake. The consequences of a single mattress wedged in the back of his van and a date willing to have sex had come back to haunt him now.

He'd never planned to hurt Mary. She was like a daisy, all sweet and pretty. Homegrown.

He'd had no idea then that a field of blooming wild-flowers was waiting for him in the big, bad world ahead. Curvy women. Tall and fine. With big boobs and a hunger for ballplayers that wouldn't quit.

So many wanted him.

He wanted them right back.

Over the years, he hadn't been faithful. No way in hell. He'd never considered himself tied down to Mary. Especially after he'd gone to college and she'd found work at Pop's Bowling Alley.

He couldn't help smiling when he told Law how Mary had a God-given talent for judging shoe size. She would hand a customer his bowling shoes after one glance at his feet. All feet except Brody's. She always teased him about them, not having shoes wide enough for his flat feet.

"While Mary served up shoes and strawberry soft serve, I got drafted into the minors." Brody pushed his plate away from him. It was common knowledge that he'd been brought up to the majors upon Zen Driscoll's retirement. "Now she's come to claim what she thinks is hers. Me."

Law cut a glance at the waitress. "Mary's pretty and she's here now," he said. "Deal with her. Don't forget who you were, Brody. Your past brought you to your present. Stop believing your own press."

Brody rolled his eyes. "Don't go big brother on me." He could tell when his teammate was about to deliver a lecture on how being a professional athlete was more about the game and the fans than the perks of having a naked girl waiting for him in every hotel room on road trips. It was so fucking hot to walk into his bedroom and find a woman spread and ready for him.

"C'mon, Law," he coaxed. "You have to admit what they say about me is true. I'm a great ballplayer. Gold Glove material."

"You walk the walk. Just back it with humility," said Law.

"Humble doesn't come with a ring on Mary's finger as well as one through my nose," he stated.

He didn't let on that Mary's arrival in Richmond reminded him of his roots. And his father. The bastard. Brody wanted her gone.

"She belongs in Plain." As Brody watched Mary, his gaze didn't flicker. She continued to work her tables, having yet to spot him.

He grew embarrassed for her. She refilled a Coke glass with lemonade. Delivered the wrong order to a table for the third time. The woman couldn't get her orders straight. Chances were good she'd be fired at the end of her shift. He could only hope so.

"Look at her," he ground out. "She's so slow you can almost hear the corn grow. Richmond will eat her alive."

"And you won't?" asked Law.

"What we had is over, finished. A strikeout," he said, ignoring his teammate's insinuation. He wanted to end this conversation before it got too personal. Like how he made it through school on his natural talent for playing ball and the occasional tutor, not on his math skills. He'd often tossed down the price of the entire meal as a gratuity rather than try to calculate a 20 percent tip.

"Mary's a walking diner disaster," Brody grunted. "She brought that couple by the kitchen door vanilla shakes and fries when they ordered senior-citizen specials."

Law narrowed his eyes. "I thought you didn't care."

"I don't, damn it. But someone has to tell Duffy his new waitress should be canned." Which would have her running back to Plain in a hurry.

Brody just might put the bug in Duff's ear.

He ignored any hot urges growing in his groin as he watched her work. She had a cute wiggle. Her ass was round and firm. He told himself he wanted that bottom gone.

"Look, Brody, I'm not here to judge what you do on your off time," Law said, throwing down enough cash to pay for his orange soda and Brody's meal. He also left a large tip, from what Brody could tell. "We're leaving tomorrow morning for Atlanta. Make it an early night. We need you primed for the series."

"Yeah, sure. You don't have to worry about me," Brody said. "I'll be on the plane before you, old man."

"The team is counting on you, Brody. Don't screw up."

Law slapped him on the shoulder and got up, leaving Brody to stew. He set his back teeth, turned slightly, and watched Mary work. She'd put his life upside down with the snap of a waitress apron.

He hung out in the diner for a while longer, noting that the people at a front table near the counter had requested the meat loaf dinner, only to be served BLTs. At a large round table, four hungry truckers ordered T-bones rare. Mary brought them chef salads. They poked at the lettuce as if it was alien to them, but the hungry look in their eyes was something Brody knew too well. Each was about to hit on Mary.

They eyeballed her up and down as if she was the blue plate special. With her ass as pie à la mode for dessert.

Although Mary tried hard, Brody knew waitressing wasn't her calling. She belonged back at Pop's with the red-and-black bowling shoes.

Her curly hair hung limp, and perspiration dampened her brow. Her face was as red as the ketchup stain on the pocket of her khaki apron. The harder she pushed, the more she messed up.

Mary was what he'd heard the other waitresses call *in the weeds.* Far behind in her service and unable to catch up.

Yet from what Brody observed, no one chastised her or minded her mistakes. He couldn't believe it. The diners smiled, encouraged her, and left enormous tips. An elderly lady took up hostess duties.

One of the truckers bused his own table. Eyeing Mary's butt and licking his lips, Brody noted.

That did it.

He stood up, snorting fire and ready to tackle the

trucker when he remembered what Law had said. *The team is counting on you. Don't screw up.*

Grumbling, he sat back down, still hot under the collar, and complained about his cold dinner instead.

"Mary, honey, can you breeze by my station and warm up the guy's mac 'n cheese?" Sally Caldwell asked, her arms loaded with plates of pot roast and chicken-fried steak.

"Sure, Sally," Mary said, wiping her face. Waitressing was harder than she'd expected. In the bowling alley, all she had to do was look at a customer's feet. Here she spent all her time *on* her feet. Which were killing her. "What booth did you say?"

"Number seven. He's fit to be tied."

Mary turned and rubbed her hands on her apron. "I'm on my way—"

She stopped, her hand flying to her mouth. "Omigod, it's—"

"Brody Jones, Mr. Baseball in the flesh," Sally answered with a smirk. "Be careful, he's an ornery cuss tonight."

"So you've said." Mary grinned from ear to ear. Brody'd never been grouchy with her. He'd always been tender and gentle when they'd kissed, his hand sliding around her waist, pulling her tight to him.

That old happy feeling came back to her when she looked at him. Broad shoulders, mussed blond hair, square jaw. How she'd missed him.

Mary bit down on her lower lip, anxious. She'd never expected to face Brody over a plate of cold mac 'n cheese. She'd hoped to have a chance to unpack and put on her prettiest dress and sweet-smelling lavender water before knocking on his door and telling him she'd left Plain. For good.

And they could be married right away.

"The man rooms here," Sally went on, intent on dishing dirt on Brody, "but you don't have to worry about him hitting on you. He only goes for uptown babes with Botox and boobs to die for."

"Wh-what did you say?" Mary played with the engagement ring on her left hand, its tiny diamond hiding its sparkle from her.

"He likes his women the same way he likes his meals. Hot."

She shook her head, not believing. Sally must be mistaken. Brody wasn't seeing anyone else. He was engaged to her. Had been since that afternoon on Jasper Bridge when he proposed, then dived into the river and wouldn't come back out until she'd said yes.

That was seven years ago. Seven long years of waiting, watching for his postcards, checking with his mom for any mention of her in his letters. He was busy playing ball and traveling with the team, Mrs. Jones insisted, giving her a comforting hug. Her boy would do the right thing when he was ready, the older woman assured her.

Mary clung to that hope. Too desperately, perhaps. She refused to believe anything had changed between them. How could it? People from Plain were a proud bunch and true to their word. They kept their promises.

No matter how long it took to fulfill them.

She had no doubt Brody would keep his word and marry her.

She squared her shoulders and grabbed her tray,

then sashayed over to him, determined to put Sally's words behind her.

"Hi, Brody," she said, putting on her prettiest smile. His piercing eyes made her shiver. "Glad to see me?"

"Sure, I'm glad to see you. You're my waitress, aren't you?" His rudeness slapped her.

She lost her smile. Fast.

"That wasn't what I m-meant," she stammered, wondering what she'd done wrong. "I'm here in Richmond for good."

"What does that mean . . . for good?"

"It means we can be mar—"

"Duffy, where did you get this waitress?" Brody hollered across the diner as the owner emerged from the kitchen, his white cook's cap askew. "I ordered mac 'n cheese and it's cold. She won't heat it up for me."

"You didn't give me a chance—" Mary blurted out.

"Look, Mr. Jones, the girl is new," Duffy said, taking off his cap, his big belly jiggling and his tone apologetic.

The cook had told Mary it wasn't easy to get renters for the old rooms upstairs, and he had to keep the ones he had happy. "I just hired her this afternoon after Leona took off two days ago with that freaky musician to get married in Vegas. Give her a chance, okay?"

It was true about Leona leaving. Mary had been sitting at the busy counter sipping her coffee after a long car trip down from Plain, trying to get up the courage to tell Brody she was here, when she decided to help out and fill her own coffee cup. Twice. And the coffee cup for the customer sitting next to her. Then all those seated at the counter.

Duffy noticed and, seeing he was short a girl, hired

her on the spot. She was thrilled to have the job and figured Brody would be proud of her.

Not dump on her like this. Making out like she wasn't doing her job. Acting like he wasn't happy to see her.

What was wrong with the man?

She held back the tears forming at the corners of her eyes. She wouldn't let him see her cry. She wouldn't.

"One mac 'n cheese coming up," she said, scooping up the dish and wiggling her shoulders like a film star. "Hot. Very hot."

"Skip it. I lost my appetite."

He grabbed his check and got up from the booth to leave, brushing by her so fast she lost her balance. Mary cried out, trying to steady herself, but she slipped on a greasy onion ring someone had dropped and skidded across the floor on her heels.

"Watch out!" she yelled, losing her balance. She tossed her tray up and the plate of cold pasta and gooey cheese spun through the air like pizza dough out of control—

And landed on Brody's shoulder.

Cheese-coated macaroni wiggled down his dark T-shirt like tiny exclamation points. Mary couldn't help herself. She started laughing.

"What are you laughing at?" he asked, his eyes fierce.

"I'm sorry, Brody, but you look so funny."

"Yeah?" he said, scooping macaroni off his shirt and handing it to her. "Here's your tip. Don't spend it all at once."

Before she could stop him, he booked from the diner.

"Brody, wait!"

"Pay him no mind, hon. Some ballplayers are like that," Sally said, laying a hand on her shoulder. "Don't let him bother you."

Mary nodded. But he did bother her. Big-time.

They were engaged. No matter what he did, she still loved Brody Jones.

And always would.

Brody shrugged off his noodle-splattered T-shirt and drop-kicked it across the floor. He drew another from a scratched wooden dresser drawer and jerked it on.

Grabbing a cold beer out of his Igloo cooler, he slammed down the lid with his foot. He couldn't take his eyes off the view from his second-story window down into the parking lot below.

Mary.

Apparently her shift had ended shortly after she'd creamed him with his dinner. She'd changed into tight jeans and a pink tank top with POP'S BOWLING ALLEY plastered across the front. Her small breasts filled out the top nicely, he noted, watching her pull a battered old suitcase secured with worn straps from the trunk of her car.

Along with a lamp and a tacky lampshade with swinging blue fringe and a red-and-blue dragon painted on it. It had *garage sale reject* written all over it.

What was with her? She'd only been here since this morning and the woman was moving in and nesting like a hen one step ahead of the chicken hawk.

He cracked the bottle open and guzzled down the brew, thinking. Damn, he'd been holed up here in this stinking room for months and the only things he'd unpacked from his van were his cooler and condoms.

Better known as life's necessities.

For a ballplayer.

And he was a damned good one. Sure, he believed his own press, like Law said. He had worked hard to get to the majors and he was going to stay on top, not wash out like his old man said he would.

His dad had lied to anyone who'd listen about how he'd been cheated out of his chance at the big time. He'd tried to take Brody down a notch, making his son believe he'd stolen his father's dream when Brody made the majors.

The truth was that Elmer Jones had had a short career in the minors because he was kicked out for illegal gambling. He had died a drunken has-been. That wasn't going to happen to Brody.

Mary had no right busting in and making him feel like he was that green rookie again from a two-bit town, with everybody making fun of his clothes and how he talked. That was all behind him. He'd damn sure improved.

It was time he put her straight.

He tossed the empty beer bottle into the tiny waste can by the door, then stormed out of his room and down the hallway with its worn carpets and peeling plaster.

The historic building had stood on this spot for eighty years and was the only rental in town that still had a community bathroom.

Brody didn't get far.

Racing down the wooden staircase, boards creaking under his big feet, he ran smack into Mary and her dragon lampshade.

"Brody, how nice of you to help me move in," Mary said, handing him the lamp. Long fringe flew into his face, nearly choking him.

That wasn't the worst of it.

She was close to him, so close he could feel the heat of her body, smell her scent. Mary was aroused.

Her need made him hard.

A pang he'd long forgotten ate at him, but he ignored it.

"You're not staying in Richmond," he said, laying his hand on the banister so she couldn't get by him.

"I most certainly am."

"You're a small-town girl, Mary. You don't know anything about men. There are all kinds of wolves here."

"Like you?" Her brow arched.

"Yeah, like me." She tried to squeeze by him, but he blocked her from going up the stairs. "Why don't you be a good girl and go back to Plain, where you belong."

"I-I can't, Brody."

"Why not?"

"Well . . ." she began, tears appearing as if on cue.

He braced himself. Here it came. The sob story.

He knew the drill. Whatever girl he was dating would give him a lame excuse about why she had to send money home to her dear old mother.

Then she'd stick out her hand and her boobs for a fifty. Or a hundred. He fell for it every damn time.

He was such a chump.

Mary had her own version.

"I lost my job," she said, trying to get a better grip on her suitcase. Her hands were sweaty, and she was breathing hard.

"You gave somebody the wrong bowling-shoe size?"

She managed a small smile. "No. They tore down Pop's to make way for a big discount store."

"Why didn't you tell me?" Brody said, relieved.

Juggling the lamp in one hand, he reached into his pocket for his wallet with the other. "I get it. You need some money to tide you over until the new store opens and you get your job back—"

Mary shook her head. Slowly, back and forth. A sick feeling hit him in the gut, like he'd swallowed a pomegranate whole.

He put his wallet back into his pocket.

She said simply, "Grandma Blanchard died."

That news set Brody back. Filled him with guilt. Mary had lived with her grandmother since she was born and her mother ran off with a used-car salesman.

She continued with, "Her last wish was for me to find you so we could get married."

"Is that why you're still wearing my ring? A ring you conned me into giving you because I felt sorry for you after graduation night when you said I was your first?"

Brody would never admit his teen crush on Mary was real. He'd never forgotten those summer days hanging out at Jasper Bridge, eating her chicken salad sandwiches and playing hide-and-seek like two kids, before jumping into the clear river to cool off.

Or those gray winter mornings before school, when the first snowflakes fell hard and fast and landed on her face and cheeks. And how he'd lick them off the tip of her nose as they huddled under the bridge to keep warm, their arms wrapped around each other.

Since then, he'd outgrown Plain. And her.

He shook off his past. Dumped it into a deep well somewhere in his mind so he couldn't remember.

"Oh, so that's how it is—you felt sorry for me." She dropped the suitcase on his foot. Hard. "You're such a jerk."

"Damn," he grunted, bending to rub his toe. The fringe on the lamp caught on his watch, tearing off a piece from the shade.

"How do you know I'm not here to give your ring back to you?" Mary demanded. "Maybe I don't want to marry you."

"But you said in the diner—"

"That was before I found out about you and your wild ways, Brody Jones. You've changed since you left Plain."

Brody began to wonder if she had shown up to dump him. "If that's how you feel," he said, "then give me back the ring right now."

"With pleasure."

She yanked on her finger, but it wouldn't come off. "I guess I've had it on so long, it won't budge."

"Doesn't matter," he said casually. "It doesn't mean anything."

"Not to you, anyway." She grabbed the lamp from him and looked dismayed at the torn fringe. "Grandma Blanchard would be heartsick to see how you've treated her lamp and her granddaughter."

"What about the way you treated me?" Brody fired back. "Tossing hot mac 'n cheese all over my shirt."

"I didn't throw it at you, and it was cold, not hot."

She pushed by him. "If you'll excuse me, I have to unpack. Duffy has me working the night shift."

"Then you're not leaving?"

She shook her head. "No. I'm a big girl, Brody. I can take care of myself."

"Duffy's is a busy twenty-four-hour diner. Creeps and weirdos roll in at all hours."

"You ought to know," she called over her shoulder as she went up the stairs, adding a sexiness to her voice that didn't go unnoticed by him.

"I bet you don't last a week," he called after her.

"Don't be so sure."

She slammed the door to her room.

Smirking, Brody went back to his room and popped open another bottle. Lying down on the bed, feet up, he drank the beer with gusto. What was he worried about? Duffy lost more waitresses than he hired. This was one bet he was going to win.

Hands down.

He watched ESPN, then grew bored. He needed some action. Richmond came alive at midnight. So would he.

Mary Blanchard wasn't used to working the graveyard shift. If it was dark outside, she ought to be sleeping. Not so last night.

She was tired, bone tired. She never knew her legs could hurt so much. She'd been on her feet since late last night, hopping tables, making coffee, and serving up the midnight special—a burger, curly fries, and a cherry soda, all for under five bucks.

Relief hit her when the sun rose and her shift was about to end. It was six AM. Only one hour to go.

The morning customers were starting to roll in.

Delivery men, construction workers.

And Brody Jones.

She blinked in surprise. What was he doing up so early? She'd imagined him sleeping until game time, after a night on the town.

She'd heard the door to his room slam around eleven thirty as she was getting ready to begin the night shift. Then his footsteps faded away down the hall.

She shrugged. What he did was his business. A smile crossed her face and made her perk up. Until they were married. Then it would be hers.

When that was going to happen, she didn't know.

She dismissed their argument on the stairs as her fault. A temporary blip in her plan to see her dreams come true. She admitted she shouldn't have been so hard on Brody, showing up like she did without warning, but there hadn't been time to let him know she was coming.

Up until a week ago, she'd never asked for his address. She'd always believed he'd come back for her. But he hadn't. She'd finally taken matters into her own hands, all very spur-of-the-moment.

Brody's mom had given her the address that was scrawled on the back of his letters, telling Mary that marrying her would be the best thing that ever happened to her boy.

With his mom's blessing in her back pocket, Mary had been certain Brody would walk her down the aisle right away.

How wrong she was.

He was arrogant, ornery, and dead set against a

wedding. Especially with her. Why? What was wrong with her?

She worked hard, went to church on Sundays, and made the best peanut butter cookies in Plain. Some would go as far as to say they were the best cookies in the county.

What more could a man want?

Sex.

She hadn't had much practice with that. Brody was the only man she'd made love to, but she was a fast learner. And how she loved to learn . . . her legs wrapped around him, his hands caressing her breasts . . .

She rubbed the calves of her legs, trying to get out the kinks. She'd get him back. She had before and she'd do it again. Like the time that snooty girl from the next town over tried to get her claws into Brody.

Gwen Gardner, she remembered, had flirted with him when they all went for a swim in the river, then pretended to drown so Brody could save her. When Mary found out the girl was on the swim team at her school, she tricked Gwen into revealing her deceit to him. It worked.

Brody hated liars.

What about that line she'd given him about wanting to give back his ring?

That didn't count. It was only a little white lie. She could have taken the ring off her finger, but she didn't want to. Not until Brody added a gold band next to it.

She pushed out her chest. Time to go to work.

She tucked stray wisps of hair under her waitress cap and licked her lips. Dry. Where was her lipstick? No time. By the way Brody was looking at his watch, he wanted to order breakfast. Fast.

"What'll you have, Brody?" she asked, strolling over to his booth, pen and pad in hand.

"Three scrambled eggs made with real butter—" He looked up. "Oh, it's you, Mary. Still here?"

"Still here." She grinned, then assumed her professional waitress stance. "Do you want hash browns with that?"

He nodded. "And coffee. Hot."

"Hot is my specialty."

He raised his eyebrows. "What is that supposed to mean?"

"Whatever you want it to."

"Too bad I won't be around to find out."

Mary panicked, ignoring the ringing bell alerting her that her next order was up. "What do you mean?"

"Didn't I tell you?" He looked smug. "The Rogues play two series on the road. I'm out of here. Ten days gone."

She excused him. "Must have slipped your mind."

His cell phone rang. A text. He read it, then grabbed his jacket. "I won't have time for those eggs. Bye, Mary. I'm still betting you won't be here when I get back."

"Brody, I'll miss you," fell on deaf ears. He'd already cleared the door.

She felt heartsick. She'd just gotten to town, and Brody was leaving her. Ten days seemed like a lifetime.

"Mary, your order's up!" Duffy yelled, leaning over the counter and banging on the bell.

Her response time wasn't quick enough for the cook. He rounded the counter and raced toward her, his eyes glaring, his belly wobbling as he delivered the food himself.

A customer was calling her, needing more coffee.

Another was waiting to be seated.

Mary's head began to pound. Her stomach tightened.

Maybe Brody was right. Maybe she couldn't cut it as a waitress. She'd give it one more hour and hope for the best.

Chapter 8

The Rogues ran the Braves into the ground. They won the first two games and were feeling cocky. Game three, and the score was 8–2 by the top of the seventh. They planned to clean house and leave Hell-Lanta.

The temperature was so high, Psycho McMillan wanted to do a rain dance. The field was so hot it could shock a lizard. The dugout was a sweat lodge.

Brody Jones sat next to Law on the visitors' bench, sweating bullets and sucking air. "My dick's roasting like a Ball Park frank," the shortstop complained.

The heat dried Law's mouth and throat, leaving him spitless. He reached for his favorite candy. "Life Saver?" He presented the roll to his teammate.

"I always get stuck with watermelon," Brody complained, but he took the candy anyway. "I'd rather have orange."

"Take what you're offered."

Brody cut Law an ornery look. The kid was on a tear, Law knew, his temper volatile. He'd been the last player to arrive at the airport, holding up the team's departure.

There'd been no apology when he'd boarded, only an angry hiss.

He'd sat in the back, he and his foul mood taking over the last four rows of the private jet. He'd brooded all the way to Atlanta.

Law had initiated conversation twice, only to be met with caveman grunts. He'd moved on to play poker with Risk Kincaid, Brek Stryker, and Psycho McMillan. Law swore Psycho had aces up his sleeve. No man won every hand, yet Psycho had. Law left the game with only change in his pocket.

Now seated side by side on the dugout bench, awaiting his at bat, Law watched as Brody clenched his fists and pushed for an orange Life Saver.

Brody never sucked Life Savers. He was on edge and itching for a fight. Any little thing would set him off.

Law had no idea what had pissed the shortstop off, but if an orange Life Saver would appease the kid, he'd give one up. Law hoped that *one* wouldn't jinx him.

He rolled down the wrapper and damn if Brody didn't take two. Law shook his head. What a punk.

"You've broken Law's ritual," Psycho called down the bench to Brody. "His strikeouts and errors are on your head now, jackass."

Brody flipped Psycho the bird, followed by a few choice words.

Psycho rose, ready to respond. Team captain Risk Kincaid stepped between the men. "You're amped. Save it for the game."

"You've got several rolls of Life Savers left," Risk said to Law. "If you need more, I'll send a batboy to the concession."

Risk understood a player's superstitions. Each man had his personal routine.

If a player valued his life, he stayed far, far away from Psycho's tub of grape Dubble Bubble.

The boxes of Junior Mints that catcher Chase Tallan stacked on a shelf next to his batting helmet were off-limits, too.

Pitcher Brek Stryker's bag of black licorice came out between innings. If the Rogues were ahead, he ate one stick. If the team was behind, he put down two. The team had scored big if only nine pieces had been eaten during the game.

Law went with his Life Savers. His ritual had started as far back as Little League. Game day, he ate only orange from the five-flavor pack. The orange *O*s gave him superpowers, or so his inner kid believed. The remaining four flavors were passed among the other players.

"Check out Dunn." Law pointed toward the first baseman, batting fifth. "He's still taped."

Rhaden Dunn had sprained his ankle during the previous series and had it taped. He'd begun hitting so well that once his ankle healed, he kept it wrapped. Dunn was superstitious, but no more so than the rest of the team.

Throughout his career, Risk never stepped on the foul line coming on or off the field. Kason Rhodes patted his helmet three times in the batter's box before taking his stance. Brody Jones wore the same jock he'd had in minor league. He'd taken a lot of ribbing from the team over that confession.

A few of the players abstained from sex on game day. However, with the race for baby daddy, no one suffered long. Those in the running had flown their wives down for both series. Someone's wife would soon be pregnant.

Law shifted on the dugout bench. He hadn't had sex for several days. He'd come close the night at Haunt with Wonder Woman. She was pure party fun and made for a damn fine fantasy.

Catherine May, on the other hand, was as real as it got. A bit uptight, but sliding-home sexy. She aroused him as much as the comic heroine. Cat had a strong work ethic and powerful sense of family. She'd want commitment. Law didn't have it in him.

It was a shame he couldn't merge the two women. He'd then have the wild side of Wonder Woman and the practicality of Cat. The comic book heroine's late-night clubbing would curb Catherine's need for emotional intimacy. The combination would be one ideal woman.

A jab to his ribs gained Law's attention. "Whoever she is, get your head out from between her legs and focus on the game," Psycho said. "Risk's sacrifice moved Rhaden to third. Brody's up, swatting air. Got the stones to bring Dunn home?"

Law pushed to his feet. "Balls to the wall."

He took his practice swings at the on-deck circle.

At home plate, Brody went down on strikes. He cursed the air blue on his return to the dugout. His expression struck terror into the cameraman who went in for a close-up, only to back off quickly. Brody's face wasn't meant for the television audience.

He looked ready to chew up the man and his camera, then spit out both bones and the FOX logo. It was not a pretty picture. Definitely not family viewing.

Law crossed to home plate. The Rogues had the largest traveling fan base in Major League Baseball. Ten thousand packed the stands in Atlanta. Their applause and cheering echoed around the field. His adrenaline pumped. His focus was intense. He widened his stance in the batter's box, letting the game take over every atom of his body.

Strike one came on a fastball over the right-hand corner. The ball had been out of the strike zone. Law tapped the tip of his bat on the edge and looked at the home-plate umpire.

The ump, known in the National League as Mr. Magoo, should have retired long ago. After that call, Law would have gladly paid his pension.

His second strike came on a foul ball.

A breaking ball gave him ball one. A fair call. Magoo must have cleaned his glasses.

A cutter dusted his nuts for ball two.

A curveball, and Law flicked his wrists and found the sweet spot. The pop-up shot behind second and had both the baseman and center fielder running for the catch.

Law tossed the bat, sprinting to first.

Scorching rays and deep shadows now marked the field. Neither fielder called the other off the fly ball. Lost in the sun, it dropped between the two players. Both Braves looked stunned.

Rhaden Dunn scored and Law was safe at first.

The Rogues' pitcher went down on strikes.

Romeo Bellisaro slammed a fastball right to the first baseman. The inning ended, the score 9–2.

Bottom of the ninth, and the Rogues were ready to close the series. To the team's annoyance, Brody fell off his game. The Braves faced two outs when an error by the shortstop stirred an Atlanta rally.

The Braves brought a man home when a ground ball shot off the heel of Brody's glove, to be recovered by Romeo at third. Angry at himself, Brody walked in tight circles and kicked dirt.

Two plays later, Brody misfired a ball to first. Dunn chased the ball all the way to the stands. The runner rounded the base and took second. The look Dunn shot Brody should have fried the shortstop on the spot.

"Shake it off, Jones," Law called to him. "We only need one."

Law could tell the errors ate at Brody. His eyes were wild, his stance tense when he needed to be loose. An infield pop-up, and three players converged. A game of seconds and inches, it quickly became a toss-up between Brody and Law. Law signaled the catch. Once made, his accurate throw to home cut off the runner, bringing the final out.

It was about damn time.

High fives were raised all around in the dugout.

Slaps on the back walked the players down the tunnel.

Brody dragged his ass to the locker room. His teammates razzed the hell out of him. It took Brody a hot shower and a long sulk before he left his errors and mistakes on the field and exhaled the game.

It was time to move on. The Rogues now faced the Marlins.

"No one shaves," Psycho shouted over the bang of lockers and loud music. Several players had their CDs cranked high, and Train, Coldplay, Daughtry, and Brad Paisley vied to be heard.

Law looked at his teammates. Testosterone wrestled for space in the locker room. A few of the players already looked scruffy, and after another few days, they'd have major stubble. If their winning streak continued, those voted onto the All-Star team would have beards.

After a day of travel, the team landed in Miami for a four-game run. The media predicted hot batters and speed runners for the Rogues and high-powered pitching from the Marlins. Numerous newspapers castrated Brody Jones for his infield errors. The kid took the field with something to prove.

Mistakes again rode Brody like a monkey on his back. That monkey was Mary Blanchard, Law later learned, as Brody spit Skoal into a paper cup. Leave it to a woman to screw a man's game.

"Play is now," Law said harshly. "Clear your head, Jones. Get it together."

"Fuck Plain."

Top of the second, the Rogues went down one, two, three. Brody snagged his glove and jogged to his position. No ball came near him, so he ended the inning clean.

Top of the third, the Marlin's starting pitcher, tagged the Colossus of Rhodes by the sportscasters, knocked cocky right out of the Rogues. The pitcher's fastball clocked one hundred. The players never touched a base.

The score remained 1–1, a tug-of-war. Bottom of the fifth, and Brody dove for an easy catch but came up empty. The coach pulled him from the game. The shortstop stormed down the tunnel to the locker room.

"Son of a bitch," Psycho snapped when the team returned to the dugout for their next at bat. "We need this win and I've got incentive."

"Money?" Kason asked.

"The title to your new Lexus?" asked Rhaden.

"The deed to Psycho Choppers?" put in Risk.

"Hell no, get real." Psycho took to pacing as he laid out the challenge. "The opening of Club Haunt under Law's ownership is five days away. Law wants us to attend as superheroes, which we are."

A few players grinned, and Romeo nearly spewed his Gatorade. "Law's claimed Captain America. Superman's up for grabs. Half you assholes want to wear the *S* and only one can. First home run claims the hero."

"You shittin' me?" came from left fielder Kason Rhodes, who'd been one of the players in contention for Superman. "I'd planned to arm wrestle Chaser, Rhaden, and Risk for it."

"Put your muscle behind your bat," said Law. Psycho's idea had merit. "Brody's the Incredible Hulk—"

"Hell, he still has lime-green streaks behind his ears from last time," said Risk.

Brody's pent-up anger would soon bust wide open and rip his uniform to shreds, he was that out of control.

"Brek, Psycho, and Romeo all want Batman. A triple, and the batter gets the Batcave, the Batmobile, and the Batplane," Law continued. "Whoever strikes out becomes a sidekick to a superhero. There's Robin, Jimmy Olsen, Speedy, Toro, Snapper Carr."

Chaser's eyes crossed. "Who the hell are they?"

Law ran down the list. He knew his sidekicks. "Robin's with Batman, Jimmy Olsen's the cub reporter that chronicled his adventures with Superman, Speedy fights alongside the Green Arrow, and Toro's with the Human Torch. Toro gained his powers as a sideshow fire-eater. Snapper Carr was mascot to the entire Justice League of America."

"You'd make a great cub reporter," Psycho taunted Chaser. "It's Jimmy Olsen for you."

"I see him more as Speedy," Risk said tongue in cheek.

Chaser's jaw set. "I'm no sidekick."

"Then pick up your big-boy bat and knock one out of the park," Psycho retorted, egging him on.

The men grumbled, but the glint in their eyes said *game on.* Motivation in any form pulled the team together and the players' competitive drive soon dominated Miami. No man wanted to show up at Haunt as a sissy sidekick.

The final score laid victory at the Rogues' feet. They'd taken game one, which amped adrenaline and spirits.

Law awarded costumes as the guys stripped off their sweaty and dirt-stained uniforms. "Risk, you're Superman." The center fielder had slammed a ball to the upper deck in right field for a home run.

"Romeo, you've got Batman," Law continued. The third baseman had landed a solid triple.

Law scanned the room. "Kason, you and Psycho doubled. Pick your superheroes."

Psycho stood buck naked, towel in hand. "Flesh Gordon," he chose.

"It's *Flash* Gordon," Law corrected.

"I'm doing the porno hero." Psycho the nudist would stand out in the crowd.

Kason untied his athletic shoes. "I'm going as Punisher."

"He's an antihero," said Law.

"Punisher doesn't always act as nice as people

expect," Kason said. "He goes to the darker side of comics."

Punisher fit Kason's personality. No team member knew the left fielder well. He was married, lived rural, and kept to himself.

Psycho told anyone who'd listen that Kason was raised by wolves. The two players tolerated each other now, but in the early days when Kason had been traded from Louisville to Richmond, he and Psycho had been team rivals. They'd hated each other's guts.

Kason had finally found his niche with the Rogues. No player was more driven or dependable. Kason could lay down a home run in the bottom of the ninth with two outs and at full count.

Law cut Brek Stryker some slack with his costume. He'd pitched seven innings with power and precision. His perfectly placed sacrifice bunt advanced two base runners, gaining him superhero status. Brek went with Wolverine.

Catcher Chase Tallan and first baseman Rhaden Dunn gritted their teeth and awaited their fate. A walk had gotten Chaser on first, but he'd struck out his last at bat.

Dunn's ground ball had rolled right to the pitcher. He'd been thrown out at first. Later, he'd popped a fly ball to the shortstop to end an inning.

Law enjoyed the moment more than he should have. Both Chaser and Dunn were slightly under six feet, yet built like bricks. He could have awarded them superhero status, but that would defeat the purpose of Psycho's home run challenge.

"Rhaden," he stated, "you're Toro, the young circus performer with an immunity to fire. He throws fireballs."

"Humbling," replied the first baseman. "Maybe the costume comes with props."

Law sincerely hoped not. "Chaser," he finished, "you're going as the cub reporter."

"Humiliating," Chaser grunted as he tugged off his baseball jersey and unbuckled his belt.

Showered, unshaved, and dressed, the team was driven back to the hotel on a luxury excursion bus. The players took dinner together at the Orange Parrot. Many of the men had invited their wives.

After a plate of fried chicken with three side dishes, Law kicked back, relaxed. Brody had split for his room, and Law was the only single man at the table. He sipped a draft beer and watched the players flirt with their women. The couples looked as if they were dating rather than actually married. They laughed, teased, and touched. A lot.

Psycho held his wife's hand from the moment she joined him at the table. Romeo wrapped his arm about his lady's shoulders the entire evening. Risk snugged Jacy so close, they appeared to share one chair. Law sensed their love, and felt odd man out. An absolute first for him.

A sexy redhead seated at the bar sent him a beer. She crossed and uncrossed her legs, signaling her availability. Law nodded his appreciation, but didn't encourage her company.

Instead, he let his thoughts drift to Catherine May. He wondered if she'd received his gift. Satin Angels should've delivered the teal nightgown by now. He hoped when Cat slipped it on, the material stroked her. She had an amazing body. And was a great kisser.

He had every plan to kiss her again.

He definitely wanted Cat at Haunt—as much, if not

more, than Wonder Woman. The realization made him sweat.

Catherine was a woman of reality, practicality, and commitment. Whereas Wonder Woman was sweet recreation. Law had been a man of amusements for a very long time.

The comic book heroine's departure from the club had disappointed and distracted him. He'd thought of little else. She'd humped and fled, a hot fantasy minus her Lasso of Truth.

But her memory wouldn't satisfy him in bed. Law wanted a moment of closure. He needed to return her golden lasso, then look at romance from a whole new perspective.

He'd had a full life. He was wealthy, well traveled, and a star athlete. Yet he'd never been part of a couple. Looking at his teammates and their wives, Law had the strangest feeling he was missing out. The emptiness surprised him, more than he was willing to admit.

The *missing* started with Catherine May.

It was early to bed for most of the Rogues. By ten o'clock, it was baby-making time. Those in the infant pool dispersed. Law went to bed alone.

The next three games against Miami left blood, guts, and attitude on the field. The Rogues battled for every hit and took the Marlins down one out at a time.

Tempers flared when the starting pitcher hit two batters in a row. Risk got nailed in the shoulder, and Psycho, the thigh. The Rogues were ready to storm the mound. Their coaches called them down. A few players grinned over Psycho's exaggerated limp to first base. The man could act.

Bottom of the eighth, and there'd been a volatile exchange of words when Romeo and a Marlin runner collided at third. The Miami player elbowed Romeo in the neck—a cheap shot. They'd have come to blows had Kason Rhodes and Law not intervened.

After ten days on the road, the Rogues sat atop the leader board in the National League East. It was time to head home.

In Richmond, the Rogues walked through the airport to massive applause. Fans had turned out for their arrival. The team's winning streak packed the terminal with banners, music, camera flashes, and a very supportive crowd.

Law appreciated each man, woman, and child. He stopped often and signed autographs. It was ninety minutes before he claimed his luggage, later yet when a parking lot attendant parked his Bugatti at the valet exit. He spent the time reading text messages.

One text from Walter Hastings nearly sent him to his knees. Auction House notification: Superman lands. $$$$$$$.

The seven dollar signs meant the comic book had sold for a million. The cost didn't matter to Law. Walter had brought Superman home. His assistant deserved a bonus. Law might even offer Walter residence at the Richmond Grace.

The man always had his back.

Law's chest expanded with instant warmth. He wanted to pump his arm and shout until his throat went raw. Instead, he held his excitement in. He let the wonder of owning the most valued comic on the planet wash over him. He felt eight years old again. And surprisingly happy.

Law waited and waited for the pain of losing his

parents to wash over him. Comics tapped memories of his mother and father. The emotional paralysis that so often followed stayed with him for hours afterward. He couldn't shake the sorrow of losing the two people he'd loved most.

Something was different today. On the sidewalk outside the terminal, Law realized his life was slowly shifting, and for the better. He now had two new comic books to frame: *Superman* and *Captain America*.

The thought of Cap took him to Catherine May. He suddenly wanted to share the news of his acquisition with her. She'd be excited, too.

He drove to Driscoll Financial in record time.

There, Zen informed him that Catherine had left early. "Another family celebration, and she never misses those. Her niece won the fifty-yard dash at a track meet. The Mays are barbecuing and dancing in the street."

Law liked music. He might have to drive out to Larkspar Lane. He could avoid the family, maybe park a block away, catch the action. He'd find a way to cut Cat from the crowd and talk to her. He was good with logistics.

"Rogues won big," Zen said to his former teammate. "You played sharp, covered twice for Brody Jones. I was sorry to see the kid get pulled from the game."

"Brody can't yet separate professional from personal. He has woman problems. He'll get back on track."

"He's a damn fine shortstop."

Law raised a brow. "As good as you, Zen?"

Zen scratched his jaw, then answered honestly. "Given time, even better."

"He believes his own press."

"We all do, at one time or another," Zen admitted.

Media built the players up, then tore them down just as quickly. Law tried to stay balanced, whereas Brody's ego was easily stroked.

"Any news on Guy Powers?" Law asked.

"Less speculation, more solid information," Zen began. "I'd planned to call you tomorrow and set up a meeting."

"I've time now." He took a chair in front of Zen's desk.

"As we assumed, Powers is deeply in debt," Zen said. "My inside source discovered that a second investor has approached Guy. A private meeting was held between the two men and an unidentified woman."

"The interested party?"

"Identities have been kept secret," said Zen. "The initial discussion was so guarded, both sides flew to Baltimore, so as not to gain media attention."

Law exhaled slowly. "I can't imagine the Rogues under new ownership."

"A harsh reality," Zen agreed. "No one likes change. Players get cut. There's also the possibility of team relocation."

Law rubbed his hands together. "Any idea on the asking price?"

Zen leaned forward, eyeing him sharply. "Why? You interested?"

"I'd like specifics."

Zen riffled through a file and withdrew a sheet of paper. "I've run some figures and would expect the market value to run eight hundred million. There's no new stadium pending or expansion on the horizon. That's to your benefit."

He pursed his lips. "The numbers I have show the

revenues are high. The operating income's in line. Gate receipts are respectable. Player expenses are a little high, but an owner gets what he pays for. The Rogues are always World Series contenders."

Zen wrapped up. "Real estate acquisitions caused Powers's downfall. He expanded too quickly. He owned the Rogues, got greedy, tried to buy the entire city. He borrowed on the strength of his name and used the team as collateral. Even if he sold off his properties, the revenue wouldn't cover his banknote."

"Not many people can afford a sports team," said Law.

"Your family is one of the few."

Law breathed deep. "My inheritance and assets are tied to my grandfather and Grace Worldwide. I've diversified my holdings through Prosper. But those investments are based on my Rogues contract. Randall is solvent and would have to cosign."

"Would he?"

"I'm not certain." Law cut a glance to the goldfish tanks. Watching the fish swim was soothing. He was quiet for a long time. In mental debate.

"Randall expects me to head the hotel chain when I retire from baseball," he said as much to himself as to Zen. "After all he's done for me, I could never let him down."

Zen understood. "You've a strong legacy to uphold."

Law flexed his shoulders. "Hospitality's in Randall's blood, while I breathe baseball."

"Good business sense is in your blood," Zen reminded him. "And you won't have to do everything yourself. Learn from your grandfather. He handpicked each member of his board of directors; they've all been with him for decades.

"Randall's a hands-on financier," he continued. "That's a major part of his success. When it comes to baseball, there are major-league owners who attend every game and those who don't know a bat from a ball."

Zen chuckled. "Remember the ditzy blond trophy-wife who took over the Ottawa Raptors after her husband died?"

Law grinned. "Charlotte Hanson."

"Right. She was asked to throw out the first ball on opening day. She couldn't find the pitcher's mound and threw from third base."

"The press ripped her to shreds."

"She posed and giggled through every article."

"When asked if she felt the Raptors could beat the Mets, she answered 'only if Mercury was in retrograde.'"

"Charlotte did like astrology."

Zen paused and steepled his fingers on the desktop. "Guy Powers is about to lose his team. Set yourself up with strong general partners, a president, a chief operating manager, and you'd be fine."

Zen's smile was sly. "You've got some teammates who will retire within the next two years. Make them general partners and shareholders. Who better to sit on the board of directors than those who've played the game? They're all like brothers. You'd keep the team in the family, so to speak. You'd trust each man to make the right decisions for the club. They'd kill for you."

As he considered the possibilities, the tension in Law's chest lessened. "I can picture Kason Rhodes heading contract negotiations. The man's tough but diplomatic. Psycho in a suit discussing revenues with the comptrollers at our annual meeting would keep the bean counters on their toes."

"The players would be on your side. That's all that matters. There'd be no bullshit or betrayal. Each man would give you his best." Zen's gaze narrowed. "Tell me, James Lawless, are you in the market for a ball club?"

Law took the dive. "Keep your finger on Powers's pulse. Find out his asking price and how soon he needs to sell."

"I'll move quickly," Zen said. "My gut feeling: there'll be no negotiations. Powers is getting the squeeze and wants out. If the right figures cross his desk, he'll bite."

"Get on it, Zen."

"I'll make some calls tonight."

West of the city, traffic was nonexistent, and Law pushed the speed limit on the back roads. The Bugatti responded to his lightest touch. It seemed like no time before he cut the car's headlights and coasted to a stop, a block off Larkspar Lane.

Dusk soon shoved the sun behind the horizon. A timer switch flipped, and lights illuminated the houses and lawns. Early Bruce Springsteen blared from a garage, and the village danced.

Law climbed from his car and stood near the hood. He leaned against the sleek bonnet and searched out Cat amid the throng. He quickly found her, and all he could do was stare.

This Catherine May was far removed from the financial world. She looked fun and free. Sassy. SWEET BABY was printed on her pink T-shirt. Her skinny jeans fit like a second skin. She danced barefoot. Her blond hair bounced. The song "Dancing in the Dark" showed off her moves.

Her father partnered her, twirling her around, until dizziness made her stumble. She laughed into her dad's concerned face, then hugged him fiercely.

Then Springsteen's "I'm on Fire" captured the beat of the night. The celebration rocked.

Law had never seen a happier family.

The Mays loved, laughed, and whooped in the twilight. The song soon ended, and Cat's mom cut in to dance with her husband. "Hungry Heart" played next. The younger kids danced apart while the married couples pressed close, choosing to slow dance.

Law caught Cat's smile as she stepped back onto the lawn. She shoved her hands in the back pockets of her jeans. She watched from beneath the lamppost. The light made her look ethereal. She could've been an angel.

"Dance, sweet baby?"

Catherine jumped. She hadn't seen James Lawless coming. He'd been on her mind, and the sight of him stepping out of the darkness seemed downright spooky. His gaze was hot and fixed on her T-shirt. His grin was a total turn-on.

Law didn't wait for her to reply. He settled her against him. Their bodies meshed, rubbed, pulsed.

The night was warm, but Law was warmer. His athletic body moved nicely. She matched his slow steps. They danced in the freshly cut grass. Gardenias scented the air.

She clutched his shoulders.

And he wrapped her in sexual awareness.

She'd worn red-heeled Wonder Woman boots the last time they'd danced. The red costume had a push-up bra that had pressed her breasts practically to her chin. The blue satin bottom covered in white stars had cut higher than any of her panties. She'd gotten a bikini wax to wear it.

This time, she swayed against Law, shoeless and fully clothed. Somehow, they still fit.

He was warm, muscled, and teased his knee between her thighs. Khaki rubbed denim, and his heat spread her legs a little wider. Had they been horizontal, he'd have penetrated her by now.

His familiarity put the fear of God in her.

"Miss me?" His breath teased against her ear.

"You've been gone?" She kept her voice even.

She felt him chuckle; knew his whole body smiled.

"Time flies." Her mouth was even with the wide aqua stripe on his dark brown pullover. "Congratulations on taking both series."

He ran his hands along her spine. "You caught the games?"

Every single second. She'd joined Zen in the conference room at the onset of play. She'd brought the hot dogs, popcorn, and sodas; and he, his expertise. Zen Driscoll had taught her baseball. She still couldn't tell a curveball from a changeup, but she now grasped the basic rules.

"I watched an inning or two," she responded.

"Did you catch Risk's home run in Atlanta?"

She nodded.

"Psycho's triple in Miami?"

"He barely made it to third."

"Brody getting bounced from the game?"

"He had his share of errors."

"How about when Kason slammed into the left-field fence—"

"He never hit—"

"No, he didn't." Law grinned. "You watched all seven games, didn't you?"

She damn sure had. "Start to finish." She'd even enjoyed the players' interviews and final media wrap-up.

"I like that you watched me play."

"Not just you; the entire team."

"I stood out, though, didn't I?"

"You made a nice catch the bottom of the ninth against the Braves."

"Nice?" He looked pained. "That play was heroic."

"You're a real Superman."

"Speaking of the Man of Steel—" Excitement tinged his voice. "The auction closed on the original comic. Walter had my proxy. He brought *Superman* home. *Captain America* and *Superman* will be framed and hung this next week."

He exhaled slowly, a plan forming. "I might move some frames around to find a place of honor for Clone Man, too."

His words surprised her, in a very good way. Law was working through his past.

She hugged him even more tightly.

Law responded with a boner.

Easing back, he looked down on her. "Did you get my gift?"

"The box of Godiva chocolates?"

"Not from me."

"The flowers? Lovely pink carnations."

He studied her. "You're not a carnation kind of woman. You're more hothouse rose."

Roses worked for her. She tilted her head back, playing him a bit longer. "The new iPod?"

He bent forward, and his dark hair fell across the

sharp cut of his cheekbones. Smugness curved his mouth, and his lips nearly touched hers. "My gift takes you to bed."

"Ah, the nightgown."

"In a way, you're already sleeping with me, sweetheart."

The thought aroused her.

She stroked his overly long hair, touched his shoulders, then ran her hands down the sculpted muscles of his upper arms. He was hard strength, a contrast to her slighter, softer curves.

Law glanced to the street where her family danced with abandon. Even the youngest of the Mays bounced in place. "Born to Run" was in their blood tonight.

"Privacy," Cat heard him mutter. He took her hand and tugged her across the lawn. They rounded the corner of the nearest house—her home, but he didn't know that yet. The pitch of the roof blocked the streetlights. They were lost to prying eyes.

He danced her back against the brick wall. They were soon as close as any two people could get and still have their clothes on.

Anticipation tingled and her knees trembled.

Desire crept up her inner thighs.

Passion brought out his warrior's kiss. A man ready to claim his woman.

Catherine May unraveled.

The strong beat of his heart collided with her own.

The hard ridges of his abdomen flexed against her belly as he breathed in and out. More rapidly now.

His hands slid around to cup her ass, bringing her against his sex, settling his erection into the V of her thighs.

She arched her back, raised her hips, deepened the contact.

The eroticism, the intensity, the raw craving took her back to their night at Haunt. Amid the darkness of the club, anonymity had stolen her judgment.

There was something about James Lawless that had her casting caution to the wind. He'd dominated her when she'd been Wonder Woman, and he was doing so again. Before they could move forward, she had to clear their past.

He needed to know that she and the comic book heroine were one and the same.

That the fantasy party girl behind the mask was the creation of a single night, not the real her.

That she was more of a homebody, and family centered.

She hoped he'd take the news well.

She broke the kiss, expelling her breath.

Law sucked his own fair share of air. "What is it, Cat?" he finally asked.

A nervous flick of her tongue, and she tasted both Law and herself on her lips. Her French vanilla ice cream blended with his sugary orange Life Savers. Their combined flavor was a Creamsicle.

Her chin felt a little tender. A whisker burn. Law appeared not to have shaved for several days.

He soon had his breathing under control, but not the rest of his body. His sex pressed her with serious intent.

She drew back to put distance between them.

"There's something you need to know," she forced out. "About me, about us."

"Beyond the fact that we want each other?"

They were two lit fuses, sparking toward the middle.

Their heat should've burned the grass beneath their feet.

"We met—"

"There you are, Aunt Cat." It was her twelve-year-old niece's voice. Ashlyn carried Foxie So Fine under her right arm, and a boot dangled from her left hand. "I caught Foxie dragging your boot down the driveway. It's three times her size and it was slow going. She's chewed down the heel and there are scratches across the toe."

Ashlyn looked at Law, smiling shyly. "You're busy, so I'll take Foxie inside. I'll return the boot to your closet and tuck it beneath your Wonder Woman costume."

"Her Wonder Woman costume?" Law was on Ashlyn in two strides. The girl's eyes went wide. He put his hands on her shoulders to calm her. "She's my favorite heroine."

"Mine too." Ashlyn visibly relaxed. "I like her red satin cape and sparkly gold headband."

"I'm a fan of her red-winged mask," said Law.

"It's a great costume," Ashlyn went on to say. "Aunt Cat let me try on the brown wig." She scratched her head. "It was itchy."

Law cut Cat a look. "I bet it was."

"I wore the silver indestructible bracelets to school last week for show-and-tell."

"I'm sure you looked pretty," Law said.

Ashlyn sighed. "Too bad Aunt Cat lost the Lasso of Truth."

"A damn shame." He apologized for swearing.

Catherine May wanted to run, needed to hide.

She reached for Foxie and hugged her niece.

Law snagged the red boot.

Cat took off for her house at a fast clip.

"Not so fast, Amazon Princess." The slap of Wonder Woman's boot against Law's palm quickened her heart. "You owe me more than an explanation."

More sounded very, very sexual.

Chapter 9

Catherine May made it to her back porch, beating Law by less than a second. He was on her, swinging the screen door wide so they both could enter. She'd left a light on, but the bulb was dim. She and Law stood in shadow.

Cat clutched Foxie protectively against her chest. She cut both man and boot a look and watched as he settled onto her red patio furniture.

He looked far too comfortable on the floral cushion, as if he'd sat on her porch his whole life and would continue to do so for the next fifty years.

His gaze held steady, holding her in place. He didn't seem overly irritated by her lie. Instead, there was heat and hunger in his eyes and a hint of revenge.

Law stroked the Wonder Woman boot, slowly, caressingly, as if she wore it now.

She could feel his fingers on her leg. Starting at her ankle, working up her thigh. Reaching higher still . . .

Her whole body shivered.

"Confession is good for the soul," he prodded.

She'd have moved if she could, but her legs felt leaden. She needed to get the lie off her chest.

"I wanted to tell you, tried to tell you—"

"But you didn't."

He wasn't going to make this easy for her. Better to come clean than stay dirty. "I visited Haunt with the eye of a financier. But somehow the atmosphere of the place pulls you in. You walk through the door not knowing a soul, yet you can feel everyone's pulse. It's one giant erotic heartbeat."

The schipperke wiggled, and Cat set her down. Foxie immediately ran to Law. He picked her up, allowed her bite, and said, "I'm yours."

Once settled on his lap, Foxie eyed Cat with the same intensity as Law. Both man and dog sought answers. Her puppy had taken his side. Little traitor.

"We're listening," said Law.

He set the heeled boot on the floor next to his chair. It stood straight, positioned so Cat could step right into it. The boot heightened the tension. A sexual tease.

"The night at Haunt got long. I absorbed the atmosphere and was propositioned a dozen times," she explained. "I was on my way out when Captain America blocked my path."

"Did he turn you on?"

"You know the rest."

"Tell me again."

He wanted to relive the night through her eyes.

He needed to know if she'd been as affected by him as he'd been by her. If the fantasy went both ways.

She squirmed but found no wiggle room.

Memories claimed her and her heart quickened.

Haunt was so easily visualized.

She'd relived the night a hundred times.

She could feel the hot, sexual rhythm of the club.

Her nostrils flared with the scent of pumpkin candles and heated pheromones.

Hidden behind masks, men and women had gyrated with sexual intent.

At the end of the night, costumes would be ripped off, sheets pulled back, and pleasure taken in bed.

"You overwhelmed me," she was slow to admit. "Your sheer size made me want to step back, yet your sexy smile, the dangerous glint in your eyes, took me beyond myself. I was no longer Catherine May. I became Wonder Woman. Her identity allowed me to let go."

"The good girl gone bad." He sank back in the patio chair, stretching his long legs before him. A man far too relaxed and comfortable while she suffered humiliation.

He arched his brow, wanting more details.

He was killing her now.

"We made small talk, we slow danced, and kissed."

"And—" he pressed. The man was insufferable.

"You seduced me."

"You lusted back, babe."

She dipped her head. "I got caught up—"

"Look at me." He wouldn't let her shy away from their night together.

She lifted her head and their gazes locked.

His face was shadowed in the porch light. His scar stood out, white and sharp. His stubble was dark. His eyes were dangerously bright.

Her cheeks warmed. "We made out, hot and heavy."

He scratched his jaw. "I remember an orgasm . . ."

Damn the man. She clenched her fists. "I humped your groin."

"How was it?"

"I . . . came."

"Was it good for you?"

Beyond good. Light had fractured behind her eyelids. She'd come apart in his arms. "I was embarrassed."

"But pleasured."

So satisfied her knees had buckled. She'd barely made it to the exit ahead of him.

"Why'd you leave?"

"I couldn't face you or myself afterward."

"Yet we met at Driscoll Financial the next day."

"You walked in, a high-profile ballplayer, and spoke of attending Haunt as Captain America. I froze, afraid if you knew me as Wonder Woman, you'd think I was easy. I wanted to be taken seriously."

He rolled his tongue inside his cheek and said, "You laughed behind my back at my attempt to find the Amazon Princess."

"Never laughed, Law. I swear." She crossed her heart. "It scared me you were so intent on finding her. I'd planned to take the secret to my grave."

He pursed his lips. "That explains your panic every time you saw the Lasso of Truth."

"I dropped it on my way out of Haunt. I never expected you to pick it up."

"It was my only connection to Wonder Woman."

"She is someone I'm not," said Cat.

"She's inside you." Law's voice was deep, husky. "She came out to play at Haunt."

"Wonder Woman's done playing—"

"Don't pack her away yet, sweetheart. She and I have unfinished business."

"What kind of business?"

Several heartbeats of silence, tense and telling. "Go put on the costume." The demand came with a predatory vibe.

"Now?" Her mouth went dry.

"Definitely now."

"I don't have the lasso," she said, stalling.

"We'll pretend you do."

The man wasn't moving. He'd sit on the patio chair until the cows came home or until she turned into Wonder Woman.

"Why?" she asked him.

"You owe me."

He'd been superhero hard at Haunt. She'd left him hanging. She'd played him with her secret, never planning to confess. She was now cornered. Big-time.

She partially blamed Foxie. The pup had dragged out the vinyl boot at the most inopportune time.

"I'll change, but it could take a while," she said in defeat.

He tapped his watch. "You have fifteen minutes, Cat."

"Then what?"

"I'll kidnap your dog."

The schipperke snuggled against his chest, almost asleep.

He tossed her the boot. "Clock's ticking, babe."

She dragged herself to her bedroom and pulled the costume from her closet. The outfit openly mocked her. Her deceit had come full circle and now bit her in the ass.

She stripped down fully, naked and vulnerable. The

bodice had a built-in bra. The blue bottom with the white-star pattern was sheer. Panties would leave a line.

Her mind felt splintered. And her hands shook.

The costume was spandex tight, as close as skin. With her first attempt, she pulled it on backward. The breast cups pointed behind her.

Reversed, the skimpy satin that covered her crotch now cut her butt like a thong. She rolled the costume down her body and tried again.

Her second attempt transformed her.

The costume shored up her confidence.

She cuffed the silver bracelets at her wrists. Wrapped her waist with the wide gold belt.

Next came the red-and-white vinyl boots.

She stood tall. Close to six feet.

She'd be eye level with Law.

The wig proved difficult. She fought with the hairpiece for several minutes. Finally got it on straight.

The golden headband added sparkle.

She slipped on her red-winged mask, studying herself in the full-length mirror attached to her closet door.

She was unrecognizable.

Gone was Cat May, and in her place stood Wonder Woman, a member of the Justice League. Confidence, power, and control settled bone deep. She had female strut and could kick villain butt.

Zam, bam, pop! No one messed with Wonder Woman. Not even James Lawless.

She returned to the porch, crossed to him, and took a superhero stance: head cocked, hands on her hips, and legs splayed over his feet. She towered over him. A true Amazon Princess.

He set Foxie on the floor of the back porch and the

pup scooted inside. Law then gave her the once-over—
twice. His gaze moved so intimately, so hungrily, her
entire body tingled.

Seconds ticked to a full minute before he pushed to
his feet and their bodies brushed. The erotic rasp of
his shirt against her leotard seduced the silence.

Cat stood her ground.

And Law crowded her.

He circled her, checking out each curve, angle, and
line.

He looked, but never touched.

Yet she still felt stroked.

After admiring her fully, he stepped in behind her.
She leaned back against him and felt him everywhere.
He was all taut muscle and warm skin. His sex strained
against the fly of his khakis. The accelerated beat of
his heart against her back sent shivers down her spine.

She turned slightly just as he tilted forward. Her
eyes were half closed and she pulled in a full breath,
waiting for him to kiss her. The anticipation almost
killed her.

His kiss was no more than a light graze of his lips—
soft, warm, fleeting. Her stomach clenched. He went
on to deepen the kiss and their tongues tangled. His
embrace became more personal, more impassioned,
with each second that passed.

Her ability to think, to reason, was soon lost. She
gave a deep sigh of pure pleasure.

Their kiss broke, yet their breaths connected in
short pants. He reached around her, securing his left
arm beneath her breast. Her hands came up to his
wrist, circling it.

"What are you going to do?" Her voice was breathy.

"I'm going to do you." He nuzzled her neck.

Her desire met his arousal and the air crackled with sexual intent. In that moment, Wonder Woman gave up her superpowers and fell to the passion of a mortal man.

He touched her with a deliberate slowness that heightened each sensation. Cupping her breast, he rubbed his thumb across her nipple. The tip puckered against his palm. His fingers trailed her rib cage with inordinate care. His hand moved lower to caress her hip, then curved over her bottom. He squeezed gently.

He went on to graze her bare thighs. Goose bumps rose. The callused pads of his fingers eased between her legs. She swayed slightly on the heels of her knee-high boots as she widened her stance, but Law held her steady.

He stroked her sex through the blue bikini bottoms. The abrasive rub of his fingertips through the satin costume was erotically sensual. His unrelenting attention taxed every nerve in her body.

A craving took hold and she moved against his fingers. He increased the pressure. She arched into his touch, grew sinfully damp. Her inner muscles contracted. She tensed to the point of snapping.

Her body flushed and her lungs compressed. Could her heart beat any faster? Stars danced behind her eyes as he brought her to climax. She let out a low moan, despite her efforts to keep quiet.

Sensations lingered, fluttery tremors that made her knees buckle. She sank against Law. Her body was sensitive, tingly, sated. The corners of her mouth curved in female satisfaction.

He held her for several minutes, until she'd recovered. Once she could stand on her own two feet, he turned her to face him. He rested his forehead against her brow and kept his voice low. "Orgasms: Cat two, Law zero."

She blushed. The man was a ballplayer—he kept score both on and off the field. She was ahead in their sexual count.

He straightened then, his expression suddenly serious. "Haunt in two days—don't disappoint me, babe. I want you. When the time comes, I'll take Wonder Woman to bed, but I'll make love to Catherine May."

She watched him leave through the porch door, a sexy guy with a killer build. He knew her body far better than she knew his. That would soon change. They had innings yet to play, and she planned to take him into overtime.

The next two days passed in a financial blur.

Randall Burton Lawless was in for the fight of his life to acquire the Richmond Rogues. He refused to let his name go public as an interested investor.

Privacy was the name of his game.

An inside corporate leak claimed Guy Powers was in desperate straits. The media had a field day.

Men of industry converged on James River Stadium, bids in hand. Ten investors had thrown their hats in the ring. Nine too many as far as Cat was concerned.

Techno-Air Dynamics had stepped up the pace. Their legal team had presented an offer that very morning, pressuring for an answer by the end of next week.

Guy Powers believed he could twist arms as well. The presentation of bids would close the following Friday. Those wanting to acquire the Rogues would meet in his boardroom. Powers would go over the offers and make his decision.

Despite his years, Randall kept pace with those half his age. Cat had gained the inside track through bank associates. Those at Richmond First kept her posted as to all corporate inquiries on the sale.

She needed to know her competition.

Randall seemed pleased by her progress.

They lunched together twice. He took her to The Brigadier Club, an establishment that catered to Richmond royalty. Most of the diners were bred and born in the city, their roots deep in founding families.

Randall introduced Cat to CEOs and presidents of large corporations. She took it all in and fully recognized her future: to rise to the top of the financial profession.

Catherine treated for their second meal. She took him to Fiesta's, a Mexican restaurant. Randall chose arroz con pollo, a dish not served at the Richmond Grace. He commented several times on the atmosphere, enjoying the mariachi music, the piñatas hanging from the ceiling, and the life-size plaster donkey wearing a red sombrero at the entrance.

Cat teased him when the waitress brought their dessert. Randall's slice of flan was twice the size of hers. The waitress liked him.

Cat admired the older man. No matter his wealth, he managed to appreciate every aspect of life. He was savvy, smart, and his stories about the early days of the Grace hotel chain took her back to the 1940s. Randall was a human history lesson.

During their time together, they never touched on

Law. Cat liked it that way. She was about to sleep with the man's grandson. More than Randall needed to know.

She hadn't spoken to Law since the night on her porch, when she'd been costumed as Wonder Woman. Being apart for two days built anticipation. Just thinking about him turned her on.

Every time he crossed her mind, she nearly had an orgasm.

She'd purposely worked late on Saturday, pushing forward with her evaluation of the Rogues organization. There'd be no surprises when she faced Guy Powers. She'd know every nuance of both man and team.

Her office clock struck six. In three hours, Club Haunt would open its doors. It was a very exciting time for Law, Prosper, and the new manager, Adrian Austin.

Walter Hastings had created a major media blitz. He had people believing Haunt was the hottest spot in all Virginia. Tonight's bash would draw the city's movers and shakers, including the Richmond Rogues.

There'd be an enormous crowd, primed for anonymity.

She'd attend as Wonder Woman—her persona bold, assertive, fierce.

She'd be Law's fantasy.

Time moved much too quickly. She was fully costumed with a spritz of spicy fragrance at her neck when the doorbell rang. No one was expected. She tugged her long, red cape around her, covering her skimpy costume.

Cracking the door, she found a liveried driver, his stretch limousine parked at the curb. The license plate: RG-5.

A Richmond Grace limo.

Law had provided her transportation.

"Wonder Woman, I'm Jacob," the chauffeur said. "Mr. Lawless felt the limousine would be easier to park than your invisible plane." He kept a straight face.

Cat's throat tightened. Law was collecting her with style and consideration. He was easing her into their evening together.

She clutched the cape over her breasts and locked the front door. Jacob tucked her into the limo. Foxie was spending the night with Cat's parents.

She was free of obligations.

And easy for Law.

Club Haunt was lit up like a motion picture premiere. Strobe lights fanned the sky, and a red carpet covered the sidewalk. Tuxedoed bouncers kept the crowd in line.

The night held excitement, promise, and James Lawless. She didn't expect commitment; only hoped for emotional intimacy.

A barbarian in a fake fur tunic, horned helmet, and leg wraps met the limo. His mask covered the upper half of his face, and his battle-ax appeared authentic.

"Catherine, it's Walter Hastings." The man offered his arm. "I'm Conan for the night."

Tonight Walter, of the three-piece suits and administrative polish, brought out his inner warrior. She never would have recognized him in the crowd.

Butterflies winged from her stomach into her chest as she entered Haunt. She was returning to a scene of anonymity and abandon. She left her inhibitions at the door.

Tonight Wonder Woman and Captain America

would take up where they'd left off. At the far side of midnight, Law would lay her bare.

A live band rocked the warehouse. New VIP lounges bordered the dance floor, offering private conversation. A one-way mirrored deck built high over the buffet gave management a bird's-eye view of the crowd.

A controlled mob, she thought. Everyone was costumed and out to have a good time. The scene was wild.

Conan the Barbarian directed Wonder Woman toward a cluster of superheroes—all big, tall, powerful men, smiling, shaking hands, posing for photographers, and signing autographs. A few heroes were being interviewed by reporters.

"The Rogues." Conan identified each player and the costume he wore. "The Incredible Hulk is the last to show. Brody Jones can't tell time."

He scanned the room, visibly pleased by the turnout. "Tonight goes beyond party hearty. The money raised at this event will be split among the team's favorite charities.

"Enjoy," Conan said as he eased into the mix.

She located Captain America among the heroes at the exact same instant he spotted her. A hundred people separated them, yet Wonder Woman saw only him.

Time slowed to the tick, tick of her heart.

The moment seemed surreal.

He took a step toward her.

And she toward him.

The crowd gave way to their meeting.

They soon stood before each other, lost to the noise and the hustle.

"You made it," Captain America greeted her.

"You thought I'd back out?"

"I never doubted you'd show. Wonder Woman wants me."

"You're pretty sure of yourself."

"I have super senses." He grinned, and his dimples flashed. "I can feel her desire."

"Feel me now."

He did. In his own way, in his own time.

There was no hurry in this man to find a private corner and press her to the wall. To kiss her, touch her, excite her. Instead he took it slow.

So slow that by their fifth dance, the physical tension between them had her so wired, she wanted him right there, right then.

He had a way of brushing his body against hers, breathing on her neck, that drove her wild. Each time, her shivers grew to the point she was actually trembling.

Captain America had game.

And he was playing her.

A slow number finally brought them into contact.

She pressed against his heat, so warm herself, they were on fire.

The club atmosphere was an accelerant for sex.

The captain kissed her forehead, her cheek, the tip of her nose. But never came near her mouth.

His arms wrapped her waist, but not as tightly as she'd have liked. The flex of his biceps proved he wanted to pull her closer, but he'd save close for later.

She sighed and eased back slightly to scan the crowd. "Haunt has a pulse tonight."

He ran his hand down her arm, pressing his thumb to her wrist. "Your heart's keeping pace with the club."

She laid a palm on his chest. "Yours is beating for me."

A flash of red cape, and Superman flew by. The *S* fit his chest perfectly. "Big-ass blast," he stated.

Chewbacca from *Star Wars* caught the superhero's shoulder. And Superman scowled. No one tugged on Superman's cape.

"Risk Kincaid," Captain America told her. Kincaid's wife, Jacy, passed next. Her mask was hot pink, feathered, and glittery, like Mardi Gras. Her soft pink jumper had BABY ON BOARD scripted just below her breasts. No wonder Superman soared.

"Risk won the locker-room baby pool," Captain America told her. "Psycho's going for second place."

Men and women making babies brought a warmth to her breast.

They'd found their mates and settled down.

The players wanted families.

Cat couldn't imagine life without children and a close extended family. She wondered if Captain America would ever stop fighting crime and find someone special.

Batman was the next to greet Wonder Woman. Romeo Bellisaro had lost his wife in the crowd. He swore the mob had swallowed her whole. He was about ready to send up the Bat-Signal to locate her.

A second slow song started, and couples danced so closely, they looked like singles. Wonder Woman went flush against her hero. She let his strength sift through her.

Their bodies fit. He was all muscle, ripped and defined. She rounded his rough edges with her curves.

It was early, only ten thirty, yet Captain America didn't know how much longer he could hold Wonder Woman in his arms and not take her right there on the dance floor. He could dance her into a dark corner for another dry hump or he could call for his limo and return to the hotel.

He decided on the Richmond Grace.

It was time to get naked.

There was no hesitation from the Amazon Princess. She took his hand willingly, allowing him to lead her to the exit. On his way out, he scanned the couples dancing.

Before the night was over, it looked like the Tasmanian Devil would bed Rapunzel. A flying monkey would do the dirty with a naughty schoolgirl. And the Lone Ranger would capture Marilyn Monroe.

Even the Pillsbury Doughboy was getting some action, his round body rubbing against a female baker. He'd be a crescent roll by morning.

Sex was in the air.

Every cell in Captain America's body craved Wonder Woman.

He held her hand in the limousine, ran the callused pad of his thumb along her softer inner palm.

He caught her intake of breath, the parting of her lips. Watched the goose bumps rise on her forearms.

He wanted to kiss her, but held back.

He let the anticipation build another twenty minutes.

The penthouse was quiet, except for Bouncer. The boxer yawned, wagged his greeting, then returned to his dog bed.

They moved down the hallway, passed the guest rooms, and entered the master bedroom.

"Last chance," he offered. "If you're not sure about

us, you can fuel your invisible plane and fly right out of here."

"I've landed."

The plush carpeting captured their footsteps.

He pulled the curtains back, knotting the ties around silver hooks on either side of the wall. Before them, Richmond sparkled with light.

She came to stand beside him. "So pretty."

"We can see the city tomorrow," he said. "I need to look at you now."

"I want to see you first," Wonder Woman responded. She was bold and confident, and took the lead. She stripped him down.

She worked his costume off slowly, as if savoring every inch of exposed skin. Gone was the blue mask with the *A* centered on his forehead. Next came the red boots that reached his knees. She dropped down, so low that her wig brushed his groin. His dick twitched, his arousal evident.

Her breath blew on his thigh, then his erection, as she worked her way back up his body. His red gloves soon cleared his elbows. He tossed his indestructible shield aside.

He needed no protection against this woman.

She fingered the spandex at his neck, then rolled it off his shoulders and down his chest. She admired as she went, her gaze as hot as his body.

The spandex caught on his sex, and she took her sweet time releasing him. If she touched him much longer, he'd fire one round ahead of her. He didn't want that to happen.

"Go lie on the bed," she commanded.

He took direction well. He lay on his bed, propped

up by several pillows. He turned his head and watched her undress.

It went beyond a sultry striptease.

She was readying his body for the night ahead.

Playing to him, keeping him hard.

She saved her wig until last. Off came the gold sparkly headband, followed by the dark curls.

She gave him an eyeful.

The lady was blond, green eyed, and nakedly beautiful.

Their night of fantasy and flirtation had come to an end. James Lawless reached out and tugged Catherine May across his bare chest.

His bed had often seemed overly large for one person. When she joined him, the mattress felt just right.

She straddled his hips. The tip of his sex strained upward. His testicles tightened, yet he didn't enter her.

He trapped her close, and his mouth descended. He teased and tasted her. Courted her with deep, hot, moist kisses.

She responded with passion and a desire to please him.

She pleased him all right.

She gave, he took, and he returned tenfold.

Her hand stroked his chest, and his heartbeat slammed against her palm. She explored him with her fingers, and his need to touch her became intense.

His fingers grazed her breasts, then squeezed her nipples. He increased the pressure, and her inner thigh muscles tightened.

He skimmed his hand across her stomach, and her soft skin shimmied.

He fanned his fingers over her inner thighs, stretching toward her curls. He rubbed her. And she went wet for him.

He fingered her more deeply. One finger, then two.

Her hips jerked.

"Sweet spot," he breathed against her mouth.

He swallowed her moan as he worked her even higher.

He loved listening to her pant.

Her breasts bore the blush of her arousal.

She neared orgasm.

He wasn't ready for her to come.

He wanted her so into him, she'd never find her way out. The idea of Cat in his bed, in his life, in his future, seemed right to him. He showed her how much she meant to him by prolonging each kiss, each stroke, every slow rock of his hips.

He scored a condom from his dresser and rolled it on.

When he finally took her, she leaned forward slightly. The position was one to stimulate them both.

She moved on him as no other woman ever had.

She raised herself up, then thrust back down.

Her hips rolled backward, forward, and she added a special little twist that made him suck air.

Their pelvic bones pressed as they sought release.

They pushed each other, harder, faster, until the bond that stretched between them took hold, this time strong and unbreakable.

They climbed—higher and higher—and then reached the stars.

Afterward, as they came down together, Cat stretched out next to him.

Law snugged her close, his energy zapped.

"Superhero sex."

He heard the smile in her voice. "But mortal recovery time."

"I can wait."

He didn't make her wait long.

Chapter 10

Brody Jones still hadn't recovered from the road trip.

He *hated* feeling like a loser.

Worse yet, he'd gotten tossed from a game.

On national television.

Once the plane landed, he'd driven around Richmond for hours. He couldn't stop cursing or mentally kicking himself in the ass. Life sucked.

It was nearing midnight and time to head home. He had a team obligation to attend the reopening of Haunt. Law was his friend. He wouldn't let the man down.

He parked two blocks from Duffy's Diner, then slunk back down the sidewalk wearing a plain black baseball cap pulled low over his eyes and a Windbreaker hiked up to his ears. He walked by the front window three times. Walked slow.

Some might have called him a stalker, but Brody didn't give a damn. He didn't want to run into Mary Blanchard.

He blamed her for his shit-poor performance on

the road. No hits, no runs, and lots of errors. He hadn't played so poorly since he was in the minors and his dad died. In an alley with an empty bottle in his hand.

He refused to let Mary ruin his game. His career. That wasn't how it was going down. He'd find her and deal with her and this time make sure he sent her packing back to Plain.

Go home, little girl. Back where you belong.

A fourth pass of the window, and there was no sign of Mary waiting tables. He cut through the diner and took the back stairs to his apartment. He needed a shower before his night at Haunt. A hot, soapy scrub that would wash his crappy play in Atlanta and Miami off his skin. And Mary out of his life.

He stripped, kicking his clothes onto the ever-growing pile of dirty laundry. He needed to stuff his sweat-stained T-shirts and torn jeans into a garbage bag and drop them off at Wash and Fold. The staff laundered by the pound. It cost him ten bucks a week.

He wrapped a towel about his waist, and smacking his scrub brush against his thigh, he lumbered down the hall, headed for the communal bathroom. He hated sharing the facility with six other residents.

He had no other choice until he moved.

A large claw-foot tub had originally stood as proud as a lion on the cracked tile floor, only to be replaced by a bright new shower. Duffy had modernized, but hadn't gotten a larger water tank. Only one person an hour could shower.

Someone was in that shower now.

Son of a bitch. He could hear the water streaming

down. Loud and fast. The hot water going down the drain.

Brody stood in the hallway, simmering at a low boil. He tapped his bare foot loudly outside the door as if that would hurry along whoever was taking his sweet time. Who the hell was taking a shower this late at night?

He needed to get to Haunt and take part in the media coverage, both print and televised. An interview would turn his day around.

Afterward, he was dead certain a sexy vamp with bite-me red lips would be hunting for the Incredible Hulk.

Him.

He ignored the cleaning lady admiring his bare chest as he knocked loudly on the outer door leading to the bathroom and shower area. The woman crinkled her nose when she passed him, then fanned her face.

He sniffed his armpit. Damn, he was ripe. He'd sweated bullets after being pulled off the field in Miami. He hadn't stopped sweating since.

No one answered his knock, so he pummeled the door.

The wood shook on its hinges.

Damn, he couldn't wait any longer for that shower. He barged in to the community bath, which consisted of a toilet, closed shower, and dressing area.

He shrugged off the realization that he was going to surprise whoever was in the shower with his half-nude appearance. Brody never thought twice about wandering around the upstairs public area wearing only a towel wrapped around him.

The other tenants were used to his getting the carpet wet after taking a shower. He went so far as to do push-ups and squats in the hallway.

A ballplayer has to be in top shape, he liked to say, both *in* and *out* of the bedroom.

But what he now found hanging on the back of the bathroom door had him scratching his jaw. What the hell?

He checked out the short yellow mini and longer red gauze underskirt. He fingered the red satin top, cut to show cleavage. His brows raised over the thigh-high white stockings with perky red bows. A pair of black patent-leather heels were so high they made him dizzy.

Who the hell would wear that kind of getup?

The sound of shower spray filled his ears and steam rolled over him in gauzy waves. He sucked the warm mist into his lungs, then breathed out long and slow.

Mary.

Who else could it be? The other tenants were not the party type. The only person on the floor to go out at night was the retired librarian in 2C. She got off on bingo.

He had to be wrong about Mary. She went to church, had morals. She had no business hanging out at a club where costumes came off at the end of the night and sex was expected.

He could imagine her lost in the crowd, dressed to tease. A werewolf would sniff out her innocence, go on to nibble her neck, paw her—

No fuckin' way. He was going to put a stop to this right now.

"I know you're in there, Mary." His voice echoed in the empty dressing room. "I want to see you. *Now*."

The shower stopped. Immediately. Then silence. *Nothing*.

Long minutes passed. What the hell was she doing? Shaving her legs, then her—

Brody cleared his throat. No, Mary wasn't *that* kind of girl. Was she?

The sexy costume made him wonder. Had she changed? Maybe he didn't know her anymore.

"Hi, Brody." Mary Blanchard opened the door, a fluffy white chenille robe wrapped around her slim body. A pink bunny rabbit with buck teeth was sewn on the side pocket. She stood barefoot, her hair plastered to her skull.

The scent of her shower gel swelled between them, the fragrance fresh and clean, while he smelled like a skunk.

He eased the breath he'd been holding. Then let her have it. "What the hell do you think you're doing?" he demanded. "Prancing around in your bathrobe—"

"It's more than you're wearing."

Her gaze was riveted to his bare chest. Was her face flushed from the hot water or his tight abs?

"Get dressed," he ground out.

"As soon as I dry off." She fluffed her hair with a second towel.

"You're wasting my time."

"You're welcome to hop in the shower."

"You'd look."

"There'd be no surprises. I've seen you naked."

He ignored that. Didn't want to hear it. Didn't want to think about those days hanging out on Jasper

Bridge in Plain, hugging and kissing. Touching each other with a hunger that made him ache.

He cut a look at her outfit. "What's with the costume?"

"It's Snow White. I plan to wear it to Haunt."

Brody shook his head. "You're *not* going to the opening tonight. Is that clear? It's late, way past your bedtime."

"You can't tell me what to do," she snapped back. "We're no longer officially engaged. I can do as I please."

He glanced at her left hand. The ring was gone.

He hadn't expected that.

"This life is not for you, Mary," he said to her. "You're not that kind of girl."

"And what kind of girl is that?"

"A girl who would wear a costume that barely covers her ass."

She reached for the white stockings with red bows, and her robe fell open. Brody got a great view of her legs, all bronzed and smooth.

His eyes shot up to her crotch.

Had she also shaved her—

He locked his jaw. What was wrong with him? This was *his* Mary, his high school sweetheart, not a baseball groupie he wanted to fuck to make him feel important.

He was a professional athlete.

A future Gold Glover and star of the Rogues.

Until that game in Miami.

When *he* took a nosedive.

And Mary had survived. She'd somehow stuck it out at the diner and Duffy hadn't fired her ass.

He moved toward her until they were nose to nose.

He was breathing fast, struggling to control himself so he could talk some sense into her—

While she remained defiant, strong. Her cheeks were pink, her eyes bright, her hair tousled.

They were pushing each other hard. Something had to give. Mary wasn't about to back down. The woman had courage.

And something else . . .

She desired him.

Her nipples poked the robe, visible points.

He caught the flex of her flat belly.

Musk captured her meadow-fresh scent.

He felt her want and need.

Rising urges pulled at him, the fierce rhythm building inside. He told himself to leave her the hell alone. But he couldn't.

Lust steamrolled him into a different kind of action—

He slammed his hands against the bathroom wall, pinning Mary between his palms. The smooth, cool tiles couldn't douse the fire seething inside him. Hot, burning. Mary's chest heaved, her lips parted, and her eyes were wide. She was frightened.

"Brody, I—" she began.

"Don't say another word." Before she could stop him, he pulled her into his arms, his hands going around her waist. Then he leaned down and kissed her.

She tensed, surprised at his abruptness. She soon relaxed in his arms and opened up to him, her lips giving way to his darting tongue.

She tasted sweet, the freshness of her just-washed

hair fragrant in his nostrils. He cupped her breasts, still covered by the fluffy chenille.

She moaned, her hands going around his waist and grabbing his butt when—

She gasped loudly, then pulled away, scooped up her bag, and ran from the bathroom.

It was only after she'd gone and he got his emotions back under control that he realized his towel had fallen off.

He was standing bare-ass naked.

His dick pointing north.

At twelve forty-five AM Mary Blanchard arrived at Club Haunt dressed as a sexy Snow White. She clasped her hands together as she took in the scene and immediately realized her ring finger was bare.

She'd lost her engagement ring.

Misplaced it?

No.

Impossible. She never took it off.

Then where was it?

Moving through the crowd, adjusting her black half mask so it didn't make her nose itch, she felt a shiver creep up and down her spine. *Wait*—

She'd taken it off before her shower. Put it down next to her toiletry bag on the shell-shaped soap dish when she'd done her nails. Candy-apple red to go with her outfit. Her fellow waitress, Sally, had given her the polish, insisting she show off her hands and well-kept nails.

How could she have been so foolish as to lose her ring? She knew the answer. *Brody Jones.*

When he'd startled her in the bathroom, she was

washing the leftover suds out of the blue-tiled shower stall and squeezing the water from her hair. She had knocked over the soap dish trying to grab her robe. Her ring must have fallen and washed down the drain.

A single tear slid down her cheek, then another. And another. She was glad she was wearing a mask so no one could see her cry. She had loved that round little diamond sitting so proud on her finger because Brody had given it to her, with love and tenderness on a summer day when the honeysuckle bloomed near Jasper Bridge.

What had happened to change him? Was it her?

Her run-in with him in the bathroom had upset her so much, she'd grabbed her things and fled back to her room.

But not before she got a parting look at his erection. Primed and ready for action. No doubt *he* had plans for tonight that included more than a hot kiss.

Her lips still burned from his mouth claiming hers. His arms had held her tightly, enfolding her in a moment of passion born out of anger.

The man was impossible. Forbidding *her* to go out and have a good time.

Talk about a double standard.

Screw him and his chauvinistic ideas. She might have come from a small town, but she believed in equal rights and being treated fairly. Especially at her job. She liked that about Duffy. *He* had given her a chance to make good. And she had.

She was proud of how her waitressing skills had improved since Brody left. She could scoot up and down the diner as if on Rollerblades. She could balance three plates at once, keep her customers' coffee cups filled with ease, and cut perfect triangles of banana cream pie without smearing the meringue.

But *Brody*. Was he fair? No way.

His attitude toward her made her so mad she'd blurted out to him that they weren't engaged anymore.

Mary looked down at her naked ring finger glowing in the strobe lighting of the club and let out a deep sigh. Seemed it was truer than she'd realized.

Before she'd had time to notice her ring was gone, Sally had popped over to help her get ready for the reopening of Haunt. Helping her wiggle into her tight costume, the gum-popping waitress insisted Mary wasn't showing enough cleavage. Rolled-up socks stuffed into her bodice fixed that problem, but they had a hard time adjusting the tight black wig over her damp, curly hair.

No sooner had they arrived at the club than Sally—dressed as a French maid—paired off with a swash-buckling pirate who promised to shake up her booty.

Mary was left to navigate the club alone.

Which wasn't easy. She hiked up her white thigh-high stockings and tottered about the club in her spike-heeled Mary Janes, looking everywhere at once.

She was intrigued by a bunch of superheroes, laughing and slapping one another on the back. The Incredible Hulk seemed to be paying particular attention to her, but the sexy vampire hanging on to him steered him away from her.

His piercing eyes made her shiver.

Putting him out of her mind, she grabbed a glass of punch and stood away from the music, trying to take everything in.

She wasn't used to all the attention she was getting

from the costumed characters—nudging her elbow, blowing into her ear, or pinching her behind.

"Hey, Snow White, where's your shiny apple?" whispered Robin Hood. "I'd like to take a bite."

She passed on the man in green tights.

"Howdy, pretty lady. Lost your seven dwarves?" asked a sexy cowboy in a Stetson, leather vest, and chaps. His mask covered both eyes and nose. "I'd be mighty glad to help you find them."

Something about his familiar accent made Mary turn around and tilt her head, thinking. He reminded her of someone from Plain who used to talk like that.

Brody?

She narrowed her eyes, taking him in. He was tall enough to be the ballplayer, thick in the chest as well. She looked down with an expert eye to judge his feet, but he was wearing boots. She walked around him in a slow circle and checked out his butt. No, it wasn't Brody.

Still, he had a nice smile. And she *was* here to have a good time. She didn't want to admit she was still hurting from the way Brody had acted that afternoon. His kiss hadn't been tender and nice like in high school. It was rough, crude. He was angry and had bruised her lips.

He scared her.

But she couldn't give up on him. Somehow she had to make him see things her way, that they were meant for each other and always had been.

"Where you from, cowboy?" Mary asked, attempting to play the game. She wasn't good at flirting, but she had to try.

"Texas."

"Big state."

"*Everything* in Texas is bigger, including my—"

"Hold it right there, Festus," a strong male voice mocked, likening the Texan to the slow-witted deputy from *Gunsmoke*. The newcomer moved between them before the cowboy could stop him.

The Incredible Hulk.

The same guy she'd seen earlier, eyeing her. His green body was buff and huge. His chest heaved and anger rolled off him. His costume stretched, about to rip down the middle.

"It's Billy the Kid," the cowboy said through gritted teeth. "Stop butting in, Hulk. Snow White's going home with me."

"Like hell she is."

Before she could cry out, the Hulk picked her up and slung her over his shoulder with ease. A cool breeze blew up her short skirt, tickling her behind.

"Put me down!" Her voice was high, frightened.

"Not until you're safe." The Hulk dropped her on a black velvet sofa in the VIP lounge. A couch so plush, she bounced before she settled.

One look at his big, flat bare feet told her what she wanted to know. *Brody Jones.*

"You're acting like a caveman," she accused. "I don't need a babysitter."

"That's debatable." He scowled. "You're going home, Mary. *Now.*"

"How *dare* you bust in and ruin my night?" she demanded as she adjusted her lopsided black wig. "You're nothing but a big hulking bully."

Bully? Brody Jones set his jaw. The woman was crazy.

"Somebody's got to take care of you," he said.

When he had seen that two-bit cowboy trying to pick up Mary, he'd lost it, plain and simple.

"You didn't want the job before," she shot back, adjusting her cleavage, also lopsided. "Why now?"

What did she have in there?

"You're just a kid, Mary," he said, ignoring her not-so-subtle reference to his recent behavior. He tried not to notice the swell of her breasts, all round and flushed.

Tried, but he couldn't help himself.

Or how her long legs stretched out on the couch.

Whoever would have thought his Mary could look so sexy?

"I'm a grown woman, Brody, and it's time you started treating me like one." Holding on to the couch, she got to her feet and, wobbling on her high heels, stared him down. "See you around, *Hulk*."

"Where do you think you're going?"

"I'm off to experience what Richmond has to offer after dark," she said, walking away without looking back.

That did it.

Spitting fire, Brody turned flaming red under the green greasepaint. Mary had barged back into his life where she had no right to be. And now she was acting like someone she wasn't.

Easy, fast. A quick lay.

That wasn't Mary.

She was like old-fashioned root beer. Its flavor was best when it was homemade. Mary was Plain born, and that's where she belonged. Back home.

He wanted to ram his fist into the wall and yell until he drowned out the hammering in his head, the wild beating of his heart.

Yet a different urge was stronger. A primal force that seeped under his superhero image in a deep, disturbing manner he couldn't ignore.

He wanted this woman in his arms again, even though there was no way in hell he would admit it. To himself. To her. To *anyone.*

He couldn't forget her kiss. Tender and loving. He would have made love to her in the bathroom if she hadn't run away.

Afterward he'd found the engagement ring he'd given her on the floor of the shower.

Had she tried to throw it down the drain?

Or had she lost it and been afraid to tell him?

Either way, he couldn't tell her that he had the ring with the tiny diamond tucked away in his room. She'd make a big scene again about their being engaged.

Brody wasn't ready for that. No fuckin' way.

Not now. Not ever.

"Have you forgotten about me, Hulk?" The superhot Victorian vampire from his first night at Haunt found him in the VIP lounge. She tapped one long, shiny, scarlet nail on his green shoulder.

He turned and smiled. "Fang me."

Who needed Mary when he had this woman ready to blow the peanut butter out of his ears and tumble with him between the sheets?

"I should be insulted after the way you took up with that little Disney," she said, chewing on the end of her acrylic. "But a threesome could be a very interesting proposition."

He raised a brow. "What did you have in mind?"

"You, me, and your little Snow White." The vampire spoke her desire. "Good girl versus bad."

"I only do one woman at a time," Brody said, all

jacked up by his confrontation with Mary and hot for sex. He was about ready to explode. "I choose you. I want your bite tonight."

"Shall we head for your van now?" She licked his neck and stroked his ass. "Then my apartment later."

Brody nodded. "Let's do it."

He followed Vampira outside. The urge to feel a woman's body up against him, hot, sweaty, and aroused, drove him nearly crazy—

Until he ran smack into a scene in the parking lot that drove him crazier still.

Mary.

Without her mask. Holding her high heels and stockings in her hand. Barefoot. Looking distressed as a guy in a cop costume stood over her, talking to her.

Somehow this creep had convinced her to leave Haunt with him. He wanted to grind the guy's bones into dust.

Minutes went by.

His gaze stayed on Mary and the guy in the police uniform standing beneath a bright streetlamp. Mary kept shaking her head *no.* Brody freaked. Damn guy in the cop costume was trying to get her into bed.

No fuckin' way.

He exhaled sharply and came to a decision. "Sorry, Vampira, this isn't going to work out after all. I have to take care of something."

Brody ignored the vampire's hissing protest and, in a few quick steps, crossed the parking lot and planted his big feet firmly between Mary and the cop.

"You wanted to see Richmond at night," he said to her in an abrupt manner. "Here I am."

"Is he bothering you, miss?" the cop asked, not too pleasantlike.

This guy played for real.

"Cut out the crap act." Brody raised his fists. "The lady is going home with me."

"Brody, *stop*!" Mary cried out. "He's only trying to help me. He's a real cop."

"What the—" Confusion pulled his punch.

"The cowboy cornered me in the parking lot," Mary explained. "Officer Davis came to my rescue."

"You know this guy?" the cop asked, his hand on his holster.

"Yes," Mary sputtered, "he's my fian—I mean, a friend."

Officer Davis smiled and relaxed his stance. "Okay. I'll be in my squad car if you need help, miss."

She said, "Thank you, Officer."

Brody led her by the elbow toward his van and settled her inside. "I'm taking you home, Mary."

She went defiant on him. "I'm only going with you so you don't get into trouble."

"You don't belong in a place like Haunt. You're too nice a girl."

"I suppose the sexy vampire is more your type."

Brody remained silent. *Never admit anything.*

Mary continued, "What's she got that I don't, besides fangs?"

"You wouldn't understand." He started up his van and drove toward Duffy's Diner, jamming his foot on the gas when they hit the open highway.

"I do . . . all too well." She let out a deep sigh. "Next time I go to Haunt, I'm putting on a tight bodysuit and going as Catwoman."

"There isn't going to be a next time," he said as he drove down the alley behind the diner and parked near the commercial Dumpster. He turned off the engine and ripped the keys out of the ignition.

Mary sat with her arms crossed, her toe tapping on the floor mat. "We're not a couple. I don't have to listen to you. You can't tell me what to do."

"Wanna bet?"

He got out of the van, circling the hood. Jerking open the passenger door, he slid one hand beneath her bottom and picked her up. He ignored her protests.

"Brody Jones, what's gotten into you?" Mary said, squirming in his arms.

"You want hot nightlife, babe, then that's what you're going to get. I'm accommodating."

"You asshole!" Mary never swore, so Brody knew she was ticked.

She tore off her black wig and beat him with it on his shoulders. She called him names and tried to kick him. She wouldn't give up.

But she didn't call for help.

She could deny it all she wanted, but he knew she wanted him as much as he wanted her. He had a boner to last all night.

By the time he kicked open the door to his room, she was breathing hard, but the fight was knocked out of her.

Her sigh was heavy. "Brody, you wouldn't—"

"Only if you say no."

The look in her eyes told him what he wanted to know. Her blue gaze was wild, fearful, yet filled with passion.

The light from a lamppost cast a white haze through the bedroom window that faced the street. He laid Mary on top of the plaid quilt on his bed and followed her down. He held her close to him, nuzzling his face in her hair and running his hands up and down the curve of her back.

"I want you, Mary," he whispered with a fierceness that surprised even him. Off came her red satin bodice, exposing her breasts.

Round, perfect. How could he have forgotten?

She blushed as red as Snow White's apple when the rolled-up gym socks stuffed in her top rolled onto the quilt. Her breasts suddenly went from a D cup to a B.

She tried to cover herself, but he wouldn't let her. His hands roamed over her breasts, plucking at her nipples, making them hard and pointy. She struggled, but to no avail. Beads of perspiration formed in her cleavage.

His mouth moved to her nipples, sucking one, then the other. He kissed her neck, her shoulders, her throat, as if he couldn't stop and would eat her alive.

Mary tried to pull back, but in doing so she pressed her breasts into his face, arousing him even more.

Brody groaned. Her bare flesh tortured him. He was close to losing it. He wanted to see all of her. He moved quickly—too quickly for her to stop him.

He lifted her yellow mini, then the red gauze under-skirt. He slipped down her white cotton panties, at odds with her sexy costume. He spread her legs apart and stroked her gently.

She was wet. Ready for him.

He sat up and ripped his costume down the middle. It hit the floor in shreds. He snagged a condom from the top drawer on his nightstand and slipped it over his dick.

"Damn, you're beautiful." He knelt, slowly sliding into her. He gave her one gentle thrust before he went wild.

Mary took him completely. She writhed and moaned, her body gripping him so tight it was as if she hadn't had a man since he'd left Plain.

Could it be true? The shock pulled his testicles tight, forcing him to ask.

Her answer sucker punched him in the gut. "There's been no one since you, Brody," she said, her words coming slow and sure, but breathy.

"*Why*, Mary?" he asked, not certain if he believed her. He gritted his teeth. His orgasm was seconds away.

"Because you asked me to wait for you." Her words were pure and true.

The truth of how she felt hit him hard. Scared him more than he would admit.

He sucked air, slowed down. His hands on her breasts were now gentle, the grind of his hips for her pleasure only.

Mary had waited for him. Believed in him.

What had he done?

He hated to apologize, but he owed her one now. "I'm sorry I lost my head tonight," he said before he could change his mind. "But I didn't want to see you hurt."

"Brody—"

"Every time we're together, Mary, I get all crazy inside," he admitted. "Like I'm a kid again and the world is throwing me a curveball and I want out."

Something in the way he said it, the pain in his voice, like a hole in his heart, touched her. She laid her hand on his arm. "I understand, Brody."

She reached up and put her arms around his neck, then pulled his face down to hers and kissed him on the cheek. Green paint smudged her chin.

"I want tonight," she told him.

"Yeah, so do I."

She arched her back and lifted her hips, opening her body to him. He found his rhythm, pushing in and out of her. He groaned her name in a possessive burst of emotion. His whole body shuddered, making her tingle.

She crossed over a moment later. All her frustrations slid away in a warm, languid rush of pleasure when—

Knock. Knock.

"Who is it?" Brody called out in a gruff voice as he got up and dragged on a pair of gray Jockeys.

"Duffy."

Brody looked at Mary as if to say, *What does he want at three in the morning?*

"What's up?" Brody opened the door slightly so the diner owner couldn't see inside.

"Telephone call for Mary from Plain."

"Why tell me?" Brody asked, blocking the door.

"Look, Brody, I'm not poking my nose into anybody's business, but the tenant in 2C heard you two come in together," Duffy said, not apologizing. "Mary didn't answer when I knocked on her door, so I just assumed she was with you."

"You can just assume someplace else, Duffy," Brody said. "Mary's not here—"

"It's okay, Brody," she said, nervous. A feeling of dread came over her as she pulled the plaid quilt around her and tiptoed to the door. There was only one person who would be calling her here in Richmond. She *had* to take the call.

She peeked through the door. "Who is it, Duffy?"

"A woman," Duffy said. She could see him wiping sweat off his face with his long apron. "Says she's your grandmother."

Her hand flew to her mouth. *Grandma Blanchard.*

Mary wanted to crawl under the bed, bury her head, and never come up for air.

She turned, afraid to face Brody. He was staring at her as if he couldn't believe what he'd heard.

"I thought you said your grandmother was dead," he accused. "She calling from the grave?"

"Not exactly," Mary mumbled, trembling. "She—she suffers from a little arthritis, but—"

"*Damn*, woman." He clenched his fists, slamming one against the wall. "You *lied* to me."

And he hated liars.

She'd stretched the truth, and had her reasons. Given Brody's expression, any explanation would fall on deaf ears. He'd never listen to her again.

He was furious.

She was fragile.

Chapter 11

"I didn't *want* to lie to you, Brody," Mary insisted, shivering, though she held the quilt wrapped tightly around her. "It just came out that way."

"Then everything else you said was a lie, too?"

"Partly true."

"Your job at Pop's . . ."

She lowered her eyes. "There is no discount store opening in Plain."

"Son of a bitch." He stomped across the room, running his fingers through hair streaked with green paint. "And what you said about waiting for me and not being with anyone else since I left. That was a lie, too?"

She lifted her chin, getting her courage back. "That was the truth. I honestly thought we were going to get married. I missed you so much, I had to come to Richmond."

"Then where's your engagement ring?" He pulled the quilt away, leaving her topless with her bottom now exposed beneath her short yellow skirt.

She heard him groan, his eyes widening at seeing her nearly nude. Then he got himself under control.

He grabbed her hand, his gaze drawn to her bare ring finger. "Did you take it off so you could go to Haunt and make it with another guy, thinking I wouldn't find out?"

"No, I—I . . ." How could she tell him she'd lost the ring? It devastated her.

She'd made such a big deal out of never taking it off, her story would sound like a lie whatever she said.

She hunched her shoulders. His face was streaked with greasepaint. The fierce look in his bloodshot eyes unnerved her. He looked like the Incredible Hulk.

He was mad as hell.

But so was she.

Something snapped in her, and she felt suddenly strong. Why was she cowering before Brody Jones like a frightened deer on a busy highway? He had openly accused her of wanting another man. When she'd only wanted him.

She'd lost her ring. Otherwise it would still be on her finger. Given the harshness of his features, her explanation no longer mattered. He believed the worst of her. So be it.

The only reason she'd gone to Club Haunt was to see how the Richmond girls excited their men in their low-cut costumes and high heels. In the end she'd learned nothing, and her feet hurt far more than after an eight-hour shift at the diner.

And Brody still thought of her as a small-town girl, not worth his time.

Was he right?

It hurt her to think he was, especially after driving all the way to Richmond, nervous about every wrong turn and clinging to the memory of how crazy in love they'd been back in Plain.

The whispers she'd overheard at the bowling alley from folks too nosy to mind their own business echoed over and over in her mind.

Brody Jones has gone big-time.

He's got women kissing more than his ass.

Mary is a fool to wait for him.

She knew now it was true.

Brody had just made love to her with a wildness that frightened her. Then he'd slowed, gone tender, once he realized she hadn't been with a lot of other men. He'd seemed almost pleased he'd been her first and last lover.

"I'm still waiting, Mary." Brody's frustration was evident in his voice. He banged his fist into his palm.

She watched him staring at her, his expression becoming more distant, as if he was withdrawing into himself.

"Waiting for what?" she said, heading for the door. He made no move to stop her. "To see me beg you to believe me? I won't do it. I did lie to you, and for that I'm sorry, but I loved you so much I would've done anything to bring us together."

She cracked the door and considered for a moment rushing back into his arms and begging him for forgiveness.

She couldn't do it. People from Plain had their pride.

So she said, "I was wrong to believe you might still feel something for me."

"That doesn't excuse the fact that you lied." There was something in his eyes that went beyond being angry at her. He seemed fired-up mad at someone else as well. Someone from his past. "You can't depend on liars."

"I don't know what's eating at you, Brody Jones, why you can't find it in your heart to forgive me. Unless you don't have a heart." She walked through the door, knowing he wouldn't follow her.

She hurried down the hallway to her room, her bare feet making no sound on the worn carpet. She slammed the door hard. Duffy was holding the call for her from Grandma Blanchard until she got dressed. She'd wasted ten minutes arguing with Brody.

She threw on a tank top over her Snow White skirt, then took the stairs two at a time. The news she received was not good. Her grandmother had taken a fall—not a bad one, thank God, but one that would lay her up for several weeks. She needed her granddaughter to come home right away.

"I'm leaving in the morning, Grandma," Mary said into the phone. Then she hung up, feeling relieved.

But miserable.

Her relationship with Brody was over.

For good.

Why did that hurt her so?

She had to shut out her feelings and get on with her life. Her grandmother needed her and that was all that mattered.

She didn't sleep much, tossing and turning, reaching out and grabbing her pillow, wishing it was Brody snuggling up to her. The pain in her was raw, and she wondered if she'd ever feel normal again.

Morning didn't change anything. She packed her bags, grabbing the lamp with the dragon lampshade—

would she ever forget the long fringe flying into Brody's face?

A strange feeling came over her. She seemed to be marking time until she was back in Plain and everything would be right again. It had to be. She had no other choice.

First, she had to tell Duffy she was leaving.

Walking into the diner, she inhaled the smell of bacon frying and fresh coffee brewing. Tears welled in her eyes. She'd miss the rows of mugs lined up on the shelf near the coffeemaker and all the greasy plates piled up in the sink. Sally chewing her gum. And Duffy, the portly cook, ringing the bell with his usual impatience when her orders were up.

"Don't feel bad about going home, Mary. I understand," Duffy told her as he opened the cash register and counted out her pay, plus extra. "Family comes first."

"Thanks, Duffy." She smiled weakly and nodded. "I'll never forget how you took me on and showed me how to be a good waitress."

The cook grinned. "You've improved. You'll always have a spot here at the diner. Anytime you're back in Richmond and need a job, look me up."

"Thank you."

Then she was off, heading up the main highway, traveling over the same roads as before. Only this time her heart wasn't filled with hope, just loneliness. A deep ache had crawled under her skin and squeezed her insides like tangled green moss snaking down the riverbank toward the old creek and choking off its flow.

You'll always have a spot here at the diner.

Those words resounded in her mind over and over again as she drove back toward Plain. She stopped at a small motel along the way, got some sleep, then was up again the next day and hitting the highway.

She could never go back to the diner. Not as long as Brody was there. He'd remind her of what she'd once had and lost.

Rain came down as she drove through the mountains of West Virginia. Heavy, slashing rain that hissed and tried to invade her car. Her windshield wipers worked overtime, but they couldn't move fast enough.

She decided to pull over and wait out the storm. She chose a burger joint with a pay phone and called her grandmother.

Holding in her emotions, she told her grandma she had stopped for coffee to get out of the rain and she'd be back on the road again soon.

"I'll be so happy to see you, child," Grandma Blanchard said. "And hear about you and Brody."

"Sure, Grandma," Mary said, panic threatening to overcome her. How was she going to tell her only relative that she and Brody were finished? Her grandmother had believed they would marry. "Are you feeling okay?"

"I had a little dizzy spell a while go, but I'm feeling better now."

What if her grandmother needed her and she wasn't there? She had miles yet to travel. "I'll be there as soon as I can," Mary promised.

She hung up and took a seat at the counter, watching the rain come down. Big drops splattered all over the plate-glass window. Her car was no more than a blur in the parking lot.

"Don't look like the storm is going to let up soon," the waitress said, pouring her another cup of coffee. "Best you sit it out."

Mary pushed the coffee cup away from her. "I can't. My grandmother needs me."

She paid her bill, then ran to her car.

She had to get home. Had to get away from Brody. He didn't love her. It was over and the sooner she faced it the better.

Her mind was so filled with rambling, irrational thoughts, worrying about her grandmother, her heart breaking, that she didn't see the orange cones and barricade up ahead. There hadn't been any road construction on her way to Richmond, yet on her way back to Plain red flashers now signaled one lane.

The day hazed in front of her like melting wax. She swerved to avoid hitting the barricade, but her wheels couldn't hold the road.

Her car went into a skid she couldn't control.

The rain pounded against the windshield so heavily she could barely see. Her arms ached as she held fast to the steering wheel. She tried to turn left, only to be jerked right.

The vehicle spun out.

The last thing she remembered was putting her arms up to protect her face as the car slammed into the mountainside.

Back in Richmond, Brody Jones took to the night and returned to Haunt. This evening, Vampira gave him the cold shoulder, all haughty and put out. He knew that, with a little coaxing, she'd fang him again. But he wasn't sure he wanted to go another round with the Victorian bloodsucker. She left scars.

He grinned wide when he saw a sexy Snow White with big breasts licking a red candied apple. Her

tongue flicked then swept, teasing him, but he didn't
get hard.

"Snow White turning you on?" asked a knight in
shining armor.

"She's got a hot tongue." He'd give her that.

Depth Charges were his drink of choice. Brody
dropped shots of whiskey in a glass of beer, swallowing
it in one long gulp. He was going for mindless and
numb. And what most would call stupid.

"Forget her." The knight's armor clanked as he
spoke. "She's mine."

There were *two* Snow Whites. Brody wrapped his
mind around them both. One for Lancelot and one
for him. His was smaller, shorter, and sweet as a glazed
apple.

He was having a hell of a time forgetting her.

He'd tossed the Incredible Hulk costume in the
Dumpster behind the diner and arrived tonight as
James Dean. He wore a black leather jacket, jeans, and
a black mask.

He wished he had a Harley.

The Rogues had a day off tomorrow and he planned
to get shit-faced tonight. He damn well had to, after
this second Snow White hit his radar.

Memories were a bitch.

Mary was haunting him.

He tried to convince himself he didn't care that
she'd run back to Plain and taken a piece of him
with her.

Something he'd thrown away years ago.

His power to forgive.

It died when his father took his last drink. Elmer
blamed everyone, including his family, for his failures.

His old man had lied so often, he didn't know the truth.

Brody had never come to grips with that. He couldn't accept *anyone* lying to him. The hurt was too deep to forgive. A man needed to be accountable for his actions.

He downed another Depth Charge and wiped his mouth with the back of his hand. He smacked the glass on the bar, and his nerves rattled. He was royally fucked up.

A turn of his head, and he caught what he feared most: his reflection in the mirror behind the shelf of booze.

Look at him. He was his father's son. The image brought his dad back to life. Brody had turned into his old man—drinking, acting like an ass, and tossing away the one thing in his life that made any sense.

Mary.

Somewhere in his inebriated state, he knew he needed to tell her he was sorry. And that he missed her.

Snow White came on to him with her big boobs and bigger smile. She was a flirt of the worst kind, using Brody to make her boyfriend jealous.

"Want a bite of my apple?" She teased his lips with the candied fruit.

"Share it with your dwarves."

"I want more than heigh-ho, heigh-ho," she pouted. "I want dangerous. Someone like you, James Dean."

"You'd cheat on your boyfriend and go home with me?"

"He's as clunky as his armor in bed."

Mary. She'd never pick anyone else over him.

The urge to get as far away from Snow White as possible moved him from the bar. Drunk as a skunk, he stumbled into the knight. Unfortunately, Lancelot wasn't about to let him off that easily.

The knight was pissed at his girlfriend for flirting with James Dean, but instead of dealing with her, he went after the bad boy. Which was ass-backward in Brody's book.

Lancelot got in the first punch. He clipped Brody's chin. But he hit like a girl.

Brody was drunk, but he was strong. He shoved the knight with his elbow and knocked him off balance. Lancelot went down in a clash of steel and medieval defeat.

Snow White dropped to her knees beside him, a woman of quick apologies and comfort. She removed his helmet and stroked his ego back to life.

"I need you to leave, Mr. Jones, before someone calls the reporters," said manager Adrian Austin. He was a tall man, built to take charge. Two bouncers had his back, the men as big as sumo wrestlers. "Mr. Lawless wouldn't appreciate negative press."

"Yeah, sure," Brody grunted, holding his head and walking, but not too steadily. One of the bouncers got him out of the club through a back exit and offered to call him a cab, but he shook his head. He needed the fresh air.

He left his van in the parking lot. Walked home.

It took him two hours. He made several wrong turns.

By the time he found his way to Duffy's, the smell of fresh hot coffee was too much for him to resist. What the hell time was it anyway? He looked at his watch. Six AM.

The sun clawed the horizon.

And he was sober.

He had a bastard of a headache.

His eye sockets felt ready to pop.

He sat down in a booth at the back and told Sally to bring him a pot of coffee. Black.

"You look like shit," she said, popping her gum.

"I feel worse."

"Where have you been, Brody?" she had to ask, sticking her gum under the black tabletop. "Getting lucky?"

"That's my business."

"And Mary's my business. She wasn't like the rest of the girls you hang out with. She was genuine." She nodded toward Duffy. "We liked her."

He rubbed his forehead. "No lecture, Sally. Just coffee."

He didn't want anyone reminding him about Mary. Desire had surged through him that night at Haunt. He'd dragged her home and played on her innocence.

He'd accused her of being interested in another man.

Something he now knew wasn't true.

"You're mighty touchy this morning." Sally didn't let up on him. "I warned Mary about you. Told her to stay away from you. But she wouldn't listen, and look what happened. You broke her heart." She looked down her nose at him. "If you weren't a customer, I'd call you a jerk. Or worse."

Leaving him to his misery, she turned on her heel and headed for the coffeemaker, muttering to herself. He could see her whispering to Duffy, who'd come out of the kitchen to see what all the commotion was about.

Duffy handed Sally a plate of steaming ham and eggs for the only other customer in the diner, then picked up a carafe of fresh coffee and headed for the booth where Brody was nursing his hangover.

"Damn, boy, man up—"

"Can it." Brody held up his coffee mug so the diner owner could fill his cup.

"I've been meaning to talk to you about Mary." Duffy put the carafe on the table and sat down.

"Not you, too," he groaned.

"Look, Brody, you may be a big man at the ballpark, but when you start messing with my waitresses, I got to say something."

"Say it and be done with it." Brody drank the hot coffee so fast it burned his mouth. He swore his gums blistered.

"Whatever Mary did to make you so mad had to be for a good reason."

"Maybe, maybe not."

"She's in love with you, Brody. And you're too much of a dumb-ass—"

Where had he heard those words before?

Oh, yeah, Law had said the same thing to him the first day he saw Mary waiting tables.

"—to know a good thing when you've got it. Mary is a sweet kid. She took a piece of my heart with her when she left, and yours, too. *If* you're willing to admit it."

Brody curled his lip. "I pay you good rent for that flea-bitten room, Duffy. I don't appreciate you butting into my business."

Ring. Ring.

"Sally, get the phone!" Duffy called out.

Brody poured himself another cup of coffee. He put the mug to his lips, blew to cool it, when—

"It's your mom, Brody."

He shook his head. "Can't be."

"She said she couldn't reach you on your cell so she called here."

He grabbed his jacket pocket, panicking. His cell phone was gone. It must have fallen out of his pocket at Haunt.

"Can't it wait?" His mother was a bloodhound when it came to his drinking. One morning lecture was enough.

Besides, he wanted to hit the sack and think over what Duffy had said. Mary did have a reason for lying to him and it was a good one.

She loved him.

But was it good enough for him?

It damn well should be.

"Your mom says it's urgent," Sally called from across the diner, covering the mouthpiece of the phone with her hand.

Brody shrugged. What could be so urgent at six AM? Unless his mom's cow, Bella, was on a milk strike again.

"Tell her to call the vet—"

Sally gave his mom the message, only to gasp moments later. She put her hands to her mouth. "Oh my God."

She turned and stared straight at him, her voice cracking as she said, "Mary had an accident going through the mountains."

Brody covered the distance between the booth and the phone in seconds. "What happened?"

"A rainstorm, road construction, her car skidded, and she lost control." Sally raced her words. "She went head-on into the mountainside."

"Give me the phone." Brody put the receiver to his ear. "Was Mary badly hurt?"

He stood there dumbfounded as his mom told him

how Mary had passed out, and when she'd regained consciousness, she found the hood crunched like an accordion. But by some miracle, the engine had turned over.

She'd weathered the storm and made it home a couple of hours ago, shaken up but okay. Mary's grandmother had called his mom and told her what happened, but Mary didn't want him to know.

Didn't want him to know.

She hated him, and he couldn't blame her.

But that wouldn't stop him from doing what he had to do.

"Rogues have a free day," Brody said into the phone, dead sober. "I'll catch the next flight out, then rent a car. I'll be back in Plain before dinnertime."

He handed the phone to Duffy.

"Thanks, man," he said, meaning it. "For everything."

Duffy nodded. "Sure, pal."

"Ballplayers," Sally said, popping a fresh piece of gum into her mouth.

"You too, Sally." Brody gave her a hug, catching her by surprise and making her swallow her gum. Then he ran up to his room to pack.

Toothbrush, underwear, clean socks—

He unzipped his toiletry bag and Mary's little diamond ring stared back at him, its sparkle dull and lonely.

Like him.

"You could get your old job at Pop's back, Mary," her grandmother said, rolling up a ball of yellow yarn.

"Though since his wife died, there's talk of him selling the place."

"I don't want to look at any more feet, Grandma."

Especially big, flat feet.

Damn Brody.

"'Course, it'll only be until you and Brody get married. Then you two can settle down and have some young 'uns—"

"I told you, Grandma, we're *not* engaged anymore."

Mary tossed down the local weekly she'd been skimming, checking off jobs. What few there were. Plain was such a small town, population six hundred twelve, and the local businesspeople weren't hiring now.

"I don't know what happened between you two, but it'll right itself," her grandmother said with confidence. "You'll see."

"No, Grandma. It's over between Brody and me." Really, truly over. They weren't meant to be.

She hadn't wanted to tell her grandmother. It was a hard subject to broach. But there was no use stalling for time. There'd be no wedding day.

"You can't fool me, child," the older woman said, tying the end of the yarn into a knot. "You still love him."

"But he doesn't love me."

"Did he ask you for the ring back?"

Mary hid her left hand. "I lost it."

She started straightening up the two-bedroom house she'd shared with her grandma since she was born.

It was a small place with a wood-burning stove that smelled of pine, a big armchair, piles of history books that had belonged to her grandfather, balls of yarn in the oddest places, and a refrigerator always filled with fresh cream, buttermilk, and her grandmother's homemade cider.

The lamp with the dragon shade was back in its place on the end table. The fringe looked tired, the shade partly torn. It looked as old as Mary felt.

"I'd hoped to see you as a bride before I go my way in peace," her grandmother softly said.

"Don't *say* such a thing, Grandma. You'll always be here with me."

Grandma Blanchard shook her head. "No, child. The time will come, and I want to see you settled before I join your grandpa."

The ball of yellow yarn fell from her lap as she got up from her chair with its faded lacy doilies askew on the armrests. She walked slowly over to a big cedar chest.

Mary picked up the yarn, but she knew that was all the help her grandmother would accept. She was independent and wanted to stay that way.

She had that same Plain pride that reminded Mary so much of Brody. Pride would be *his* downfall.

She noticed her grandmother walked slower, her gait different, a sharp pain etched on her face as if every step hurt.

Her grandma's pain was Mary's own.

What would she do if anything happened to Grandma Blanchard?

"Come here, Mary." Her grandmother opened the chest, and the smell of camphor balls filled the room. "I have something for you."

Grandma Blanchard pulled out a long, white satin dress, the purity of its color enriched by her memories. She had worn it at her own wedding, its beauty timeless.

Gauzy layers of ivory tulle covered the white satin skirt with its tiny waist. The tight bodice with its high neck was covered with handmade lace and had sheer fitted sleeves that ended in a point on the back of the hand.

A filmy train trailed across the wooden floor when her grandmother held it up to the late-afternoon sunlight.

"Your mama eloped, and I was never able to hand down the dress. I saved it for you, Mary," her grandmother said.

Damn Brody. A wedding was not in her future.

"It's beautiful, Grandma," she said, bringing the soft satin to her face, praying the tears rolling down her cheeks didn't stain it. "Just like you."

That made her grandmother smile. "You are such a joy to me, Mary. I want to see you happy."

"I am happy, Grandma, being here with you."

"Your young man will come back to you. You'll see." The older woman put the dress away in the chest. "And when he does, the wedding gown will be here for you."

"Brody is stubborn. He's got this idea in his head that he wants to forget his roots and where he came from." She sighed. "I can't fight that."

"But you can."

"How?"

"Show him what you're made of, Mary. Stop brooding and reminiscing about times gone by. Go out and get your self-respect back."

"You're right," she agreed. "They liked me at the diner in Richmond. Duffy said I was a good waitress. I bet I could get a job in the coffee shop at Pop's."

"Then do it, girl."

"What about you, Grandma?"

"I'll be fine. I need help for a few weeks till the old bones mend, and then I'll be my old self again."

"Seeing how the rain has stopped, I'll walk into town." Mary opened a window and breathed in the air. The late-afternoon heat hovered in the clear sky overhead. "I'll take the path that goes around the creek and cross there. The old wooden bridge may be weakened from the storm."

Her grandmother's eyes twinkled. "Didn't you and Brody often meet after school at Jasper Bridge?"

Mary smiled. "How'd you know?"

"I was young once, too, child. I do understand."

A strange look came over her grandma's face that told Mary she was keeping something from her. Did it have anything to do with the phone call she'd placed early that morning?

Mary had gotten up for a glass of water, still shaken from her accident, when she saw her grandmother whispering into the phone and looking over her shoulder to make certain Mary wasn't around.

There were no secrets between them.

The phone call had troubled Mary, but she would let it go, for now.

"I'm tired." Grandma Blanchard returned to her big chair. She lowered her frail body onto the cushion, then straightened the doilies on the armrest. She liked things neat. "Get along with you. I'm going to rest now." She closed her eyes.

Mary kissed her on the forehead, then closed the door behind her. She started down the path to the creek.

Mary's memories were strong. She and Brody had made out under the bridge, and later made love. She'd blushed a deep pink when he'd unhooked her

bra and touched her breasts. Dusk had loomed behind
them, the bordering forest thick and lush, the oak trees
standing tall and still.

The only sound was their heavy breathing.

Then her breathy moans . . .

Mary suddenly knew where she had to go.

She headed down the road toward Jasper Bridge.

She needed to cleanse herself of the past before she
could find the future. The time was now.

She cut across Suttman's Field, owned by a farmer
but used by both Little League and the high school
baseball teams. The diamond was quiet, except at the
hours when teams held practice. Two batting cages
bracketed the stands.

The ground was wet and soggy now, keeping the
players away. She trudged on. The arch of the wooden
bridge was dead ahead.

Brody Jones arrived in Plain tired but pumped, his
need to make sure that Mary was okay driving him on.

He'd dropped off his overnight bag at his mom's
and gotten the whole story from her about Mary and
Grandma Blanchard. His mother was long on detail. It
took her twenty minutes to recount the accident that
had left Mary bruised and sore yet glad to be home.

He was home now, too.

He needed to set things right between them.

Brody told his mom not to hold dinner; that he'd
return in his own good time. He climbed into his rental
car and took a drive down Main Street, then over to
Grand Avenue, the two-block business district. Memories busted his ass—some good, some bad.

He passed the old barber shop where he'd gotten

his first haircut, then Tom's Hardware Store next door. The First National Bank occupied the corner of the block.

He didn't need the GPS navigation system to locate the Blanchard house. He could drive there with his eyes shut. The clapboard looked as old as Mary's grandmother. He parked the car and stepped out, then walked the narrow path to the porch steps. The steps creaked beneath his weight.

The boards on the short porch were weathered and worn, yet swept clean. Purple and yellow petunias filled the window boxes. When he knocked on the door, no one came. A kick in his gut told him he was wasting his time. He'd been mean to Mary. What if she didn't want to see him?

Why did that thought hurt so much?

He rubbed the back of his neck, turning to leave when—

"I've been expecting you, Brody Jones," Grandma Blanchard said, opening the door. "I was napping and didn't hear you knock at first."

No doubt his mom had called her and told her that he was back in town.

"Is Mary—"

"Come in, boy. What you need is a glass of cider and a piece of sweet corn cake." She pulled him inside before he had a chance to object. "*Then* we'll talk about Mary."

Brody smiled. No one could argue with Grandma Blanchard when she invited you in for a snack.

She insisted he sit in the big armchair with the lop-sided doilies and put up his feet. Only when he swore he couldn't eat another bite did she mention Mary.

"What happened between you two, Brody?"

He told her straight. "She lied to me."

"I don't mean that, son," she said quietly. "You were gone so long. Why didn't you come home to marry her? Isn't my granddaughter good enough for you?"

She was too good for him, Brody had come to realize. "Mary's a wonderful girl—"

"But she reminds you of everything you want to forget—is that the reason?" she asked.

"Yes. I can't change that."

"No, but you can accept it." Grandma Blanchard looked thoughtful. "That's all I'm asking of you, Brody. Mary's a small-town girl. Accept her for who she is. Not what you want her to be."

He had every plan to do just that.

Many times Brody had thought about Mary while he pursued other women. He remembered her pretty smile and soft lips. Her gentleness, her innocence. Her unconditional love.

Why he'd pushed her out of his life, he didn't rightly know. Maybe it was because he was a coward, and that possibility bothered him most.

The elderly woman picked up the ball of yellow yarn and started unwinding it. "I've got some knitting to take up. Get on with your day."

"Tell Mary I stopped by." He rose from the chair.

"Why don't you tell her yourself?" she said simply. "She's down by Jasper Bridge."

Where they'd hung out after school. Where he'd proposed to her when he was still a shy kid with a big dream and a lot of promise.

He liked that kid. Too bad Brody didn't know him anymore. The boy was lost to the man.

"Good-bye, Grandma Blanchard."

"Bye, Brody."

He let himself out, his emotions as scattered as the afternoon breeze. Maybe the older woman was right. It was time to man up. He couldn't change where he came from, but he owed Mary an explanation. He prayed she'd accept his apology.

He patted his jacket pocket and felt the circular outline of her tiny engagement ring. Should he win her back, he would take her shopping for a new diamond ring of her choice.

The walk down the road toward the wooden bridge was tough on him, his heart pounding, the scent of honeysuckle strong after the rain.

Then he saw her, standing on the edge of the bridge. She was wearing jeans and a tank top and looked beautiful in the setting sun, its ever-changing reds and golds highlighting her silhouette in a shimmering halo.

He watched as she kicked off her sandals, then looked down into the water. The surface rippled and swirled.

Concern gripped him when he realized she was going to jump. What if she'd suffered a concussion and wasn't thinking straight? She wasn't a strong swimmer. She'd be pulled under.

She could drown.

God Almighty. "Mary, don't . . ." But she couldn't hear him.

Splash. In she went.

He raced to the edge of the river and dove in after her. Down, down he went, moss swirling around him and threatening to choke him. His eyes strained, burned, as he looked for Mary in the murky mess.

He fought to remain calm. If he could hang on,

he'd find her. Had to. He'd been a fool. *A crazy fool.* He wanted her to know that.

Don't give up. His jacket and athletic shoes weighed him down. He felt clumsy and waterlogged.

When he thought he couldn't hold his breath any longer, he grabbed on to her slim body, dragging her to the surface. His arm wrapped her waist as he swam her to shore.

They collapsed on the bank. He immediately noticed the big bruise on her forehead and the smaller one on her chin. Her wet curls stuck to her pale cheeks. She looked fragile and broken. All because of him. He hurt for her.

"What were you trying to do?" She coughed. "Drown me?"

"The river was moving fast." He drew air into his raw lungs. "I saved you."

She rolled her eyes. "The river is poky. You saw the breeze blowing on the surface. I knew right where to jump. I could've managed without you."

That's what concerned him most, her not needing him. Ever again. He stared at her now, remembering all they'd once shared. He wondered if Mary believed in second chances. He damn sure hoped so.

She sat very still. The deepening shadows stretched between them. Night would soon usher out the day. "What brought you home?" she finally asked.

He adjusted his jacket, then removed the little diamond ring from his zipped pocket. He held it out to her. "I needed to see you. You forgot this when you left."

"My ring." There was relief in her voice.

"I found it in the shower drain the day we—"

"And you never said a word?" she said accusingly. "How could you do that to me?"

"I'd rather do this." He pulled her to him, tilted her face up, and kissed her, long and with feeling, then released her.

She touched her lips, swollen from his kiss. "I'm not sure I understand."

"I know who I am, Mary," he told her. "A guy from Plain who can play ball. No more, no less."

"I've waited so long to hear you say that."

He slid the ring on her finger and looked deep into her eyes. "I love you, Mary Blanchard. Will you take me back?"

"You never really left me."

Brody picked her up and Mary put her arms around his neck. Their wet clothes clung together. "We need to change," he said. "And tell your grandmother our news."

Mary laughed. "I have a feeling she already knows."

He nuzzled his face in her wet hair as he carried her down the country road. The breeze that had earlier ruffled the river now hurried them along. The sweet scent of honeysuckle welcomed him home.

Chapter 12

The fragrance of Asiatic lilies and alstroemeria in shades of green, peach, and yellow rose from the centerpiece on a square table at Callum's Café. James Lawless recognized the blossoms, once grown in his grandmother's hothouse nursery on the roof of the Richmond Grace. The sun would beat on the glass structure in the summer and snowflakes whitened the panes in winter.

Grace Lawless had loved flowers, no matter the weather. His grandparents' suite had once bloomed like a florist shop. His grandmother had had a green thumb. She grew everything from exotics to Christmas cactus.

Law favored bamboo. Tall stalks were clustered in his penthouse living room. He'd discovered the plant as a young child during a family trip to China. The bamboo grew wild around the koi ponds and water gardens at the Shanghai Grace. He'd brought a little bit of Asia home with him.

He loved to travel.

Someday he would like to show Catherine May the world. He might get around to it, if she'd allow him five minutes.

After their incredible night together, she'd taken to her office. She'd locked herself behind closed doors.

She said she had a top-priority project on her desk and she couldn't see him for a week.

He'd promised to give her space.

Seven days was seven days too long.

He debated going back on his word.

His heart was into the woman.

He wanted to propose.

But he'd like to do it face-to-face and not by text message.

Lawless men were known to fall in love quickly and for life. In 1955, his grandfather had met his grandmother at Grand Central Station in New York City. He'd been in town on business, and she'd been visiting relatives.

She'd had a ticket on the 20th Century Limited for Chicago. And he'd had his private Pullman attached to a train heading south. His lifelong journey with Grace Morgan began with his purchase of a ticket to the Windy City.

Randall had had no reason to visit the Midwest other than to be with Grace. Their travels extended for fifty-two years.

His father had picked out his mother in the football stadium at the University of Virginia. A running back for the Cavaliers, his dad had scored a touchdown, then tossed the football into the cheering crowd. The ball had bounced around among the fans until his mom caught it.

Law now wanted to catch Cat May.

At that moment Randall Burton Lawless entered the café. He sported a three-piece suit, polished wing tips, and a fresh haircut.

His persona was as old-world as his cane.

The hostess directed Randall to Law and laid down a second menu. Randall patted Law on the shoulder. The strength in his greeting was less vital than in previous meetings. His features were drawn. Fatigue darkened his eyes.

"Perfect health," Randall reassured Law as he settled on the café chair. He leaned his cane against the table. A cane Law admired, although there appeared to be tiny holes near the bottom by the hand-applied horn tip.

"I haven't seen you in several weeks," Law began. "I thought getting you away from the hotel might be a nice change."

"A break is always welcome," Randall agreed. "I've been busy."

"Hotel business?" Law was always interested in the renovations and expansion of Grace Worldwide.

"A bit more diversified." Randall was evasive. He picked up his menu and studied the items.

Law narrowed his eyes. Randall was running down the menu as if this were his first time here. They ate at Callum's often. Both knew the menu by heart. Law always ordered the double cheeseburger.

Randall favored the Waldorf chicken salad.

Today his grandfather chose huevos rancheros. Extra salsa and sour cream. "A special order, please," he said to the waitress. He then rattled off the ingredients and how best to cook the dish.

"Mexican food?" Law hadn't seen that coming.

"I enjoy it on occasion."

What occasion might that be? Law wondered. Who accompanied Randall when he dined out?

Friends in Randall's age bracket were health conscious. Many were on special diets. A combination of chili peppers, garlic, and salsa would give most older people heartburn. Cheese and sour cream would clog their arteries. Eggs would up their cholesterol.

The waitress turned in their order and returned with their drinks.

Randall had black coffee, Law an orange soda.

Their meals arrived shortly thereafter.

They talked business as they ate. Law let his grandfather tally the profits on Grace Worldwide before he mentioned acquiring the Rogues. He couldn't throw his hat in the ring without Randall's backing.

"I've reviewed the monthly spreadsheets on the Atlanta Grace," said Law. "Reservations are up ten percent from last year. It's going to be a good summer."

"All the hotels have maximized," added Randall. "Even the Venice and Madrid Grace hotels are showing substantial profits. They've been slow in past years."

"Your mark is on the chain." His grandfather's international reputation was platinum.

"*Our* mark, Law," emphasized Randall. "Grace Worldwide is family."

His grandfather's voice held pride and hope as he waited for Law to step up to the plate and take over the hotels. The man had built the largest and most prestigious hospitality conglomerate in the world.

It would be handed down to Law. Someday.

He looked at his grandfather, seeing strength, perseverance, and the position of his heritage. Kindness shone in the older man's eyes; his caring had been evident throughout Law's life.

At age eight, following his parents' death, Law had been a broken boy. Randall had raised him. And Law owed him.

His grandfather needed him now.

Law was loyal. He wanted to give back.

He'd had his career in baseball.

He'd give up anything for Randall.

Including the Richmond Rogues.

He'd call Zen and pull out of the bidding war. Zen had yet to put forward Law's initial offer. Law could withdraw without repercussions.

Zen would understand; he'd told Law the acquisition battle would be brutal. Ten initial investors had begun the negotiations. Four were left standing.

His grandfather meant more to him than the sport.

Law's contract ended with the season. His sports agent would soon negotiate with the new owner. Barring injuries, he'd like to play another year, maybe two, and retire with those teammates who'd weathered fifteen years together.

He hoped he wouldn't get traded when the dust settled. And that the team wouldn't be moved to another city.

He ran one hand down his face, clearing his head, putting baseball behind him for the moment. "I've met someone," he told Randall.

His grandfather didn't appear overly surprised.

Randall was as omnipresent as God. He predicted circumstances and situations before they happened.

He had edge.

"Her name's Catherine May," Law continued. "She's

a financier, works with Zen Driscoll. She closed the deal on Club Haunt. She's helping me build Prosper."

His grandfather nodded. "Catherine is Zen's protégée and soon to be his partner."

"I want to marry her."

Randall sipped his coffee. "Is she aware of this?"

"She will be shortly," Law said. "Cat has a heavy workload this week. By Friday, it's back to the two of us."

"An engagement celebration would be in order," the older man suggested. "Just close friends, family."

"Cat was born to a village."

"Well, we've a ballroom at the hotel that can accommodate large parties."

"You have no objection?" Law asked.

"How long have you known Catherine May?"

"A month."

The older man's lips twitched. "That falls within the Lawless time frame. We men have a sixth sense about our women." He looked at Law. "You didn't know sooner?"

"I met her in costume at Haunt. She had me at Wonder Woman."

"And you had her at Captain America."

Law suspected his grandfather knew every detail of that night. But he let it pass.

"Good luck against St. Louis." His grandfather also knew the team's schedule. "Their rookie pitcher is so undisciplined the media calls him ER because of the batters he sends to the emergency room. Last week against Ottawa, he hit a batter in the neck. Damaged his windpipe."

That he had. The kid had power, but lacked precision. And when his pitches went wild, they were dangerous.

Even the mascots feared for their lives.

The Lawless men talked more baseball while they finished their meals. Randall paid the bill.

Law left the tip. "Next time I buy."

"Next time we go Mexican."

The Rogues dropped two of their three games to the St. Louis Colonels. The losses were the result of distraction and irritability.

A new team owner would soon be announced.

Both players and fans were touchy, jumpy, unsettled.

The Rogues paced the dugout fence. It was their last game in the series with the Colonels.

Crowd support proved halfhearted. The occasional cheer rose and quickly died.

The CEOs from Techno-Air Dynamics attended the series. Gerald Addison and Blaine Sutter sat in the owner's box. Their visibility broke the players' concentration. No man could fight the inevitable.

Guy Powers was out.

A new regime would soon be in.

Five o'clock, and there'd be a new front office.

According to the media, Powers had narrowed the field to three investors. Two were familiar to Law, but the third remained a secret. The media had pressed for the names of all involved. Yet one investment team refused to disclose.

Law was impressed they were able to maintain secrecy.

Someone had the press in his pocket.

The game rolled on. The Colonels' pitcher taunted the batters. Fastballs whistled by their ears, tipped their noses, blew behind them, and dusted their balls. It was both intimidating and maddening.

Tempers were barely kept in check. A man at bat wanted to hit, not take a fastball to his body. A deeply bruised shoulder or thigh was painful.

Law's walk down the baseline was a letdown.

Brody Jones was the first player to get nailed by ER. He took a cutter to the wrist. His face twisted. He swore.

Law felt the sting all the way in the dugout.

"Prick," Psycho McMillan muttered, cursing the pitcher.

Brody said worse as he stormed the mound. He landed a solid punch.

The crowd roared their approval.

ER folded like an accordion.

The benches emptied, and the Rogues released their pent-up anxieties. It took security thirty minutes to break up the fight.

Medics took to the field and an ambulance was called.

ER was taken to the hospital.

Brody Jones had broken ER's jaw. And was ejected from the game.

Back in the dugout, Psycho massaged his knee. "Anyone see who kicked me?" he asked.

Romeo shook his head, then lifted his arm. "I got bit." He showed off teeth marks near his elbow.

Risk Kincaid rubbed his side. "I've got a broken rib."

Law knew Risk wouldn't seek treatment until the game ended. He'd play hurt.

Law had taken a knee high on his inner thigh. Any higher, and he'd have had the voice of an adolescent girl.

The game continued, and a St. Louis veteran now pitched. The series soon came to an end.

As soon as the game was over, the Rogues took to the locker room. A celebration should've followed their 5–2 win. But after just a few nods and low fives, the men showered, shaved, and dressed. An eerie silence lingered.

They'd lost two games.

The superstitious scruff was gone.

They gathered, no one wanting to leave.

Not until the new owner was announced.

Psycho slammed his fist into a locker.

Brody kicked a garbage can, upending it.

Law sat on a bench, elbows on his knees, hands holding up his chin. He looked at his teammates. They'd gone the distance together, but their futures were now in jeopardy.

"I'm headed upstairs," he finally said. "There's a media gallery toward the back of the boardroom; it seats thirty."

Romeo straightened. "We could catch the action."

"Make our presence known," added Risk Kincaid.

"Kick some Techno-Air ass." Psycho was in.

"Sit, Psycho, sit," Risk instructed.

On the sixth floor, fifteen players entered the gallery. The seats were situated twenty feet from the enormous rectangular table where the final negotiations for ownership of the Rogues were in progress. Law claimed a seat in the first row between Risk and Brody. He looked at Guy Powers.

Disapproval shone in Powers's eyes as he scanned his team. He didn't appreciate their disruption, even though the men sat quietly. Even Psycho.

Powers sat at the head of the table, flanked by his advisers, attorneys, comptrollers, brokers, his general partners, and two major stockholders. His business team would have kept him focused had he heeded their advice to avoid expanding so quickly in a shaky real estate market.

He'd left his baseball team to suffer the consequences.

The CEOs from Techno-Air Dynamics sat to the right. Their smiles were smug.

Representatives from Langhardt International, an import-export conglomerate, filled six seats on the left. Law recognized the executives from a picture in the newspaper.

But it was the two people seated at the back of the table who drew Law's stare. They'd distanced themselves from the corporate greed at the opposite end.

They sat with poise and control.

With experience and purpose.

An older man and a blond woman . . .

Law couldn't believe his eyes.

He wanted to stand, to cross to them. Give his support. But the code of the boardroom kept him seated.

"Your grandfather." Risk elbowed him.

"Catherine May," added Psycho.

"Damn, dude, why didn't you tell us Randall was the silent third party?" came down the row from Romeo.

Because Law hadn't freakin' known.

Cat's week of silence became clear.

She'd needed her privacy.

She'd been secretly working with his grandfather.

She'd been prepping for this meeting.

Law was so stunned, he couldn't breathe.

He could only listen.

Catherine May sat stiffly in her black skirt suit. She wanted to shift on her seat and cross her legs, but was afraid to move. Afraid it would show vulnerability among these titans of industry.

Randall held his position, intent and stoic.

Cat followed his lead.

She'd attended the meeting at his request.

She hoped her aggressive preparation would pay off.

The boardroom gave her the chills. Powers had purposely pitted the corporations against each other. The atmosphere was hostile.

Negotiations had been heated, yet Grace Worldwide had made it to the final three. The high-powered acquisition discussions had run six hours as each large-scale investor laid out its financial intentions.

She'd been prepared to defer to Randall during the Grace Worldwide presentation, yet he'd let her run the show. The men at the table had snickered and initially blown her off. They'd seen her only as a woman, a weak link, next to go down.

But Cat had done her homework. She'd presented facts and figures, and her comments had been solid. She'd hit on areas the other two financiers had overlooked. She'd caught several of the men jotting down notes.

Now, Guy Powers opened the floor to initial offers. He scoffed at Langhardt International and soon sent them packing. The corporation wasn't playing in the same ballpark as Techno-Air and Grace Worldwide.

After a second round of bids, Powers curled his lip, then left the room in a huff. He was demanding more than the team was realistically worth. He was deep in debt, yet wanted to walk away clean, clear, and ready to rebuild. He had his eye on another block of skyscrapers.

Powers returned to the boardroom, a tumbler of whiskey in hand. He toasted the room and said, "How badly do you want the Rogues?"

The CEOs from Techno-Air Dynamics bumped shoulders as they crunched final numbers. Their offer was soon slipped into an envelope and passed to Powers.

Randall Burton Lawless slipped Cat a note. *Bring it home. Now.*

Catherine May shook on the inside.

Outwardly, she kept her composure.

She opened her financial binder, slowly removing a piece of stationery with the Grace Worldwide letterhead.

She stalled for time as she recalled her research on the Techno-Air team. She knew their net worth, outstanding notes, and liquid assets, as well as their personal histories. She'd done background checks.

Gerald Addison was six times divorced; he owed alimony that could settle the national debt. He also gambled heavily in Las Vegas. His good times were coming to an end.

His partner, Blaine Sutter, was filthy rich, yet lived beyond his means. He was stretched nearly as thin as Guy Powers. His comptrollers kept two sets of books. Sutter's debt was well hidden.

Cat touched her bracelets for luck. She was wearing the silver indestructible Wonder Woman bracelets to give her power, however imaginary.

Her love for Law and her admiration for Randall came together. The team meant so much to each man.

Randall loved his grandson and wanted him happy. Even if it meant Law would stay with sports instead of taking over Grace Worldwide.

It was time to play in the big leagues.

She took a chance and wrote down their bid.

She rose and took the longest walk of her life to the head of the table. Every executive followed her, their curiosity evident.

She faced Guy Powers, meeting his gaze squarely. She placed the stationery facedown, then returned to her seat.

She nearly stumbled on her way back to Randall.

She'd been so honed in on Powers and the acquisition that she hadn't heard the team arrive. Fifteen men had snuck silently into the gallery.

James Lawless sat a mere twenty feet from her.

Their gazes locked for a heartbeat.

His eyes were hot, hungry, and full of pride in her.

An image of their night together came to mind.

She relayed her own feelings: she loved him.

He nodded, message received.

Randall stood and held her chair.

Cat settled in for the verdict.

Powers took his time. He gave the Techno offer a full fifteen-minute review.

He took five seconds with Grace Worldwide.

A very bad sign.

Cat's stomach clenched. This wouldn't end well. She'd failed both Randall and Law. She fidgeted, didn't know how to fix—

The warmth of Randall's palm covered her hands.

He silently asked her to be still.

She forced an outward calm.

Smiles broke on the faces of the Techno team.

They were ready to shake hands, ready to throw an acquisition party. They were that sure of the outcome.

Guy Powers shut down their celebration.

He looked down the table. His gaze touched Cat, then held on Randall. His words would stay with her for the rest of her life. "She's good. Congratulations."

Cat sat stunned.

Randall showed little emotion.

He rose and indicated Cat should stand as well.

Her legs barely held her.

She took his arm, needing the support.

They made their way across the boardroom.

A handshake closed the deal.

Techno-Air Dynamics were poor losers.

The CEOs hit the door without a backward glance.

Guy Powers and his staff soon followed.

Once the room cleared, shouts broke from the Rogues in the media gallery. En masse, they charged Randall and Cat.

Law reached Cat first. His hug lifted her off the floor. She clung to him tightly.

His kiss made the boardroom blur. The commotion

faded. For a full minute they were the only two who mattered.

The team congratulated Randall, careful in their exuberance. Randall was a vital man, but he was also eighty-six. No player wanted to knock down the new team owner.

"The Rogues stay in Richmond," roared Psycho as he invaded the boardroom bar.

Psycho handed out imported beer, high-end whiskey, world-class wine, and vintage Dom Pérignon.

Cat stood beneath a champagne shower.

The celebration drew toasts and warrior whoops.

Cat hoped the positive momentum behind them now would take them to the World Series.

After an hour, the players realized Law needed time alone with his grandfather and Catherine May.

Psycho packed up several cases of booze.

Risk, Chaser, and Romeo shouldered the boxes.

Kason Rhodes offered his acreage for a party.

Their celebration would go long into the night.

Law took her hand and squeezed it.

His strength flowed into her.

The pressure of her day fell away.

She leaned into the man she loved.

He supported her.

Law spoke first to his grandfather. "I had no idea you were a contender for the team. When I saw you, I nearly shit a brick."

Randall raised a brow over the brick. "I was aware of your interest, and not through Zen Driscoll. The president of Richmond America notified me that you wished to borrow against your trust fund. Before I could intervene or show support, you'd backed out of the bidding. Why, Law?"

"I realized you and Grace Worldwide meant more to me than baseball."

Catherine caught the hitch in Law's voice.

"I bought the Rogues for you." Randall's own voice deepened with emotion.

Tears came to Cat's eyes. There wasn't a selfish bone in either man's body. They'd have sacrificed a great deal for each other.

Cat eased back, expecting the two men to hug.

They didn't. Fisting their hands, they went through a series of fancy hand bumps. Randall chuckled with the last knock of their knuckles. "Play ball," he said. "We both owe Catherine our gratitude. The deal wouldn't have gone down without her."

Randall looked down at her heels. "A bunch of wing tips walked into the boardroom, but a pair of black suede pumps ruled the day. Your lady has edge, James."

The compliment warmed Cat's heart and she hugged the older man.

"What was our last bid?" Randall finally asked.

"You don't know?" asked Law.

"I let Catherine bring it home."

Cat smiled at the older man. "I pored over spreadsheets on Techno. They weren't as solvent as they let everyone think. My gut told me that they'd maxed out and made their final offer. They were straining and couldn't go any higher. Guy Powers seemed to recognize that as well. Our bid read, 'Grace Worldwide will top Techno by one million dollars.' I knew it would still fall within the range of what we'd discussed earlier."

Law rested a hand on his grandfather's shoulder.

"We'll make this work," he promised. "I'll split my time between James River Stadium and the hotel chain."

"You won't have to shoulder it alone," Randall told him. "You'll delegate. You'll place top people in the front office, executives who will have your back."

"I've eight starters in mind as we speak," said Law. "I expect you to live another fifty years, if not longer, Grandfather. No one knows Grace Worldwide like you do."

"Someday you will know as much as I, perhaps even more," Randall assured him. "Give it time."

He glanced at his watch. "The dinner hour approaches. I'm meeting Walter Hastings at Fiesta's. Tonight's special is chicken chimichanga. Walter goes for the dessert. He likes the *tres leches* cake topped with maraschino cherries. I have flan."

"Mexican food again?" Law looked surprised.

"Not so much the food as the waitress," Cat gathered, smiling. "Bella Anna spoils your grandfather."

"I see a Cancun Grace in our future," Randall said as he walked toward the door. "Let's consider the expansion." He left the boardroom.

Law exhaled. "Randall's happy."

"So am I." She sighed. "Today was as exciting as it was frightening. The negotiations were so tense and stressful, I don't remember breathing. Through it all, your grandfather trusted me." She'd found that humbling. "I didn't want to let him down. He did this all for you."

"And I want to do something for you now."

He left her, heading for the door.

She heard double clicks as he locked them in.

He returned to her, a man with swagger and a

wicked smile. "Ever made love to the owner of a ball club?" he asked.

She licked her lips. "I like major league."

James Lawless lifted Catherine May onto the long, rectangular table and they initiated the boardroom.

Epilogue

The Rogues won the World Series that year. Their power, stamina, and cockiness kicked New York Yankee ass.

The people of Richmond threw a parade in their honor. The mayor gave each player a key to the city.

Two weeks later, James Lawless married Catherine May on Larkspar Lane, right in the middle of the street. His grandfather, Walter Hastings, the Rogues, and Cat's entire family were in attendance.

The reception that followed at the Richmond Grace welcomed her as a Lawless. She'd never been happier.

Law had planned their honeymoon. He wanted to recapture his childhood memories and travel where his parents once vacationed. They took off for Europe. For a month.

Once they returned, he took his place as principal owner and chairman of the Richmond Rogues.

Zen Driscoll made Cat his partner. She was on her way to being one of the top financiers in the city.

Cat had agreed to move into Law's penthouse, a transitional home until they could agree on a residence.

Bouncer and Foxie bonded.

They were never more than two paws apart.

Brody Jones continued to play baseball. He wasn't ready to retire. Law had offered him a place in the front office, but Brody leaned toward coaching. Someday.

Back in Plain, he'd bought the land near Jasper Bridge and built Mary a two-story house. Every room had a view of the old bridge. The townsfolk put up a new concrete bridge farther upstream, but tourists who headed to Plain always came out to see the old wooden bridge where Brody had once proposed to Mary, then, years later, jumped in to save her. The media had picked up the story and it spread everywhere.

People thought it romantic.

Mary was not a girl to sit idle, so Brody took over Pop's Bowling Alley when the old man was ready to sell. She enjoyed running the place and was especially interested in making sure every kid in town had the right size bowling shoe. She handpicked the waitresses for the coffee shop.

Brody's mom helped out when Mary spent the baseball season in Richmond with Brody. Grandma Blanchard prepared for her great-grandbabies. She knitted blankets, sweaters, and booties.

During the off-season, the Joneses returned to West Virginia. They had Plain pride.

* * *

Risk Kincaid fathered four boys in five years. And still wanted two more.

His wife, Jacy, compromised and agreed to one more. She became pregnant with twins. Twin boys. Risk was ecstatic.

Risk invested heavily in the ball club and became the managing general partner/cochairman.

Psycho McMillan didn't wait for Law to appoint him to the front office. He claimed the title senior vice president/general manager. He moved into an executive suite and ordered a desk nameplate before Law had signed off on the banknote.

His wife, Keely, gifted him with a baby girl on his own birthday. He couldn't stop staring at the tiny pink bundle with the peach-fuzz hair. He cuddled and rocked Camilla "Cami" McMillan for hours on end, giving her up only for breast-feedings. He even changed diapers.

Psycho refused to allow Cami playdates with Risk's boys. They were too damn rough for his little princess.

Facing a future of Barbie and ballet, he made sure Cami's first word was *ball*.

Romeo Bellisaro and Chaser Tallan landed in the front office, also as vice presidents: Romeo for baseball operations; Chaser for strategic ventures.

Romeo's wife, Emerson, suffered complications during her pregnancy and delivered prematurely. The team gathered in the waiting area outside the delivery room.

The hall overflowed with ballplayers until word

came down that baby boy Bellisaro was out of danger. The men later lit cigars in the parking lot in little William Liam's honor.

Jen Tallan owned and operated three concession stands at James River Stadium. During her pregnancy, she ate so many grape snow cones, her lips were stained purple. Jen sucked so much ice, Chaser was afraid his son would arrive frozen.

He brought three baby blankets and a hot water bottle to the delivery room to welcome Christopher John.

Kason Rhodes took his place as senior vice president of international scouting. His wife, Dayne, worked in player promotions. They drove to work together.

The Rhodeses had yet to have children, but added a menagerie of breeds to their household. Fenced acreage allowed the dogs to chase and play. Eight furry faces met them at the gate every day.

Law appointed Rhaden Dunn vice president of corporate and community events. Rhaden and Revelle were social, visible, and supported the city. They participated in every Rogues charity event.

They were frequent winners of the Great St. James Canoe Race. Revelle always blushed profusely when her husband threatened to paddle her behind if she didn't stroke faster. She could paddle like a paddlewheel even if her arms ached for days.

One year their drawing placed first in the Chalk Walk.

Psycho swore they'd brought in a ringer to sketch

the local war memorial. Fifty names were neatly listed on the monument. The public donated hundreds of dollars in support of their fallen heroes.

Brek Stryker joined his wife, Taylor, on several extreme sporting events before settling in the front office. Taylor owned Thrill Seekers. The two of them went paragliding in New South Wales and skied downhill in La Grave, France.

After rafting down the Brahmaputra River in India, they returned home. Administration seemed a breeze to Brek after nearly being thrown overboard while experiencing legendary drops, thirty-foot standing waves, and class-six rapids.

Under the new regime, the Rogues remained contenders. The executives and officers played fair with the team because the men in the front office had their roots on the field. They understood and protected their own.

Across town, Walter Hastings had Law's back at Grace Worldwide. Randall had promoted Walter and given him stock options as well as a permanent suite at the hotel. Walter worked as hard as ten men.

Retirement was within Randall's reach, but he never fully grasped it. He had wealth, his health, and a daughter-in-law he adored.

He never admitted to handpicking her for Law. But in his mind, he'd played his part. His grandson had found love.

Randall's only regret was that his wife, Grace, along

with Law's parents, weren't around to see his grandson's transformation.

James Lawless thrived with Catherine May.

Sometimes tragedy ended with blessings.

He couldn't wait to meet his great-grandchild.

Law had hinted at starting a family the following year. Zen had agreed to a nursery at Driscoll Financial.

The Lawless name would continue for generations to come. That was the greatest gift of all.

If you love Kate Angell, you're in luck!

No Tan Lines,
**the first in a new series about
life and love at the beach,
is coming this June!**

There's a place where the ocean meets the shore, where kicking off your shoes and baring some skin is as natural as sneaking under the boardwalk for an ice-cream cone and stolen kisses.

But life isn't all a beach for Shaye Cates, even if her idea of an office is a shady umbrella at the water's edge equipped with cell phone and laptop. Steely-eyed Trace Saunders is the incredibly irksome fly in her coconut tanning oil. And running a kids' softball team with her longtime rival is going to have everyone in her little Florida town buzzing. Her scads of laid-back relatives and his whole uptight clan know that Shaye just wants to play ball while Trace thinks only of business. But beneath the twinkling lights of the Ferris wheel, the magic of sea and sand can sweep away every inhibition . . .

Suddenly, it's summertime, and the lovin' is easy.

Read on for a sneak preview . . .

Prologue

"We've got customers." Kai elbowed Shaye Cates in the side. Their summer job placed them behind the candy counter of the Snack Shack on the Barefoot William Pier.

Tonight's outdoor movie, *Babe*, was being shown on the outer wooden wall of the concession stand. The family film flickered through the open window above the popcorn machine as a pink pig raised by sheepdogs learned to herd sheep with the help of Farmer Hoggett.

Shaye straightened from behind the counter. She brushed her hair out of her eyes, then tugged down the hem on a T-shirt that had started life five years ago a much brighter shade of blue. Her jeans were bleached white. She was barefoot and her pomegranate nail polish was in need of a fresh coat.

She'd been stocking oversized boxes of Jujy-fruits, red licorice whips, and snow caps when Trace Saunders, the hot boy with the cool name, walked in. He carried two black vinyl beach chairs under his arm, as moviegoers were required to supply their own seats.

His date trailed behind him. Crystal Smith was sixteen going on twenty. She appeared relaxed, whereas Trace looked restless and bored by the midnight feature. He apparently wasn't into talking farm animals.

Shaye despised him. Her dislike surpassed cooked cabbage, alarm clocks, cold weather, and shoes. Trace was an ass.

What did she expect from a hotshot jock? He was the star of a rival high school team, a sophomore who played varsity. He'd gone through a growth spurt and now stood six feet tall, all lanky and smug. He was big enough to play major league baseball. If he ever did, that was one bubble gum baseball card she'd trash. And fast.

That very afternoon Shaye had sat on the bleachers at Gulf Field and watched Trace hit a line drive between the shortstop and the second baseman in the top of the fifth. His team was already ahead by four runs, yet Trace rounded the bases as if his hit would win the game.

The boy could sprint, long strides, pumping arms. Not that she noticed. She was more interested in her cousin, Kai, who played catcher. He'd crouched low for a throw from the center fielder as Trace slid home. Trace's shoulder caught Kai in the chest and sent the catcher flying. Kai sailed several yards, slamming into a metal post. He'd bruised his spine.

Trace's fan club applauded his run. Ten clueless teenage girls bounced on the bleachers like booby pogo sticks.

Shaye was a tomboy and broke the school rule of nonplayers on the field. She'd climbed the chain-link fence and raced straight for Kai. She dropped to her knees and asked, "You okay?"

Kai fought to catch his breath. "Wind knocked out of me."

She placed a comforting hand on his shoulder, then glared at Trace. The boy dusted off his uniform pants, all smiles and puffed chest. Shaye *despised* his cocky smile, and wanted to wipe it off his face. He'd hurt Kai. The incident was unforgivable, and she'd let him know it with a dirty look. Which Trace had ignored.

Trace topped Kai's shit list as well. Kai had always been the athletic superstar until Trace moved to town, coming from a private boarding school. Trace was Kai's chief competitor in both sports and dating. Trace had gone as far as to steal Kai's girlfriend, which was unacceptable to Shaye. Crystal belonged with Kai.

Shaye's hatred of Trace was born in her blood. He was a Saunders and she was a Cates. The century-old feud killed all pleasantries between them.

Over a hundred years had passed since her great-great-great-grandfather William Cates left Frostbite, Minnesota. He'd been a farmer broken by poor crops and a harsh, early winter. He'd sold his farm and equipment, then hand-cranked his Model-T and drove south. The trip was long and hard, yet he pushed on until the Florida sunshine thawed him out.

On a long stretch of uninhabited beach, William rolled up his pant legs and shucked his socks and work boots. Once he experienced the warm sand between his toes, he vowed to never wear shoes again.

He put down roots, married, and named the fishing village Barefoot William. The town expanded slowly, as family and longtime friends moved to the Gulf Coast.

Even after he was elected mayor, William walked barefoot through City Hall, as did the other city officials. Back then, life existed on a man's word and a solid handshake. For two decades, the village remained small and laid-back.

Until the day Evan Saunders disrupted the peace. He was a capitalist with big-city blood. He wore three-piece suits, a bowler hat, and polished brown oxfords. It was rumored the man never broke a sweat in summer.

Evan set his sights on real estate. He contacted Northern investors and, within six months, the Saunders Group began to buy up land. Evan wanted to citify the small town. He sought to turn Barefoot William into a posh winter resort.

William Cates and Evan Saunders sparred for sixty years. William battled zoning and expansion. He was comfortable with the short boardwalk and long fishing pier. He valued friendships and a sense of community, whereas Saunders was a developer. Evan built his own boardwalk and yacht harbor and snubbed the barefoot mayor.

Hostility flared between the two men, and Barefoot William became a town divided. On an overcast day with thunderheads roiling, the conservative and the capitalist drew a line in the sand, which neither crossed during the remainder of their lifetimes. The line later became Beach Street, the mid-point between Barefoot William and Saunders Shores.

The Cates' Northern cement boardwalk linked to a wooden pier that catered to fishermen, sun worshippers, water sports enthusiasts, and tourists who didn't wear a watch on vacation.

Amusement arcades and carnival rides drew large

crowds to the boardwalk. The specialty shops sold everything from Florida T-shirts, ice cream, sunglasses, sharks' teeth, shells, to hula hoops.

A century-old carousel whirled within a weatherproof enclosure. A wall of windows overlooked the Gulf. The whirr of the Ferris wheel was soothing, while the swing ride that whipped out and over the waves sent pulses racing.

Barefoot William was as honky-tonk as Saunders Shores was high-end. Couture, gourmet dining, and a five-star hotel claimed the southern boundaries. Waterfront mansions welcomed the rich and retired. Yachts the size of cruise ships lined the waterways. Private airstrips reduced commercial travel. They were a community unto themselves.

In Shaye's mind, Trace Saunders didn't belong on the Barefoot William Pier. Not tonight. Not ever. He was like gritty sand rubbing against her skin. She wanted to wash him off.

She leaned her elbows on the candy counter and gave him a hard look to let him know where she stood. "You're trespassing."

Trace crossed the wide wooden planks of the candy shack and came to stand before her. Her breath caught. He was tall. "I'm slumming." His boy's voice was manly deep, a baritone that gave her goose bumps.

She looked him over with careless indifference. His hair was short, black, and spiky. His eyes were a blue-gray as pale as the crest of a wave. Movie night was casual, tank tops, T-shirts, shorts, yet Trace wore a white button down and dark slacks. She wanted to kick sand on his polished loafers. No doubt he'd kick it back.

She felt Kai tense as Crystal joined Trace. She wore

a pink sundress with a narrow turquoise necklace strap. Shaye tried not to stare. Crystal was all girly and hot, everything Shaye was not. From the corner of her eye, Crystal glanced at Kai for all of two seconds. Kai, on the other hand, glared a hole through her.

The two had a history. They'd grown up together. Crystal had claimed Kai as her boyfriend in the third grade. She'd pulled his hair on the playground until he agreed. They'd hung tight for seven years, up until her sixteenth birthday, when Crystal decided she looked too much like a kid.

The Scissorhands Salon in Barefoot William no longer suited her. She'd called the stylists juvenile and silly. Crystal crossed to the dark side and booked an appointment at Zsuzsy, an exclusive day spa in Saunders Shores. The spa achieved the desired effect. The girl entered through the mint green-and-gold double-doors and emerged a young woman. Shaye and Kai hardly recognized her.

Crystal had cut her long brown hair, dyed her eyelashes, then gone on to purchase a wardrobe from Eclipz, a new teen designer.

Kai made the mistake of saying he missed Crystal's ponytail. Crystal had yet to forgive him. Shaye kept silent when it came to Crystal's lashes, which were so sooty and thick her brown eyes appeared black.

Trace Saunders was the only one to compliment Crystal's haircut, a style as geometrically sharp as her tongue when she later dumped Kai.

Kai still suffered a broken heart. It was painful for him to see Trace and Crystal together now. Shaye needed to move them along.

She tapped the top of the candy counter. The colors

of her mood ring shifted from calm blue to midnight dark. She loved retro jewelry and shopped the local flea market every Saturday.

"Buy something or say good-bye." She was being rude to Trace, but didn't care. He'd never given her one good reason to be nice to him, so why start now? Besides, business was slow and she needed a candy sale.

Trace raised an eyebrow. Tonight he looked more amused than affronted. He was used to her behavior. She constantly blew him off, and, on occasion, openly cheered when he struck out at baseball, missed a hoop in basketball, or came in second at a track meet.

He wasn't crazy about her, either. His girlfriends had boobs and hips. Shaye was an A-cup and all legs. Trace had called her "Toothpick" for as long as she could remember. She hated the nickname.

"I'd like cotton candy," Crystal placed her order.

"We're sold out and the machine's being cleaned," Shaye took pleasure in telling her.

"A bag of popcorn, then," was Crystal's second request.

"All that's left is unpopped kernels," Shaye said. "You could chip a tooth."

"Hot dog?" Crystal tried a third time.

"Steamer's turned off."

Crystal pouted until Trace suggested, "Candy bar?"

His date perked up. "We can play Sweet Treat," she was quick to say. "Shaye created the game. She asks a question and, if you answer it correctly, the candy's free."

"Free sounds good," Trace agreed.

Shaye preferred that he pay. Her family owned Snack Shack, and any item given away cut into their profits. Even something as small as a candy bar. She was annoyed that Crystal had shared a game played only by close friends. Trace was her enemy. She must never forget that.

"I'll go first," Crystal said.

Shaye had always liked Crystal, until the girl dumped Kai. Crystal was an average student, more into appearances than schoolwork. She often got confused by the wording of a question. "How is cotton candy made?" Shaye asked.

"In a cotton-candy machine."

Shaye shook her head. "Sorry, wrong answer. I was looking for either corn syrup or granulated sugar."

Crystal's shoulders slumped.

Trace frowned and took his date's side. "Technically, her response was correct." He gave Shaye a disapproving look that made her uncomfortable. "If you'd wanted ingredients, you should have said so."

"I was certain she'd say the candy was made from cotton," Kai muttered from behind Shaye.

"She deserves another chance," said Trace.

Shaye didn't like where this was going. He was determined to see how far he could push her. She didn't like being pushed.

"I want to go again," Crystal pleaded.

Shaye debated. Second questions weren't part of her game. But whatever she asked, chances were good Crystal would botch the answer. "Superman's other identity. Name the candy bar," she said.

"Jimmy Olson."

Shaye didn't look at Crystal; she met Trace's gaze instead. She was surprised by the sympathy that darkened his eyes. He seemed embarrassed for his date. If it was anybody else, she would have admired that in him. Not

Trace. His expression sought Shaye's help to ease the situation.

She scrunched her nose. This boy was a Saunders; she owed him nothing. But because of his genuine concern for Crystal, she gave him something. "Clark Bar. Clark Kent was Superman. Both Kent and Olsen were reporters at the *Daily Planet*. You were close, Crystal."

Crystal sighed. "Close is good."

"Correct would've been better," said Kai.

Shaye removed a pack of gum from a shelf beneath the counter. "Bubble Yum Cotton Candy?" She offered the girl. It was her favorite flavor.

Crystal opened the pack and removed four pieces. She unwrapped each one and popped them in her mouth. Her cheeks bulged as she started to chew. "I can blow a bubble as big as my face," she bragged.

Trace leaned left. "What if it pops?"

"Have fun getting the gum out of her hair." Kai was aware of the consequences.

Crystal ignored her ex-boyfriend. She blew a small practice bubble, sucked it back into her mouth. "It's Trace's turn to play Sweet Treat."

Shaye shook her head. She was done for the night. She'd wasted two good questions on Crystal. She wanted Trace and his bubble-blowing date to move on. "We don't have time."

"Make time." Trace reached into the back pocket of his slacks, removed his wallet, then a twenty-dollar bill. He set the money on the counter. "I'm buying five minutes."

Shaye bristled. Did he think she was that hard up for a sale? Even if she was, she'd never admit it. Still, she debated taking the bill.

Kai, on the other hand, had no such qualms. He snatched the twenty and put it in the cash box, a box with five singles and a handful of change.

Business was slow. Too slow to give Trace back his money. Kai had polished off six hot dogs, eating the profits as he shut down the steamer. Bored herself, she'd eaten a bucket of cheddar cheese popcorn.

Shaye had several tough questions she could ask Trace. She'd love to stump him. She went with the one that made most people draw a blank. "Name the colors of candy corn, base to tip."

"Candy corn." He rocked heel to toe, his stance tense and competitive. "Give me a minute, I'm thinking."

Shaye rolled her eyes. Trace was such a dork. He didn't have an answer, yet he drew out the game. Was that a hint of a smile? No, she was imagining things.

The silence within the shack grew as hot and heavy as the humidity on the pier. A full minute passed. Sweat gathered on Kai's forehead and at the crease of his neck. Moisture slickened Shaye's palms. She rubbed the flat of her hands down her blue-jeaned thighs, then curled her fingers into fists.

She soon nudged Trace. "Your answer?"

"Candy corn celebrates a lot of holidays," he slowly said. "Which seasonal colors do you want? There's gingerbread, candy cane peppermint, reindeer, patriotic raspberry lemonade, Indian corn, and eggnog to name a few."

Shaye's jaw dropped. No player had ever named *flavors*. Put to the test, she couldn't name the colored stripes on holiday corn. Trace Saunders was either a candy connoisseur or a bullshitter. She clamped her mouth closed, grew uneasy. "Your basic corn," she said.

"Yellow, orange, white."

Damn. Her stomach sank. She was dealing with a candy corn fanatic. What else would he try to put over on her?

Crystal giggled. "Isn't he amazing?"

Amazing wasn't the word Shaye would've chosen. Asshole fit him better. She eyed him with suspicion. "You know a lot about candy corn."

He shrugged, admitted, "Jelly beans and holiday corn are my two favorite candies."

"Trace gave me a gourmet box of jelly beans last week for my birthday," Crystal bragged. "You could eat the jelly beans individually or toss an assortment in your mouth and mix the flavors. Jelly beans are the new birthday cake."

"I'd rather have cake and ice cream," Kai said.

"And candles." Shaye hadn't meant to speak her thought aloud. Candles sounded childish. Not that she cared what Trace thought of her.

Behind her, Kai yawned, scratched his stomach. His camouflage T-shirt was as wrinkled as his khaki shorts. It was getting late.

Shaye tapped her finger on the countertop, avoided looking at Trace. "Pick your free treat," she said.

"Select one for me."

She went for Lemonheads, only to change her mind. A solution came to her, and she dipped her head so he wouldn't see her smile. She had no conscience where this boy was concerned, so she grabbed a box of Skittles from the lower shelf instead. She passed it to him.

He accepted the candy. "We'll play again, Toothpick."

She hated the humor in his eyes and the fact he teased her. "Not on my pier we won't."

"You don't want to get even?" he called over his shoulder as Crystal took his hand and tugged him out the door. The girl was so possessive.

Shaye grinned now. He'd soon realize she'd gotten him back. He just didn't know it yet. The Skittles were a year old, left over from the previous summer. They'd be stale, hard as rocks. She'd only kept the box around as a reminder to order a new case.

Taste the rainbow, Trace Saunders.

Chapter 1

"Skittles?" Kai offered Shaye a handful of candy as they walked the length of the boardwalk. The majority of kiosks and colorful wooden storefronts stood open to the public. Customers were far and few between.

She shook her head. "I can't stomach them."

Fifteen years had passed, yet Skittles still reminded her of Trace Saunders. The man was on her mind today. They were scheduled to meet for lunch. A meal she dreaded.

He was now CEO of Saunders Shores and she presided over Barefoot William Enterprises. Trace had only recently inherited his position. He'd previously worked from New York City, where he oversaw his family's real estate holdings.

It was rumored the Saunders family owned a block of skyscrapers and several hotels as well as holding stock in companies that owned national landmarks.

Trace had returned home following his father's unexpected fall from a ladder. Brandt Saunders's attempt at replacing a shutter on a window had landed him flat on his back. He'd dislocated his shoulder and broken his hip. He was homebound for six months.

Gossip spread with Trace's return. He went on to surprise everyone by staying on after his dad's recovery. He'd sold his summer house in the Hamptons and closed his eyes to the bright lights on Times Square. He'd left the rapid pulse of the city for the slow, changing tides of the Gulf Coast. He'd been home two years now.

Shaye had never left southwest Florida. She couldn't imagine living anywhere else. As a kid, she'd followed her grandfather and father around town, learning the business from the moment she could walk. Her very first steps had been on the pier. Her heart belonged to Barefoot William.

Today, she and Trace had business to discuss. A proposed professional/amateur beach volleyball tournament required his approval. Trace still straddled the fence.

Her dozen phone calls and countless e-mails hadn't changed his mind. Trace remained noncommittal in sharing *his* beach with her for the event. What was wrong with the man? The tour players would draw a huge crowd and boost slow summer sales for everyone.

That very morning he'd requested a meeting at his office, no doubt surrounded by a bunch of suits. She declined. Her idea of an office was sitting under a shady umbrella on the sand with her cell phone and laptop.

They'd argued for thirty minutes on a location. He'd finally agreed to lunch at Molly Malone's. The diner was located on North Beach, on *her* side of the street.

Shaye's aunt owned the restaurant, known for its

home cooking. Molly was as round as a hamburger bun and happy with her shape. She relished food and life and offered a free slice of pie with each luncheon special. Shaye hoped coconut cream was on the menu today. It was her favorite.

Kai adjusted his black baseball cap with *HOOK IT, COOK IT* scripted on the bill, an advertisement for two of his shops. *HOOK IT* sold bait and tackle and *COOK IT* stood next door, a small chef's kitchen where fishermen could have their daily catch cleaned and filleted for a small fee, then baked or fried for lunch or dinner. A salad, hush puppies, and fries came on the side. The tourists found it a novelty to eat their meals fresh from the Gulf.

When times were slow, Kai worked as a handyman. He remodeled the boardwalk shops when they changed hands among the family. He'd worn a tool belt much of the spring.

Beside her now, he shifted his stance. "When does Dune expect an answer on the event?" he asked.

Dune was her older brother. He'd played professional beach volleyball for seventeen years. He was a dominant force and a major voice in the sport. He planned to use his popularity to draw players south for a weekend.

Volleyball had very loyal fans. This wouldn't be a sanctioned tournament, but with media coverage, Barefoot William could turn a profit. This was exactly what she needed to keep the family businesses in the black after a slow start to the summer season.

"Time has run out. Trace needs to make up his mind today." She cleared her throat, swallowing her guilt. She was not looking forward to this meeting. "I, on the other hand, have already made up mine. I called Dune late last night and we set dates. The players will be in town over the Fourth of July. He will guarantee top seeds from both the women's and men's tour. He'll send a list of names for promotion."

Kai rolled his eyes. "You make crazy look sane."

She had crossed the line, and she knew it. She'd set the date without Trace's consent. She hated the fact that she desperately needed him. All she required was two hundred feet of his beach to set up the final volleyball net, concessions, and bleachers.

Saunders Shores would benefit as much from the competition as Barefoot William. However, her southern neighbors weren't as financially strapped as her own family businesses. Her side of the street was sucking summer air.

She hated dealing with difficult men. Trace was a royal pain in her ass. He rated no more than a blink of an eye in her book, if that. She released an expansive sigh. "He has to agree."

Kai wasn't so sure. "There's a lot of planning around an event this size. Saunders is formidable. He could ax the tournament out of spite."

Kai was right, as always. It was no secret she and Trace barely tolerated each other. Ill will slapped between them like high tide against cement pilings. She'd cross a street or take to the alley to avoid the man. He rubbed her the wrong way.

She stood as still as her thoughts until a light breeze blew her hair across her cheek. She tucked the curls behind her ear. Overhead, seagulls squawked, circled, and dived for fish. The sun's climb was slow, lazy. The Gulf waters were as pure a blue as the cloudless sky.

High humidity stuck her red tank top to her back.

The cement beneath her bare feet grew hot. Shaye hopped to a spot of shade near the entrance to the carousel.

The hand-carved purple-and-white horses were motionless while the workers wiped them down. Each mount had jeweled amber eyes and a gold saddle. Their legs were bent, ready to race. The wooden platform was polished, the driving mechanism oiled. The ride opened at noon. The calliope music would soon echo across town.

She waved to Oliver Ray, who managed the merry-go-round. Oli was replacing lights along the outer rim of the orange scalloped top. He nodded from his ladder, a thin, gray-haired man of few words. His mechanic's overalls never showed a sign of dirt or grease. Only the heels on his steel-toed boots were scuffed. Pushing sixty, he'd never missed a day of work.

Shaye wished her younger employees had Oliver's work ethic. They, unfortunately, did not. A midnight beer bash or beach bonfire had someone calling in sick every other day and Shaye scrambling to replace them.

The day before yesterday, she'd helped out her uncle at Hooper's Hoops. The kiosk sold hula hoops in a variety of colors from hot pink, sand tan, to metallic silver.

Shaye had entertained a few perspective buyers, twirling a fiery orange hoop until her hips got sore. She swore her waist had a permanent indentation from six hours of twisting.

But all in all, she knew she was fortunate to work with her immediate and extended families. The Cates family owned every shop, arcade amusement, and carnival ride along the boardwalk and down the full length of the pier. Barefoot William needed to stay in the black. The volleyball tournament would save the summer. And her sanity.

The only thing wrong with the event was that it involved Trace Saunders. A fact she couldn't change. She hoped their meeting wouldn't be filled with awkward silences or worse yet, angry words.

She wracked her brain. She needed some assurance having lunch with him wouldn't turn out to be a bust.

She looked down on her mood ring, now a dark gray. The color reflected her tension and stress. She needed to relax, loosen up. Take charge.

Next to her, Kai leaned his forearms against the bright blue pipe railing that separated the boardwalk from the beach. He looked out over the surf. "Trace is a challenge. What's your plan of attack?" he asked.

"I'll charm the man."

Kai couldn't help himself. He laughed, as she'd known he would. "Good luck. You're sarcastic as hell and always snub him."

"Not always."

"Name a time you've been nice to him."

One moment came to mind, which she'd never shared with Kai. It had been late January, and she and Trace were at City Hall for a Beach Erosion Meeting. They'd collided in the doorway of the conference room, as she was going in and he was coming out. She'd bumped his chest with her shoulder. He'd been all starched white shirt and solid muscle. He'd loomed over her, a big man with a bigger presence.

His cologne was subtle, yet masculine. The scent reminded her of early mornings down by the pier when the air was fresh and the sand was free of footprints.

Neither of them had moved until the chairman of

the committee arrived. Trace took a polite step back then, allowing her to pass. She'd forgotten the snide comment she was going to make about him crowding her. She'd let their closeness slide. That one time.

"You need to change your tactic," Kai said, breaking into her thoughts. "Find his weakness and exploit it. A pretty woman is the best weapon against an unsuspecting man."

She frowned. "Trace is always suspicious. He never lets his guard down."

"Neither do you," Kai said. "Saunders likes the ladies. You clean up nice, Shaye. Distraction could work in your favor. Show up in something besides a T-shirt and cutoffs. Wear shoes. Flirt a little."

She blew raspberries. "Bad idea. He'd see right through me. I'm not that good an actress."

"You may dislike the man, but you need him," Kai reminded her. "Both your signatures are required on the recreational permit. You can't forge his name."

He nudged her with his shoulder. "You're doing this for family, and we love you for it. None of us wants to close up shop."

Her cousin was right, as always. He was her voice of reason when she was being unreasonable. Her parents, siblings, and relatives meant everything to her. Without the proper paperwork, Trace could bust her for trespassing. He wouldn't think twice about pressing charges.

The sun beat down, and her shadow grew short. She looked down on her toes, freshly polished a Peruvian orchid pink. Her pedicure would be wasted by wearing shoes, although flip-flops might work.

Flirting, however, was out of the question.

She couldn't force what she didn't feel.

Over the last year, newspapers and magazines had profiled Saunders with curvy brunettes. Shaye's high metabolism kept her thin. Her hair was white blond.

She wasn't Trace's type. Neither was he hers. She preferred bare-chested men in boardshorts, whereas he wore tailored shirts and trousers.

He was all business and she was all beach.

She scrunched her nose. There had to be another way to force his hand, beyond breaking his fingers . . .